Lethal Abandon
by
Kallie Lane
Shadow Soldiers Suspense
Book 4

LETHAL ABANDON: A Shadow Soldiers Suspense Novel

Publishing History

First edition published 2014, The Wild Rose Press, Inc.

Second edition published 2019, Kathryn Donaldson

Third edition published 2021, Kathryn Donaldson

Digital ISBN 978-1-7779233-5-8

Print ISBN 978-1-7779233-4-1

Published in the United States of America

Dedication

To Joan and Greg,
Thank you so much for moving out while Micah and
Remy moved in!
And to those who serve and protect.

Acknowledgments

Here's to my incredible support team: the people who help breathe life into my novels by providing essential information, critiquing, and bolstering yours truly whenever I feel I've drifted off course. You know who you are Coreene Callahan, Fred Donaldson, June Gauld, Lesley Lawrence, Hélène Ste-Croix, and JJ Wilhelm. I'd be lost without you, and any mistakes are entirely my own. To Chris and Dave, my family, my anchors in a storm. I love you.

Author's Note

L ife sometimes hands us curveballs, and this was one of those years for me. I want to thank my readers for falling in love with the Shadow Soldiers and urging me to write the next book. I'm so glad you did, because you reminded me of what's important, and LETHAL ABANDON is here!

The main location of this novel, Silver Lake, is one I know well. I have a cottage there. It's very peaceful, although never when the Shadow Soldiers are in residence. But I love my characters, even with—or maybe because of—their rough edges. I learn more about them with every book I write in the series. I also believe in happy endings, which is why each Shadow Soldier will find his soul mate as the series unfolds.

And so, I raise my glass to you, my readers. Thank you for your wonderful encouragement. And thanks for believing!

Chapter 1

Remy Renaud wanted out of the Everglades. She hated the swamp so much she begged Saint Christopher, the patron saint of travellers, to *please* get the lead out and transport her somewhere else. Make that anywhere else. And could he manage it *before* the crocodile bumping her canoe killed her? Because *now* would be a really good time.

The whopping croc stared at her through yellow, iridescent eyes. Toyed with her like a cat with a gerbil. No doubt enjoying the game before it flipped her out of the canoe and dragged her under in a death roll. One swish of its powerful tail, that's all it would take.

Please, whoever's listening up there, find this frickin' carnivore something else to eat and make him leave me alone!

Inhaling a steadying breath, Remy attempted to center herself, knowing she had to get out of this mess on her own. Not easy to do. Everglades National Park was nothing like the nature reserve where she worked as a wildlife biologist. The bogs here overwhelmed her, not to mention the reptiles—alligators, crocodiles, water moccasins, and rattlesnakes to name a few. And would she ever forget the roughly fifteen-foot python she'd seen slithering through a cypress grove that afternoon? It had shattered whatever was left of her Pollyanna sense of adventure, never mind the croc currently stalking her every move. She was unnerved and fresh out of brilliant ideas. Could life possibly get any worse? *Don't even go there,* she decided.

Instead, she reminded herself how she had gotten into this mess. It hadn't been difficult, not after she refused Pete Mandel's offer to be her guide. Her obstinate streak rearing its carrot-topped head, she'd insisted she could find her own way in almost twenty-four-hundred square miles of protected acreage with only a map. Well, it had seemed logical at the time, but now, not so much.

Still, why would she allow the head park ranger to babysit her when she was trained in wilderness survival herself? And she was, just not *this* kind of wilderness. Pete had tried to tell her this before she'd paddled off alone in the canoe, and forgotten the two-way radio on the dock. So this was her mess and her fault.

A swarm of mosquitoes mocked her, dive bombing in the fading light, reaffirming how much she loathed this place and situation. She was here to gather information on the Canadian Sandhill Cranes that normally migrated north, and discover why some of them had summered with their Florida cousins instead. But the cranes hadn't cooperated with her visual headcount, flying farther inland. Drawing her deeper and deeper into the Glades, a bonafide suicide mission for a greenhorn. She knew she needed to make tracks out of there right away. She sighed, eyeing the crocodile. If only she knew which way to go.

No one else was around. Nature seekers and hikers weren't allowed in restricted areas of the park, which made perfect sense considering predators roamed the wetlands. The eerie sounds—a deep-throated panther growl being the obvious one at the moment—the smell of decay, the stillness in the air all caused her to sweat with fear while her insides froze with dread. She should have headed back an hour ago and hadn't, a rookie mistake of disastrous proportions. There was only a little daylight left, barely enough time before she lost the sun under the thick canopy of trees.

She paddled in a wide arc away from the prehistoric beast tailing her. He wasn't fooled, turning along with her as she altered course. Alone in the marsh with only a meat-eating stalker for company, the irony hit home. She normally preferred being by herself, enjoying the science of the job, the peacefulness of nature. Not today.

Give her bears, wolverines, and mountain lions any day of the week. At least she was armed at her own park in Alberta. But here? She imagined the dinner bell clanging as the massive reptile kept even with her, its eyes and snout skimming the algae-slicked water. She was lost in a strange place with night closing in, and hope fading to a whisper inside her head. A pitiful scream worked its way up her throat. She swallowed it back.

Forget it. I will not shriek like some scared-y-cat, little girl.

She would never live it down if someone heard her cries for help and park rangers rode to the rescue. They would inform their boss and Pete was a family friend. Crap, he'd tell her brothers and she'd be a laughingstock by the end of the day. So, no, she'd use her compass, her skills, and find her own flippin' way back to civilization.

She heard something in the distance. The drone of a motor broke through the sounds of frog ribbits and crickets chirping. Another few minutes and a beat-up boat crossed her bow. An old man hunkered at the throttle, a faded ball cap on his head. A cigar bobbed between his cracked lips. Definitely not a lost tourist, she decided, waving her paddle to flag him down.

He cut the engine and doffed his hat. "Evenin' miss. They call me Papa Joe."

Remy studied the lean face tanned to the consistency of shoe leather. White whiskers stubbled his chin, gray hair tangled to his shoulders. It was his blue eyes that held her attention, though, their gaze razor sharp. She judged his age to be somewhere between sixty and a hundred. It was impossible to tell. "My name is Remy Renaud."

"That's a right fine French name. Cajun, are ya?"

"I don't think so. I was born in New Brunswick, Canada."

"Acadian roots then. Explains the red hair and freckles." He stroked a palm along his jaw. "Ain't none of my business, Remy, but you should be headin' back afore nightfall. Lots of unfriendlies out here in the Glades. Are ya lost?"

What the heck, there was no point in ignoring the obvious. "A little. Do you think you can help me?"

"I reckon I could, since I'm headin' back myself." He grinned, chomping on the unlit cigar. "You follow me and I'll have you home in the time it takes to cut off a rattler's tail. I won't go too fast."

The tension drained from Remy's muscles, although she wasn't quite sure how long it took to "cut off a rattler's tail." Still, she instinctively trusted the man. He instilled confidence, and...

"Walter! Get the hell away from her before I bop you with the bang stick!" The old man grabbed an elongated steel rod from his boat, thrusting it in Remy's direction.

She followed his gaze to where her hand rested. The crocodile's jaws were an inch off the gunnel heading for her fingertips. *Holy hell in a hand basket!*

"Get out of there, ya filthy beggar!" The croc recoiled after a shot from Papa Joe's weapon and moved off. The man tossed the pole in the bottom of his skiff, shaking his head. "Rubber bullets. They won't kill him, but they sure pack one hell of a wallop. Just don't pay him no mind, missy. Old Walt has been livin' in these parts goin' on forty years. He likes to fool with the tourists some, but he ain't chewed on nobody yet, far as I know. And he won't follow you no more."

"Th-thank you." God in heaven, please get her out of there in one piece. She needed a stiff drink, a hot bath, and room service to shore up what was left of her sanity.

"Here, hang this around your neck." Papa Joe tossed her a battery powered lantern with a lanyard attached. "I'll be watching for that there light so I know you're still behind me. Otherwise, I'll double back."

As darkness closed around them, Remy did as he asked, picked up the paddle, and followed his slow-moving boat heading west out of the swamp. She backed off enough to stay out of its wake, not difficult to do after Papa Joe picked up a little speed. Before she knew it, he was quite a bit ahead, her arms churning to keep up and losing the battle. Still, she could see the stern light on his skiff, so she knew he hadn't left her alone. And while distances could be deceiving at night, she thought she recognized a grouping of trees on an upcoming beachhead. If so, then she was only ten or fifteen minutes out from the boat docks.

A flash of movement caught her eye in the nearby shadows. An alligator slid down a bank tossing its head back and forth. Something glittered in its jaws. What was that? Remy held up the light. A woman's hand flopped between the reptile's teeth, a diamond ring on a finger. The gator dove beneath the surface and disappeared before her next breath.

Sweet Jesus! Did I see what I think I saw? She might still be alive!

Remy swung into shore, landing the canoe on an embankment beside a fancy power boat. She leapt out and tried her cell phone. No signal.

Damn it, the woman needs help now! With nothing but a couple of finger-size bandages stuffed in a pocket of her cargo shorts, she grabbed the paddle and backtracked after the claw marks and tail tracks heading down to the water from a group of mangroves up ahead. She had to find the owner of that hand before she bled to death.

Pulling her belt from its loops to use as a tourniquet, she braked to a halt after clearing the trees, stumbling across something so grisly her mind refused to accept it. The blood drained from her head, the paddle slipping from her grip. She sagged against a tree to support herself as the horror around her sank in.

A man with a shovel stood over a mound of earth. He lunged at a gator. The reptile hissed when the spade swooped and bashed its head. It charged him. Dropping the shovel, the guy pulled a gun. Shot the alligator between the eyes. The *boom* of the weapon ricocheted, birds screeching in treetops as the sound rolled through the swamp like cannonball fire.

He swung his weapon toward another reptile. "Get out of here, you fucker!"

"Stow the firepower before the park rangers zero in on us!" A second man stepped from the darkness; stocky, sallow complexioned, a machete gripped in a meaty fist. He swung the blade, slashing the gator through the neck. Blood sprayed, landing on his silk shirt and designer jeans. The stench and sight of gore sickened Remy.

"Wha—?" Her brain finally kicked in and registered what stared her in the face. A slim arm stuck out of the ground. The hand was missing.

No, no, no! This can't be happening!

Other body parts were strewn across loamy earth, too many to belong to one person. Someone, or something, had dug them up. Remy's heart slammed in her ribcage.

Oh, dear God, this is a body dump!

Her stomach twisted in knots. Two pairs of eyes drilled her as she swallowed bile, covered her mouth with her hands, and backed away. Not much of a strategy, considering the men had her outnumbered.

"I'll be damned. Looks like the gators brought us a present, Sig." The man with the machete leered in the lamplight as he advanced, tossing the blade from one hand to the other. "What do you think? Should I gut and filet her? Or do we have time to play?"

"Right," the man with the gun said, grabbing his crotch through his pants. "Like I want some gator ripping off my wanger while I'm shagging the bitch. Cut her fucking head off and be done with it."

Remy inhaled and exhaled as best she could while Machete Man closed the distance. Martial arts—she was trained to defend herself. It was all about breathing and using her opponent's strength against him. *I can do this.*

He lunged.

Remy kicked his knife hand away, dropped her leg, and hooked him behind a knee. He fell hard, but still managed to slice her with the blade. She disengaged and backed off, feeling a stab of pain in her thigh. Uncertain how bad the injury was or how long she had before she fainted from blood loss.

Ignore the pain. Breathe in, breathe out. Focus on his next move.

She didn't have long to wait.

"Freaking cow. I'll slice you to ribbons and leave you for the wild boar to eat!" The psycho sprang to his feet, charging her head on. When he lunged, she twisted by him. Clamped her fingers around his wrist and pushed his arm into the front of his body. She rammed the heel of her other hand into his shoulder blade. The machete arced upward, slicing across his throat. He collapsed at her feet, dead almost before he hit the dirt.

Remy froze, horrified by what she'd done, knowing she didn't have a choice.

"You killed him!"

Whirling too late, a gun slammed into her forehead. She crumpled in a heap, dizzy and disoriented, blood streaming from a cut over an eyebrow. Swiping at the blood, she stared into the soulless eyes of the man above her. Prayed he'd take a clean shot and kill her outright. He aimed for her knee instead.

Bam!

Papa Joe stood over him like a wild man when he collapsed across Remy's legs. "I got him with the bang stick, but he won't stay out for long. We gotta move."

"I'll call 9-1-1," Remy pulled out her cell phone with trembling fingers as the old man wrapped her thigh with a bandanna he'd tugged from around his neck.

"That there phone won't work." He dragged her to her feet. "There ain't no cell towers on state protected land. Confuses bat radar or some such thing."

"But—"

"No time for buts, Remy." Papa Joe put an arm around her waist. Much stronger than he looked, he was able to haul her out of there and down to the water. "Get in my boat afore you pass out."

"Don't worry about me. Are the keys in the power boat?"

He shook his head. "No time to check. We gots to get out of here afore he wakes up. Turn off the lantern so he don't follow us."

Papa Joe pulled on the starter cable. He shut down the running lights and gunned the throttle. "Hang on, girl. You're gonna be fine."

"I know, Papa Joe." Her world rocked on the waves for a few seconds, the drone of the boat motor soothing her before darkness closed in.

MICAH RIVERA SAT AT the open bar on the pier nursing a longneck. Pete Mandel, his buddy since kindergarten, sat across from him with a Perrier in hand.

"Thanks for driving out here, Mic." Pete toasted him with the water bottle and took a deep swallow. "Sorry I couldn't make it to Miami like we'd planned."

"Don't sweat it, pal." Micah rotated his shoulder and felt the tug. Getting shot a few weeks ago had messed with his plans, although he was almost healed now. Still, recuperating with his folks in that retirement village in Miami had almost done him in. He loved them, they were all the family he had, but playing shuffleboard and bridge weren't exactly on his list of favorite things to do. But with the injury, he couldn't do a whole lot of anything else. Not until the muscle damage healed completely. "It's great to have a change of scenery before I head home."

"Already? You sure that's a good idea?" Pete shot him the big brother look, the one he reserved for kickass occasions when Micah refused to listen to reason. "Didn't your CO tell you to take another few weeks off?"

Like that would happen. "From my Special Ops reserve unit, yes. But I have a business to run, my friend. I can't stay here indefinitely. My customers demand the best in security, which means I have to be there to make sure my employees keep them smiling."

"Bullshit. Your company practically runs itself with all the ex-forces talent you've got on the payroll." Pete laughed. "I get it. Your mama's been introducing you around again and scaring the bejesus out of you. Only a woman batting her eyelashes with marriage on her mind could make you bolt like a jackrabbit. Who is it this time, the daughter of some Puerto Rican dignitary?"

"More like the state representative herself and Maria is both smart and beautiful. I'm just not interested." Micah leaned across the bar and grabbed a handful of nuts out of a bowl. "What about you? Do you ever have the urge to settle down?"

"Hell no, especially not since Remy Renaud landed back in the Glades." Rolling his eyes, Pete signalled the waitress for another Perrier. "Damn pretty woman, but she's a royal pain in my ass."

"How so?" Micah added another longneck to the order. Any woman who could rile Pete—the epitome of laid-back and who-gives-a-shit—sounded interesting to him.

"The family bought a vacation home here after you moved away. Her four brothers are friends of mine from way back. Remy is the youngest." The waitress brought their drinks and Micah paid the tab. "Anyhow, she's a wildlife biologist now, spending a few days at the park to study the migrating patterns of birds."

"So? How does that equate with her being a pain in your butt?" Micah took a swig of his beer, settling in to get the rest of the story.

"Remy wouldn't let me act as her guide while she's in the park. Stuck her stubborn little nose in the air, shot me a stiff middle finger, and went off on her own." Pete glanced at his watch. Micah had noticed him doing that ever since they'd sat down. "That was twelve hours ago. She's not back yet."

"Hell, it's been dark over an hour now." Micah didn't like it. A lot could happen to a woman alone in the Everglades, and none of it good. "Did you send out a search party?"

"See, that's the problem." Pete ran a hand over his buzz cut, a frown riding his eyebrows. "If I do that and there's nothing wrong, Remy will skin me alive. On the other hand, if anything happens to her, the Renaud brothers will kill me and bury me deep in the swamp. I'm damned if I do, and damned if I don't."

"Yep, I'd say she's a pain in your ass." Micah felt the grin forming on his lips. "May God protect us from strong-willed women."

"I'll drink to that." Pete tapped his bottle with Micah's. "This is why we're sitting here instead of whooping it up in some steamy Miami hotspot. I'm afraid to take a piss until I get Remy on a plane back to Canada. See, she didn't hang with the rest of us when she was a kid. Hated the Glades and stayed clear, lacks experience with what's out there. Anything happens to her and it's on my head."

"You sure there's nothing romantic going on between you two?" Yeah, Micah was playing devil's advocate and enjoying the hell out of it. On the other hand, he couldn't deny his interest was piqued, which made no sense at all. The last thing he needed was a female who sounded like a firestorm. Still, he couldn't help the twinge of jealousy when he thought Pete might be hooking up with her. "It sounds to me like you have some chemistry brewing."

"More like bad mojo." Pete shot him a disgusted look. "She's the ornery kid sister I never had. I feel sorry for any dumb bastard who decides she's worth a second look. 'Cause if Remy doesn't send him to an early grave, those brothers of hers sure as hell will."

Micah shook his head. "All kidding aside, someone has to look for her. If you don't want to grow some balls and do it, get some of your people on it. But do it now."

Pete's walkie-talkie screeched to life. "Chief?"

He answered the call. "What's up, Luke?"

"The Renaud woman is back. Papa Joe brought her in. You'd better get here quick."

"It's about damn time. What's her story?"

"She's hurt, Chief."

"What?" Pete jumped to his feet and tore for the stairs down to the dock. Micah was right behind him.

"Papa Joe says she ran into some men burying a body in the swamp. They tried to kill her."

"Holy Christ! Where is she?"

"We just carried her off Joe's dinghy. It's in the last slip down by the picnic area."

"I'll be right there. Alert the sheriff's office and paramedics."

"Already done, Chief."

Pete raced along the wooden pier, hit the ground at the other end and kept on running. Micah spotted a throng of park rangers gathered around a picnic table in the distance. A slim woman sat on top. Fiery-red hair tumbled past her shoulders in thick waves. Blood dripped down the side of her face and her expression was wild. She couldn't seem to focus on the questions being asked of her by the rangers. *Shit.*

He nudged Pete's arm. "Let me handle Remy while you corral your staff. They're scaring her."

"Good idea. She'll balk if I try to help her anyway, won't want me telling her brothers she couldn't handle things herself. See what you can do for her while I question Papa Joe."

They broke through the crowd, Pete giving Remy's hand a squeeze before moving off with an older man and some of his rangers. Micah stayed with her, lightly cupping her chin to catch her attention. She jumped at his touch and tried to pull away. "Easy, honey. You need to lay down so I can look at your injuries."

"I-I don't need any help." She was white as a sheet. A nasty gash oozed over an eye, a bitch of a knife wound creasing her right thigh beneath a bloodied do-rag.

Man, she was out of it if she thought she could walk away with those injuries. "You're probably right, but humor me. Okay?"

Grabbing a bedroll from one of the park rangers, Micah eased her on her back and tucked it beneath her head. She struggled at first, her breathing ratcheting up a notch. She was clearly afraid and confused. "That's it, just try to relax. You're doing great."

Violet eyes blinked wide at him through thick, auburn lashes. He pulled a mini Maglite from his belt and flashed it in her pupils, trying to ignore the pull of those gorgeous peepers. Her gaze reacted to the light, her pupils contracting normally. A good sign for eliminating potential head injuries. But damn, a man could lose himself in her eyes.

Micah refocused on the three bulkiest guys standing close by, figured he'd use them to protect her from prying eyes. Whoever had attacked her could be watching. "You men, move to the far side of the table and block the view from the water. And someone find me a first aid kit."

Grabbing the case a park ranger handed him, Micah went to work. "How are you holding up, Remy? You still with me?"

She jerked when he poured peroxide in the open gash on her leg. "I know it stings, but hang in there."

Pushing the edges of the wound together, he secured them with strips of tape. Next he covered it with a dressing.

"W-who are you?"

He placed some gauze pads over her eye to stem the blood flow. "The name's Micah Rivera. I'm a friend of Pete's."

She laughed, the sound bordering on hysteria. "That's not much of a recommendation."

Micah could see the signs. Shock was setting in, her skin clammy to the touch. Sweat streaked her temples while her teeth chattered. He found a blanket and tucked it around her, touching her wrist to gauge her pulse. Her heartbeat was rapid. *Where in hell are the paramedics?*

Sirens echoed in the distance, lots of them. No surprise there. A body buried on park land was big news. It would attract a lot more attention than just the sheriff and his deputies. Any TV crew worth its salt had already picked up chatter on the police band and was on its way. Not to mention the forensics unit, coroner, and FBI, since Everglades parkland was their jurisdiction.

Pete clamped a hand on Micah's uninjured shoulder, drawing him aside before he could patch up Remy`s head wound. "I need you to stick with her, Mic. I'll have to show the cops and FBI where the body's buried. Papa Joe gave me the location."

Micah gazed at the old man who was back talking to Remy. He had a hunch he wasn't that old and far from feeble. He watched as the guy doused some paper towels in bottled water and cleaned off her face. Then he dressed the cut over her eye like an expert. Military trained, that was for sure—a medic, maybe?

He nodded to Pete. "Remy should leave now, before this turns into a full-blown media circus. The last thing she needs is some reporter plastering her name and face on a late-breaking news bulletin."

"I'll tell her." Pete leaned in close, his jaw tight with concern. "I'm scared for her, man. We've had a serial killer running rampant in Florida for over three years, with no leads. Nine women are missing from this area alone, never mind the rest of the state. If this is what she stumbled onto, Remy's life is in the crapper. Papa Joe told me he saw body parts, and not just from one corpse. And there were two assholes out there in the swamp. One of them got away, Mic. Papa Joe didn't see his face, but he says Remy can identify him."

"Shit. What happened to the other guy?"

"Joe says Remy killed him in self defense."

Micah was stunned. How could a small woman like her protect herself from a killer and get the upper hand? "And you believe him?"

"No reason not to. She's trained in martial arts—Russian Systema. Her parents died when she was ten. Her brothers raised her after that, making damn sure she could handle herself."

"Jesus H. Christ." Micah's gaze slid back to Remy. He knew how it felt to take someone's life. Not something you ever forgot, especially when it was up close and personal. His heart ached for her. She watched him, fear and sadness in her eyes. "Let's move her before the FBI gets their hands on her then. If the dump site holds more missing victims, they're liable to hang her out like a red flag to catch this asshole. And don't kid yourself, he'll come after her."

"My feelings exactly." Pete's gaze cemented with his. "I need you to keep her in the wind until this is over, man. I don't want to know where she is. It's better that way."

Didn't that sound like fun? The pain in the ass woman who gave Pete nightmares had just become his personal problem. Micah mulled it over, wished he could walk away but knew he couldn't. If he didn't make the Renaud woman disappear until the danger was over, who the hell would? Besides, Pete was like a brother, and Micah couldn't refuse him. "Here's the deal. I won't turn her loose until I know she's safe, but after that she's on her own."

"Fair enough."

Remy didn't take the news well when Pete dropped the bomb that Micah was hauling her out of there. She glared at him, a stubborn tilt to her trembling chin. "I don't know you. I don't need medical attention. And I'm staying with Pete!"

Micah understood. She was injured, outnumbered, and feeling coerced. Only God and Remy knew what had happened to her in that swamp, but he was certain she'd paid a terrible price. He didn't want to force her to go with him, but her life could depend on it. So... "Papa Joe, are you willing to tag along with us for the ride?"

The other man glanced at Remy and then back at him. He had to know she wouldn't go without a fight. Glancing at the approaching

SUV's, it looked like old Joe had already figured out the score. He had a protective streak where she was concerned and maybe wouldn't want her used by the law to bait a dangerous trap.

"Get your butt in gear, girl. We're taking this here fella up on his offer."

"But, Papa Joe..."

"No time to argue, missy. We gots to beat boots outta here." He sliced Micah a glance. "Follow me."

Micah scooped Remy up in his arms, pulling the blanket over her face so no one would get a visual if they were spotted. As patrol cars and unmarkeds screeched to a halt and killed their sirens, they pounded for the boat and pulled away. Papa Joe drove under the pier, skimming around pylons as they made it to the far end of the dock past the bar. Reaching his rental SUV without incident, Micah settled Remy on the back seat and secured her seatbelt. Papa Joe slid in beside her.

She whispered to the old man as Micah angled behind the steering wheel. "I hope you brought your bang stick."

"I did. And it ain't loaded with rubber bullets. This time it's the real deal."

Joe's gaze challenged him from the rear-view mirror, grinning around his chewed up cigar. The smile didn't reach his eyes, and Micah figured Joe's weapon was already aimed at his spine through the bucket seat. Yep, there was nothing like riding with an armed ex-military man who felt the need to protect his sidekick—especially when the battered lady's brain wasn't firing on all cylinders.

Not much he could do about it without drawing attention to his vehicle and Remy, since they were sitting in the parking lot of the bar. He cranked the key, deciding Joe wouldn't risk shooting him once he floored it for the exit. The Denali spun on gravel as the tires grabbed and pulled out on the highway. He hit speed dial on his cell phone, splitting his attention between the road behind and cars in front of him, waiting for the line to pick up. Nick Rizzoli answered on the third ring. He was an ex-marine with ties to Micah's Spec Ops squad in Canada.

"Yo."

"Rizzo, I have a friend who needs off-the-grid medical attention in the Miami area. I`m talking X-rays, stitches, shots—nothing that requires surgery as far as I can tell."

"Hold on." Rizzoli came back on the line a minute later and gave him an address in Little Havana. Micah could practically hear his grin over the phone. "Drive around back and someone will let you in. You know, for a guy already on the injured list, sounds to me like you're mixing it up down there."

"It's one of those things that can't be helped."

"Sure it is, you crazy bastard. Wish I was there to join in the fun. I have friends in the area if you need backup."

Micah thought it over, lowering his voice. "If they're anything like Blue and his team who gave us a hand with Rocket's goat-fuck situation in Hereford, it might not be a bad idea."

"I'll reach out. Give me your wish list."

"I'll get back to you from the clinic. There are a few things that come to mind." Micah disconnected the call, looked up to see Papa Joe staring at him in the rear-view. "Is something the matter?"

"Not so far." Joe pulled the cigar out of his mouth, removing a piece of tobacco stuck to his tongue. "You better pray it stays that way."

THE DARK SEDAN KEPT pace with the Denali from three car lengths back. They rolled east out of the Everglades on Highway 41. Sig's best guess? Miami was their next stop. Anger consumed him for the woman riding in the SUV. Did she think she was invincible? That there wouldn't be payback for what she had done? Taking Blade's life was a huge mistake and she had no idea who she was up against. Otherwise, she would have done herself a favor and begged Blade to kill her outright, a no brainer to Sig's way of thinking. But the bitch wasn't smart. She also wasn't aware of the number of men available to avenge Blade's death.

Just like the boys in *Lord of the Flies*, their own group had formed fifteen years earlier at a private boarding school in the Alps. A lifetime ago and so far away—Sig thought of those days as a beloved fairy tale. A case of like meeting like, recognizing in each other the darkness growing within themselves—the desire to maim, torture, and kill. Without being caught, of course.

A bunch of spoiled, troubled kids thrown together by moms and dads who thought 'boot camp' would straighten them out. Make men out of them. And it did, just not the kind of men a woman wanted for her next door neighbor.

As adults—moving on to obtain degrees from the finest universities money could buy—they maintained close contact. Because success in the eyes of the world wasn't enough, and couldn't provide the thrills they enjoyed most.

A smile touched his lips. A great leader needed his team to focus on a common cause, victory being the end result. The woman who slaughtered Blade would be their ultimate prize, her deathblow being the *coup de grâce*. He'd take pleasure in her suffering when the time came, and so would his associates.

Sig laughed, the sound mingling with the piano concerto pouring through audio speakers. He lowered the volume and hit speed dial on his throwaway phone. "Inform the others, Blade was murdered tonight. We're going after the woman who killed him."

The line stayed quiet for a few seconds. "You want us to fly out there?"

"Not yet. I need the tags run on a vehicle first. It's a rental. Find out who's driving it." He gave him the plate number of the Denali and disconnected.

The highway became SW 8th Street in Little Havana. The Denali turned off and hung a left onto 12th Street. Sig hung back, pulled over, and parked when the SUV streaked into the alley behind an emergency clinic.

He reached into the glove box, pulled out his Sig Sauer—the gun that gave him his nickname—and checked the clip, shaking his head. Not enough ammo and too many people inside. Besides, he never worked alone. Better to watch and wait. Find out where they crashed for the night and who he was dealing with. Once he knew that information, he'd contact the rest of his team.

And the game would begin.

Chapter 2

Remy lay on the examination table in a small room of the clinic watching paint peel. Moving on to the cracks in the plaster, she listened to the air conditioner gasp and moan while waiting for the MRI results. Not that she thought anything was wrong with her brain, but Micah Rivera seemed unduly concerned. He told Dr. Sanchez she'd been gun-smacked on the head, and the doctor had ordered the scan at his insistence. Which begged the question; how could a dilapidated clinic afford a state of the art MRI machine? Did most of their clientele come through the back door like she had done and pay top dollar for anonymity?

Her leg and head wounds were already cleaned, her thigh neatly sutured, and bandaged. The cut on her forehead had been glued. Antibiotic and tetanus shots were also done. As soon as the X-ray results were in, she would catch a cab back to Everglades City and her hotel. She could drop Papa Joe at his boat on her way. Once she was dressed, of course. The flowered hospital gown with her fanny catching the breeze wasn't how she wanted to cross the hotel lobby, especially if the police waited to question her.

And they *would* question her, of that she was sure. That's if they didn't haul her off to jail for killing a man, although it had been in self-defence. Still, they might hold her until they completed their investigation, and how long would that take? Her eldest brother, Frank, was a lawyer. Maybe she should swallow her pride and have him go with her to the police station. Oh, wait a second, she couldn't phone him because Micah had pulled the battery from her cell phone and pocketed it. The big bully.

Closing her eyes, she tried to shut out the world and get herself on track. Her body ached. A sick feeling churned the pit of her stomach. Her physical injuries would heal. But what she'd seen in the swamp? Knowing what those men had done—and then killing one of them?

Jesus on a dashboard, how will I sleep at night with those images inside my head? She should have stayed with Pete, like she'd wanted. He would know how to handle this...this nightmare. And lend her a brotherly shoulder to cry on when she fell apart.

A broad hand closed over hers, holding firm when she tried to slide out from under it. When had Micah entered the room? He moved soundlessly for a big man. She'd heard the bass of his voice out in the hall a while ago, wishing she could make sense of his words as he talked on a cell phone.

"You did what needed to be done, Remy. Make peace with it and move on."

Blinking back tears, not her usual way of handling crisis situations, she breathed deep. She had once read it was impossible to cry when inhaling and hoped she wouldn't hyperventilate before she got herself under control. But she was exhausted. It had been one hell of a day.

"I-I took someone's life tonight. How can I move past it?"

"What choice do you have?" Dark eyes burned into hers. His fingers cupped her chin when she tried to look away. "Besides, you know in your heart he'd have done the same to you. Not to mention, how many other women would he have targeted if you hadn't stopped him?"

Micah's expression was intense; the taut set of his square jaw a sharp contrast to his symmetrical, almost pretty boy features. A small scar etching one of his eyebrows offset her initial impression of him—The Good Samaritan—in the right place at the right time to help her out. No way. He wasn't what he appeared to be, was definitely more warrior than Latin lover, or maybe a lethal mixture of both. Who was this man? And why would Pete hand her off to him?

She hadn't needed medical attention so badly she couldn't have waited for Pete to take her to the hospital himself. So something else was at play here. Both men had kept her in the dark, which royally pissed her off. "Are you one of those shoot'em up guys? All guts and glory after you blow someone's head off?"

He shrugged a shoulder. "Why? Because I don't lose sleep over the death of murdering vermin like the one you took down tonight?"

"Yes, that and the fact I really don't know anything about you."

"Honey, I'm just a man trying to make the world a safer place."

"Oh, golly gee. I guess that explains it all." Remy stared at him, pulling herself up to a sitting position on the table. "If you've finished the lecture, please pass me my clothes. I need to get out of here."

Micah reached for the neat bundle stacked on a wooden chair. Her wallet slid from the cargo shorts and fell to the floor with a thump. He scooped it up and flipped it open, staring at her driver's license. His lips curved. "Remington Rose Renaud. That's quite a handle for a small spitfire. It suits you."

She clutched the clothes to her chest, felt sick when she saw the bloodstains on them and smelled their coppery scent. Swallowing hard, she tried for flippant when she still had the urge to burst into tears. "It's what happens when your father's a gun enthusiast, your mother's a botanist, and they choose your name over a bottle of bubbly."

"You mean to tell me your dad named you after a gun?" Micah's smile caught in his eyes, a chuckle rising from his throat. "I'll bet you were born with a hair-trigger temper. *That's* why your father named you after a firearm."

"Maybe, but most people call it colic when their baby fusses and cries. They don't saddle her with the name from hell."

"It could be worse. He might have been into Howitzers or Benellis. Besides, I like it."

"I don't *care* what you like. Now leave me alone so I can get dressed."

"I'd hold up on that." Good grief, a nun sailed through the door and closed it behind her, a very pretty one wearing a drab gray dress with buttons marching down the front. A matching wimple covered her hair, thick stockings and black oxfords completing the uniform. A large crucifix hung from a chain around her neck.

Remy was stupefied. Had someone sent the sister to offer support because she'd killed a man? "I don't know why you're here, but I didn't ask for religious guidance."

"Praise the Lord, 'cause I'm rusty on the scriptures." The nun laughed, holding out a hand to Micah. "Graciella Gonzalez. Rizzo sent me."

Rizzo? Hadn't Micah talked to someone by that name on his cell phone in the SUV? "What's going on?"

Micah ignored her question, shaking hands with the other woman. "You packed up the hotel room?"

Graciella raised her eyebrows. "Of course. Once we exchange outfits, you're good to go. Everything's in the van out front. The keys are in the ignition."

Micah nodded. "Can you get Dr. Sanchez and Joe in here while I explain things to Remy? And tell the doc to bring his auto-injector. He'll know why."

The nun wrapped a hand around the doorknob. "By the way, you were right. You picked up a tail. One guy—he's parked out front in a dark sedan. You want us to handle him?"

"No. He might be FBI. If all goes well, he'll follow you instead of us when we leave. Give us a few minutes?"

Micah swung back to the gurney, placing his hands on either side of Remy's thighs. "I promised Pete I'd keep you safe until they catch the other animal who buried the bodies in the swamp. I don't want any arguments. You need to change clothes with Graciella so we can beat it out of here."

Remy pushed against his chest. Rock solid, he didn't move. "Forget it. I'm going back to my hotel."

He ignored her words, effectively boxing her in with his arms. "We'll leave with some other 'clergy' members, straight out the front door, while Graciella and a few of her associates head out back to the Denali, pretending to be us."

"I don't think so." She shoved him again. He still didn't budge. His face was an inch away from hers. He smelled of sea breezes and clean sweat, an appealing combination if she wasn't so frightened. Where did he plan to take her? Her mind was scrambled, her limbs too weak to use self-defense moves to send him flying. Still, she'd make her own decisions regarding her life, thank you very much.

"I'm not going anywhere else with you, not that I don't appreciate what you've done for me. But I can take care of myself from now on."

"This isn't up for debate, Remy." He held her in place when she tried to ease off the table, a hand tipping her chin until their gazes locked. "You don't have a choice. You're coming with me. So is your pal with the bang stick. He was skulking in the hallway when I was on the phone earlier. He knows too much."

As if on cue, Papa Joe plowed through the doorway, shoving him away from her. "Back off, jerk face!"

Micah had him in a headlock in an instant while Joe cursed a blue streak. The doctor advanced on them both with something in his hand. Remy shrieked, the sound of her voice turning Micah's attention her way, his arms locked around Papa Joe's neck. His gaze said it all, cold and hard. He meant business. "How do you want him, Trigger? Dead or alive?"

"Alive," she whispered.

"Good choice. If he behaves himself, he just might stay that way." Micah nodded to Dr. Sanchez, who injected Joe while Graciella pinned his arm. Remy heard a hiss as something released from the doctor's auto-syringe into Joe's body.

MICAH RELEASED HIS hold and watched Joe stagger and catch himself, barely managing to stay upright. He swayed on his feet, the cigar tipping from his lips. He bounced into the far wall, got this dreamy look in his eyes, swallowed several times, and...burst into song.

"Well, hell. Joe's a Vietnam vet."

Remy nudged him in the back. "What's he singing?"

"*Fortunate Son.* The Creedence lyrics hold special meaning for him. And no wonder. It was a lousy, unpopular war. Those who served didn't exactly return stateside as heroes. In fact, many of them were treated like crap for serving their country."

At least it solved the puzzle about Joe's military background. But while Micah empathized, now wasn't the time for Joe to break the sound barriers and blow their cover.

Graciella and one of her men managed to snag him, tugging priest's robes over his head and switching out his army boots for sandals. She struggled to gather Joe's hair in an elastic band at his nape while he belted out the chorus.

"Joe, shut it!" Micah ran a hand across the back of his neck. Jesus, it was bad enough Remy glared at him like he was Freddy Krueger. But how the hell would he get them out to the street unnoticed with Joe screeching his fool head off?

Dr. Sanchez smirked, palming the wad of cash Micah handed him. "Diazepam. He won't give you any trouble for a while."

"This wasn't part of our deal, Doc." Micah growled. "He needs to turn down the volume."

"Hey, he's feeling relaxed now and found his happy place," Sanchez laughed. "I can't help it if he's running off at the mouth."

"Right." Micah rolled his eyes, watched the doctor exit the room while shoving the Glock Graciella handed him into the waistband beneath his own robes. Not much good if he had to draw it fast, but better than nothing. He gazed at Remy, her face pale and hands trembling. He knew he'd scared her with his move on Joe, but it couldn't be helped. Hell, nothing about this op was normal.

He'd rather be tossing back beers and looking at pole dancers with Pete than operating blind. He missed his team, was used to a well-oiled machine with no surprises. In contrast, this smacked of disaster. Yeah, he'd be glad when he got Remy back on his home turf. Still, he was grateful to Rizzo for sending him Graciella and her boys.

"You'll do." Graciella gave Remy the final once over, satisfied she would pass inspection in the "sister" outfit. She gave her own bloodied costume—Remy's clothes— a pat. Donning a long, curly, red wig over her black hair, she smoothed a bandage on her forehead, another on her thigh, and turned to him. "Carlos and Dom will handle Joe while you focus on Remy. They'll accompany you to the extraction point. Good luck."

"Same goes." Micah shook her hand and eased Remy off the table to the floor. His gut tightened at the contact. He thought about what she wore beneath the "nun" getup, probably nothing but the flimsy hospital gown and her panties. Jeez, the last thing he wanted was to get turned on by Pete's so-called pain in the ass. He was here to do a job. Keep her safe. That was it.

He silently cursed his body for having other ideas, for damn sure she wasn't his type. Too feisty and independent. But those big violet eyes of hers, that tight little body and the curliest long, red hair he'd ever seen packed one hell of a wallop.

"Take your hands off me, you jackass!"

Of course, when she opened her lips, she reminded him of all the reasons she should be off limits and in a faraway galaxy. It had nothing to do with their mutual friendship with Pete. The woman had a mouth on her as well as a stubborn streak, so *not* his kind of woman.

"Don't hold back, Trigger. Tell me how you really feel." He wrapped an arm around her shoulders, his senses wading through her faint, swampy odor to the woman beneath, a touch of lemongrass, field flowers, and class. *Shit.*

"Behave yourself. Or didn't you hear Graciella? There's a creep outside who wants to get his hands on you. You don't want to draw his attention."

"Fine, but as soon as we're out of here, I'm gone."

He didn't say anything, focused instead on moving her out to the hallway. She shuffled more than walked; her injuries must be stiffening her joints. She had to be experiencing some pain. Dom and Carlos snagged Papa Joe between them, the five of them heading to the front door dressed as Claretian missionaries.

Micah scanned the waiting room. It was almost empty. No one pinged his radar. A mechanic—the name of a garage printed on his shirt—held a bloodied hand to his chest while speaking in rapid Spanish to the intake nurse. A family with a glassy-eyed child sat patiently waiting their turn with the medical staff. A couple of gangbangers, one of them with an icepack pressed to his jaw and a gash on his cheek, lounged against the wall in a far corner. He breathed easier. So far, so good. That is until Joe opened his big mouth to sing again, and all eyes turned to them.

For the love of God! He'd blow their cover if he didn't shut it. Micah turned, grabbing Joe by the shoulder while maintaining a grip on Remy's arm. He whispered, "Joe. We're surrounded by tangos, man. Zip your lips."

Searching the room looking for terrorists, Joe hissed. "Where are they? I'll blast 'em with my bang stick."

"We ditched the weapon. It wouldn't fit under your priest's robe. Just keep it cool until we reach the van. Can you do that?"

"Watch me." Joe held up both hands, making "V" signs with his digits as they passed through the lobby. "In the name of the Father, Son, and Holy Spirit, let's all ride the peace train."

Amen to that.

Hot, humid air packed a wallop when they opened the front door to the street. Micah scanned their surroundings, listening to the Cuban rhythm pouring through speakers from a nightclub next door. No one caught his attention when their happy gang continued to the curb. But as they neared the van, Remy balked, attempting to move past the vehicle. Micah tightened his hold. "Settle down."

"This wasn't part of our deal!" She strained against him, almost wiggling free.

Good God, did she really think he'd turn her loose to sashay down the streets of Little Havana on her own? Not a chance. He slid the side panel open on the van and scooped her inside. Carlos tossed Joe in after her, hopped in with them, and pulled the door closed. Micah took the shotgun seat while Dom slid behind the wheel to drive.

Listening to Remy chew him out with a string of curses, Micah grabbed a water bottle from a cooler at his feet—compliments of Graciella—and tossed it to Remy. "Here, rehydrate yourself. You can complain after we're out of here. Right now, I need you to stay quiet."

Reaching under his robe, he eased the Glock into his palm and glanced in the side mirror. The Denali drove out of the ally a few seconds later, hung a left, and headed in the opposite direction. Headlights came on behind the van. The car made a U-turn and followed the SUV.

They were home free. For now.

REMY DIDN'T WANT TO wake up. She was bone tired. Every muscle in her body ached. But the tires hit something with a thump and bounced, the whine of the engine screeching to a fever pitch. The van shook and rattled so much her teeth clanked together. A loud boom crashed overhead. Her gaze flew open and landed on the window, to see nothing but lightning slashing through thick fog and black water churning below them.

Oh, God, we must've hit a guardrail on the highway! We're going to drown!

Hands gripping the armrests—*armrests?*—it took another streak of light to realize she was buckled in a seat on a small aircraft, hurtling at breakneck speed for a wooden dock. The plane landed with another smack on the water. Pontoons fought pitching waves with Micah at the controls, backlit by the eerie lights shining from the cockpit. "Hold on back there! This could get rough!"

Another fire bolt lit the cabin followed by a clap of thunder. The only other passenger Remy could see was Papa Joe, trussed up like a Thanksgiving turkey on the seat beside her. Wild eyed, he mumbled something unintelligible behind the duct tape covering his mouth. She stretched out a hand and ripped it off, her own gaze riveted to the windshield as the plane rocked and reeled to a shuddering halt at the pier.

"Ouch! You dang near tore my lips off." Joe glared at Micah. "And *that* fool laced our drinks with somethin' and hauled us aboard this here flying deathtrap. Quick, untie me!"

Remy wanted to do what he asked but was too afraid to move. Micah shut down the engines, the whine of spinning props silent except for the echo ringing in her ears. The door unlatched from the outside and a hulk of a man boarded the plane. Scooping Joe up in a firefighter's carry, he backed out again. While Papa Joe cursed in his ear, he shouted at Micah. "Let's boogie Mic."

What? Remy didn't have time to think as Micah came out of the pilot's seat toward her, unsnapping her seatbelt and lifting her to her feet. "You too."

Desperate to shake loose from the hand clamping her wrist, Remy kicked him in the shin with her good leg. "Let go of me!"

His expression tightened. "Do that again and I'll return the favour with my steel-toed boots. Now move."

Edging her to the door, Micah handed her off to another man. "Go easy on her, she's been injured."

The man nodded, scooping her up in his arms. He jogged through swirling fog and pelting rain to tuck her inside a waiting SUV. Micah grabbed their gear from the plane, raced through the storm, and slid in beside her, the other man taking the passenger seat alongside the driver. Sandwiched between Papa Joe—who again had tape over his mouth—and Micah, she flinched as the driver gunned it for a muddy track winding between trees bending in the gale. Micah leaned across and snapped her seatbelt in place while she pounded him in the chest. "Let me go!"

"Believe me, I would if I could." His dark eyes met hers for an instant as he brushed raindrops from his hair, his brows locked in a scowl. "We're stuck together like glue, Remy, until we find out what went down in the Everglades. Right now, you're the only witness who can identify a killer."

"The police will protect me," she argued out of desperation. "Take me to them and let me give a statement. Once that's done, the freak has no reason to come after me."

The driver glanced in the rear-view mirror and rolled his eyes.

Micah leaned forward, tapping the other man on the shoulder. "Law, how much time do we have?"

The guy glanced at the dashboard clock. "Twenty minutes to a private airstrip east of here. The airport owner is indebted to us, since we saved his son's life in Afghanistan. He offered us unlimited use of his runway, no questions asked. Hawke's waiting on the tarmac in the Challenger."

"Nice." Micah turned in the seat, scanning the woods behind them. Remy followed his gaze. More lightning flashes, more rumbling thunder, and fog blanketing the forest in every direction. "Stay sharp, fellas."

Remy punched him in the shoulder. "What's going on?"

He ignored her, focusing on their surroundings, the insufferable jerk. Still, she needed answers. Micah frightened her. Yet Pete trusted him. Surely, she could reason with him? "Why won't you take me to the police? I *killed* a man tonight, and they will want to question me. Shoot, they probably want to arrest me!"

Micah's grin flashed white in the shadows of the SUV. "They'll have to find you first."

"What?" She inhaled a breath of fresh air flowing through the vents. Not the Glades, she realized. The air smelled too pure, no swampy odor. It was also too cold, goose bumps rising on her skin. "Where are we? How long have I been sleeping? Let me out of here, you son of a—"

"Let's leave my mother out of this. You've been out for six hours, give or take." Remy continued to struggle and Micah captured her flailing fists, securing them in one of his big hands. "We've just left Lake of the Woods...the Canadian side. We flew across from Minnesota into Ontario. And someone else is flying the plane back to cover our tracks."

Remy stared in disbelief. "You smuggled me out of the U.S. to Canada? *Without* using my passport?"

"No choice." He pulled off his jacket and bundled her into it. His clean, spicy scent in the folds did nothing to calm her nerves. "Besides the fact Papa Joe doesn't own a passport, you need to be out of the spotlight until we have more intel on those swamp murders. I don't want the feds using you as bait to catch their serial killer."

"So? What? You drugged me and dragged me across the border against my will?" Remy wanted to sock him. If only she could free her hands from the jacket to do it. "That's kidnapping and it's illegal!"

"Yeah, well, so is killing women, dismembering them, and dumping their bodies." Micah gazed out the window again, searching the sky. Lord, he was probably scanning for border patrol helicopters. "Hunt? You getting anything?"

The man in the front passenger seat danced his fingers over computer keys. "Nothing, Mic. Looks like the weather blocked infrared and satellite images, just like you planned."

Micah nodded. "And border patrol can't fly in this deluge. So no matter what they think they saw on their radar before we swooped over the water and got swallowed up in the squall, they probably lost us fifty or so miles back."

Hunt logged off his laptop and stored it in a bag at his feet. "Yeah, and the pilot you paid to jockey the plane back to the U.S. will say he was blown off course."

"That's the plan." Micah glanced at his watch. "He's already taken off."

"In a thunderstorm?" she asked.

Micah shrugged his shoulders. "He's a bush pilot. It's what they do."

Hooking Remy's chin with a finger, he turned her gaze to his. Lightning captured the sardonic smile on his lips, the one that didn't reach his eyes. "Face it, Trigger, I've just erased you. Like it or not, you're mine now."

Chapter 3

It had been the perfect ending to a mind-fuck night—fleeing with Remy over the border, the trip in Hawke's private jet to Ottawa, and then the two-hour ride in the SUV to Silver Lake. The only good thing was Papa Joe rode in the second vehicle with Law and Hawke for the final leg of their journey into the Laurentian Mountains. Yeah, it was a big plus, because Micah hadn't heard his nattering after the duct tape was removed from his mouth and been tempted to knock him flat. Instead, he'd had his hands full dealing with a spitfire, worried Remy would jump from the SUV if given half a chance. Lucky for both of them Hunt drove while Micah kept his gaze on her. Luckier too she'd passed out from exhaustion before he'd been forced to restrain her with flex cuffs. It really wasn't in his gene pool to frighten or hurt a woman.

Wired from the trip, Micah carried her down the hall to the first bedroom he came to and laid her on the bed. Slipping her out of the "nun" outfit was no easy task, given she never woke up to give him a hand. Still, he couldn't help but appreciate the muscle definition of her arms and legs in the flimsy hospital gown she wore under the habit, stockings, and serviceable shoes. She packed a few pounds of solid power on her frame for such a small woman, he realized, which had saved her life in the godforsaken swamp—at least long enough for Papa Joe to arrive with his bang stick and get her out of there. Micah's jaw tightened. Thank Christ, Remy was skilled enough in martial arts to kill one of her attackers. Otherwise, she would be dead.

She moaned, curling into a more comfortable position on the mattress and snuggling a pillow beneath her cheek. Micah covered her with a quilt, ignoring the urge to climb in beside her and watch her sleep. He was a red-blooded male, after all, and Remy was a beautiful woman...at least when she wasn't opening her delectable mouth to hurl insults his way.

Forget it. It made more sense for him to hit the rack in another room while she slept, since he'd already been up for more than twenty-four hours.

Cold air pumped through the vents, and Remy suddenly shivered, yet her forehead burned beneath his fingers when he swept the hair away from her face. He also noted beads of sweat gathering at her temples. Neither was a good sign. Jeez, something was definitely off. Had infection set into the stab wound she'd suffered last night?

She needs a doctor.

He about-faced and double-timed it to the living room. Hunt and Law sat in the dining space off the kitchen shovelling food into their mouths, Hunt waving a syrup pitcher over his plate. "Great stacks, Mel. I could eat ten more of these."

"Coming right up." Melena Salera, Theo's little pixie—at least that's what they called her given her diminutive size—poured pancake batter on the griddle, flipping bacon with her other hand while shooting them an impish grin. "Just let me carry these downstairs to Hawke and Papa Joe and then I'll make you another batch. I can't have you guys fading away from lack of food."

Right. Micah snorted. There wasn't a man on his Special Ops team who was less than six-feet tall or weighed less than a water buffalo. They all had enough muscle on their bones to survive for a week living on roots and berries. A hand squeezed his good shoulder, his buddy Theo Sauvage coming up behind him. He nailed him with a concerned glance. "How is she?"

That's how his team worked. No reproach. No beat down over the fact he'd kidnapped a woman and smuggled her into the country, making them all accessories to the crime. Fact was they trusted his decision and would back him up, no questions asked.

"Not good. She's burning up with fever."

Theo pulled out the cell phone clipped to his waist. "Doc Finley can take a look at her."

"Tell him to get here fast." Micah sighed with relief, turning to the front windows while Theo connected the call. He looked out past the wraparound decking, down to the wide expanse of Silver Lake below. Waves rolled into shore from the wake of a passing speedboat, the sleek Tahoe tethered in his boathouse alongside Theo's Bayliner bumping against its moorings.

He supposed it was his boat, given he had bought the place as a package deal, almost sight unseen. An impulse buy after he'd touched down at Melena's cottage with the rest of the team when she'd been threatened by some very connected bad asses, as in joined at the hip to a Las Vegas cartel. Dark times for all of them, ending with a happy conclusion for Melena and Theo, thank the saints. He also remembered the doctor who had tended Mel's wounds at the time. A good man who would zip his mouth shut to keep Remy safe, once he knew her situation.

Remy. She belonged to Micah for now, at least that's what he'd told her, but what to do about her? She butted heads with him at every opportunity, balked and bristled at every turn. Surely, she was smart enough to know she needed him as her bodyguard? But no, Remy Rose Renaud opted to do things her own way, every damn time, while giving him a king-sized headache in the process.

Stubborn. Obstinate. Why didn't she understand the trouble she was in?

"Doc will be here soon." Theo joined him at the bank of windows, handing him a steaming mug of coffee. A hulking man packing lots of muscle and a gun at his hip, Theo was the team's lead sniper as well as a top-notch lawyer. Micah looked at him over the rim of his cup and couldn't help wondering if both his friend's skills would be required on this op.

"It wouldn't hurt to have him take a look at your shoulder while he's here, Mic."

"No dice." Micah rotated the shoulder in question, a smirk twisting his mouth. This was Theo's way of seeing if he was up to the task of protecting Remy. Otherwise, the rest of his team would take over. Give him a pass to head back to Miami and play shuffleboard until his medical leave was up. No fucking way. "Remy's my responsibility and I'll handle whatever needs doing. The rest of you can clear out and cut your involvement. I don't want any of you facing charges because of what I've done."

"Spoken like a true jackass. Did you forget we were there when you took the hit at the rodeo? We know the extent of your injuries," Theo snapped, grabbing him by the folds of the priest getup he still wore. "Brothers in arms, remember? So don't shovel that pile of shit our way because it doesn't fly worth a damn. We're here for you, just like you've always been there for us. In other words...we've got your back...no matter what. So get it through your thick skull before I mop the floor with you in front of Mel!"

"Hey, I'll help with the pounding," Melena said, a sparkle in her cobalt-blue eyes. "Just don't hurt his pretty face."

Theo laughed, backing off only when Micah's cup sloshed coffee down the front of his shirt. He raised both his fists.

Oops, that must burn. "Okay buddy. You guys want to join me in a prison cell, that's up to you. But you're right. I may need your help on this one."

Theo scowled. "Mind telling me why you kidnapped a woman and smuggled her across the border?"

"I can give you the condensed version." Micah swiped a hand across the back of his neck. "It's probable Remy can identify a serial killer in

Florida. She stumbled across a body dump in the Everglades, and one of the perps got away."

"And?"

"Pete Mandel asked me to keep her off the grid. He's worried if the FBI gets hold of her, they'll use her to draw the killer out in the open. That's all I've got, Theo. I can't exactly ask the Feds to keep me in the loop, but Pete will keep tabs on them, let us know what's happening."

Theo still glared at him, holding the shirt away from the skin on his chest. "So, we keep her safe until this bastard is caught?"

"Right, which I'm hoping will only be for a couple days." Micah thought about it, a smile curving his lips. "When is Rocket due to arrive?"

"Tonight. He's bringing Billie with him. They can bunk in with us at Melena's. Sully and Breeana will stay at my place, directly across the bay from here. They can leave their vehicles with you and I'll drive them down the lake when they're ready to settle in."

Yeah, Micah had forgotten his was one of the few houses on the lake with road access. Most people had to park their rides at the other end at the public docks and boat to their cottages.

"That'll work." He crossed to the landline perched on an end table and got a dial tone. He punched in the numbers and waited for it to connect. "Rocket? It's Mic. Just calling to check on your ETA."

Reece "Rocket" Morgan's voice boomed through the line from Alberta, clear and strong. "Hey, man. Glad to hear you're up on your feet again. Billie's in the process of tying off a couple loose ends at the ranch and then we'll head to the airport."

"Listen, can you stop by Rizzo's on the way? See if he'll loan us a dog for the duration? Some of his associates helped us out in Miami, and I'm hoping he'll come through with a guard dog as well." Nick Rizzoli was the best damn dog trainer and handler Micah had ever met. He could use one of his beasts to help protect Remy.

"No guarantees, Mic." Rocket laughed. "But it shouldn't be a problem since I've worked with some of his *kids* before. You have a preference in dogs or will any of his pack fit the bill?"

"Bring me a killer, Reece. Remy's life could depend on it."

REMY STARED AT DOC Finley through dry-as-dust eyes. She had a feeling her lids would crack if she so much as blinked. Skin stretched tight over muscle and bone, her throat was parched, and her head ached. Still, she didn't want to take medication from someone on Micah Rivera's speed dial. She couldn't afford to trust him. "Why do I need more antibiotics when the doctor in Miami already gave me a shot?"

Doc sighed, nudging his fishing cap back on his head, the hair tufting along its edges badly in need of a trim. She thought it a miracle he hadn't stabbed himself with the barbed hooks attached to lures on the hat. "Think of the Glades as a cesspool, Remy, as well as the knife that cut you. I already spoke with Dr. Sanchez in Little Havana, and he gave you a shot of penicillin, which was great for starters. But it's not doing the job and that's why you're running a fever. You need stronger antibiotics to kill the infection."

He pulled a vial of pills from the breast pocket of his *Fish or Cut Bait* khaki shirt and plunked it on the nightstand. "Take one every twelve hours. Don't skip. Be sure to finish the ten-day prescription. Do that and you'll feel better soon."

Resigned, Remy accepted the glass of juice he handed her. She managed to swallow one of the caplets under his watchful gaze, as well as a couple of aspirin. What he said made sense. Refusing his help could land her in the hospital and she wouldn't take the chance. "Thanks Doc."

A knock sounded on the door and a pretty, blue-eyed blond sailed into the room with a knapsack in her hands. "How's the patient, Doc?"

"She'll live, Mel, although she's as stubborn as you were back in the day."

"Well, a hot shower and change of clothes might improve her outlook on things." The woman crossed the room, moved into the bathroom, and turned on the taps. "Be with you in a sec."

Doc winked at Remy, packing up his medical bag. "That's my cue to leave. Don't get the gash on your leg wet. Wrap it in plastic. I'll stop by tomorrow to check on you."

Melena peeked around the corner as soon as Doc left, a huge grin on her face. "Isn't he the greatest? Doc's very old school, but he sure knows what he's doing. He patched me up not long ago, which was very nice of him, considering I practically knocked him unconscious before I realized he and Theo were trying to help me."

She paused for a beat, probably because Remy stared at her in shocked disbelief. Since the attack on her in the Everglades, her life had taken a decided left turn into central casting on a bizarre movie set.

Who is this woman? Where the heck am I and why is everyone acting as if this is the most natural thing in the world?

"Look...I don't mean to be rude, but I don't know you. And I'm confused about what's happened to me since I was hauled out of Florida last night."

"Oh, that." Melena dismissed her concern with a wave of her hand, coming back into the room and plunking herself down on the comforter. "It's simple, really. Micah brought you to Silver Lake because he believes you're in danger. And the rest of the guys are here to make sure you stay safe."

"*That* doesn't tell me anything." Throwing off the covers, Remy tested her legs as she slid out of bed. Still shaky, her muscles hurt, most probably from fighting for her life against a killer. "And what *guys* do you mean? Who the heck are they?"

"Darn, will you look at the time?" Melena glanced at her watch, popped up and almost sprinted for the door, hesitating a moment before pulling a disappearing act. "Um, you should talk to Micah if you have those kinds of questions. I'm sure he'll fill you in as soon as you're feeling better."

"Right. Thanks for the tip." Remy's head felt woozy, whether it was from the fever or her conversation with this nut-bar woman, she hadn't a clue. But one thing she did know, washing the last of the swamp from her body could only help. "I'm going to shower now."

"Good idea!" Melena angled her chin. "I left you some things to wear in the backpack in the bathroom. They should fit. Micah called me from the clinic after sneaking a look at the labels in your clothes to get the sizes. The stuff I found in your own suitcase is running through the washer and dryer. Everything will be ready this afternoon."

"Really? Th-thanks." Okay, so Melena was nice to help her out and so was Doc. But, Micah had taken her against her will, and that said it all. The nerve of the man. While she was being stitched and prodded last night, he was already planning her disappearance, taking her measurements on the sly for a new wardrobe and then cleaning out her hotel room without her knowledge. Graciella had probably done it for him. Could anyone say conspiracy?

She didn't trust any of them. For all she knew, they were a kidnap ring and she would be sold to the highest bidder. Well, that might be stretching things a bit, but she couldn't go along with Micah's plans after he'd pulled the rug out from under her without batting an eyelash.

The water was hot, the shampoo and body wash pure heaven when Remy stood under the spray. And forgot to wrap her thigh in a plastic bag. *Damn*!

Once the water ran cold she towelled off, slipped on underwear, black shorts, and a tank top, thanks to Melena—and yes, the sizes fit her like a second skin. Found a fresh toothbrush, toothpaste, face cream, and a little makeup in the bag with the clothes, and almost felt human again when she left the bathroom. Until she crashed into Micah, who leaned against the wall on the other side of the door.

He steadied her with a hand, seemed to take her in from head to toe with one glance of those mysterious brown eyes. His dark hair hung to his shoulders in wet strands, a sheen of water glistening off his bare chest and powerful legs. He wore soaking wet cargo shorts. All in all, an amazing looking man. Too bad he's a criminal. And a jackass. "Sorry to startle you. Apparently, this is my room. I just came in to shower and change."

"What? You're not sure if this is your room or not?" She felt her eyes narrow and her temper flare. "You know, I might still be wobbly on my feet, but my mind is working fine. You're already wet, and if you don't know if this is your bedroom, then maybe you're the one who needs medical attention."

He arched an eyebrow, the corners of his mouth tightening. "I'm wet because I just swam fifty laps in the lake to get your screaming out of my ears. It was one hell of a night, Remy. And I didn't realize this was my room when I tossed you on the bed because it's the first time I've been in the house since I bought it. Theo says he stored my gear in here and I need my shaving kit and pants."

"Gosh, my heart bleeds, Mic." She moved past him, a glare in her eyes. "Did you ever stop to think if you hadn't kidnapped me, I wouldn't have blown out your eardrums with swear words?"

"You're an ungrateful piece of work, you know that?" His hand shot out, lightly gripping her arm. "If it wasn't for our mutual friend, Pete, I'd toss you back in the swamp in a heartbeat."

"Do it!" He was too close to her now, too masculine, too...everything. Remy didn't know why, but she sensed he always came out the winner, no matter who he went up against. Well, not this time. "Fly me back and let me take my chances. I don't need you interfering in my life!"

Micah pulled her to him, his minty breath fanning her cheek as he whispered in her ear. "You need me, Trigger. You just don't know it yet."

Releasing her so fast she almost toppled over, he strode into the bathroom, slamming the door between them. He left her with smoke pouring out her ears and unsettling thoughts on her mind. No way did she need him, not as her protector and not as a man. *Especially* not as a man.

"Insufferable jerk! I hope you like cold showers!" Remy couldn't help the satisfied smile edging her lips. That is, until she walked by the open cupboard and saw her 'nun' garb hanging alone on the rod. Vague memories of last night's fiasco mingled with humiliation. Micah had done a lot more to her than toss her on the bed when they'd arrived at the house. She'd been too sick to push him away, and she remembered. He had undressed her.

THE HOUSEKEEPER TOPPED off Sig's coffee, gathered up the remains of his lunch, and wheeled the tea trolley inside, closing the patio sliders behind her. She knew his demand for privacy was sacred, that he wouldn't tolerate anyone listening at keyholes. Hell, even his wife walked on eggshells around him, which was as it should be.

A powerful man had the right to control his environment, didn't he? Just as hunting women for sport was necessary to him and wouldn't be denied. After all, his hobby allowed him to be who he was meant to be. And no one would spoil it for him. Not the bitch from the dumpsite, and not anyone protecting her. He'd allowed her to get away after killing his partner. A huge fucking mistake he needed to rectify.

Below him, the ocean glittered with the jewel-toned sails of catamarans tacking across the bay. Waves pounded the rocky shoreline, the muffled roar carried up on the salty sea breeze. He watched a ship heading for open water outside of Miami, its smokestacks glistening in the sun. Perhaps he'd take a cruise with the missus when this was over. She'd like that, and he'd been ignoring her lately.

Sig rolled up his cuffs with a smile and fired off a text message to his assistant—reserve a Caribbean cruise for two, departing a month from today. Then he scooped up the other phone, the one he used to communicate with his hunting buddies, hit speed dial, and waited for the connection. "What have you found out?"

The Dentist—his skill with pliers and a drill was something to be admired—answered in a raspy whisper. "The cops haven't identified Blade yet."

"They won't, unless his wife reports him missing. She thinks he's away on business for a few weeks."

"And he never calls when he's gone." The Dentist paused for a beat. "You're sure the feds can't trace him?"

"We've got nothing to worry about." Sig pulled a gold lighter from his pocket and lit a cigarillo, filling his lungs with smoke. "My source tells me Blade's prints and DNA aren't in the system. Either way, it doesn't matter. Nothing points back to a bunch of school boys from his past. No, the only possible link was his throwaway phone."

"You destroyed it?"

"Of course."

"So once we dispose of the witness, we're home free."

"We're already in the clear, because she can't possibly recognize me. You know my flair for theatrical makeup. Trust me. I was in full *goombah* costume that night, including a wig and face putty."

"Christ." The Dentist laughed. "The chickie probably thought she was staring at John Travolta, straight off the set of *Saturday Night Fever*."

"You got it." Rolling ash from his cigarillo in the ashtray, Sig focused on the reason for his phone call. "What have you got on the car rental?"

"Hold on." The Dentist paused to yell at one of his kids, telling him to leave the room and close the door. "The Denali was a rental registered to a Canadian...Micah Rivera. I did more digging and found out he owns a high-end security firm in Ottawa. He protects government officials and their real estate holdings. Our source up there says he's a big tough bastard and not one to be messed with. Apparently, he's with Special Ops in a reserve capacity when he's not on the job."

"Big whoop—like I'm shaking in my shoes." But Sig appreciated the challenge this guy could offer. Yeah, hunting down the woman had just become interesting. "You got a location where he's keeping her yet?"

"Working on it, Sig. One of our guys is watching his house and says the place is deserted. I called Rivera's office. The guy's totally off the grid. Or if anyone knows where he is, they're not saying."

"Find him. He's hiding her somewhere." Sig stubbed out his cigarillo. "Meanwhile, I'm working on another lead, the forest ranger she was cozy with."

"By the way, you got a name for our lady friend yet?" The Dentist chuckled. "I can't wait to get started on her dental work."

It was Sig's turn to grin. "Our man at the bureau identified her as Remy Rose Renaud. And from what he was able to dig up, she's a feisty piece of work."

"Sounds to me like she's an emancipated bitch who doesn't know her place."

"Well, she will soon enough," Sig said. "We're going to have ourselves a real good time when we run her to ground."

Chapter 4

Papa Joe sat beside Remy on the wraparound deck of the huge cedar and fieldstone cottage. They watched the sun set behind distant mountains, its dying rays sparkling off the bay. The boats moored below them bumped gently against the dock. A fish jumped in the water, ripples flowing outward from the spot where it landed. A ski boat zoomed by towing children in an inner tube, their excited giggles floating on the breeze.

"Well, I guess if the damn fool had to drag us somewhere, it might as well be here." Papa Joe leaned back in a lawn chair, nursing a beer. "Not bad digs, even if it ain't the Glades. I miss the wildlife though."

Remy couldn't help but smile. In spite of his rough demeanor and cagey ways, she had a soft spot for Papa Joe. Maybe it was because he had saved her life, but once Micah pointed out Joe was a Vietnam vet, she knew he was also an honorable man who had somehow gotten lost in the system. Yet, he had risked his life to save hers.

She chuckled, which felt good, since she hadn't had much to laugh about lately. "You mean you'll pine away for the crocs, gators, and snakes while you're here?"

"Them too." He cast a grin her way, blue eyes dancing beneath his white, bushy eyebrows. "I was thinking more of the strippers in the girlie bar I go to on Saturday nights."

Remy held up a hand to halt the conversation. The sounds of vehicles, barreling up the road behind the house and braking to a stop, caught her attention. Car doors slammed and Micah exited the French doors on the level below her to stand on the flagstone path. Hawke and

Theo suddenly materialized on either side of her as Hunt and Law came around a corner of the house with the new arrivals and mile-wide grins on their faces.

"Tubbs! Knock it off!" A big man tugging on what she could only describe as the beast from hell angled his chin at Micah by way of greeting while fighting to control the animal tethered to him by a short, leather leash. Two-hundred-plus pounds—*plus* being the operative word—of snarling jaws resisted the forward momentum and plunked its ample rump on the path.

That is until the dog saw Micah and charged him like a runaway freight train. The leash slipped off the man's wrist. "Look out!"

"Oh. My. God!" Micah barely got the words out before Tubbs knocked him flat on his back and slammed on top of him, jowls shaking and saliva dripping. A menacing growl filled the air as teeth the size of bowling pins closed around Micah's neck. "Rocket, do something! Freaking...hell!"

Remy leapt from her chair, taking the stairs at a hobbling gait to reach Micah. *Please, Jesus, don't let the dog kill him!* She heard distinct clicks as guns were drawn and aimed at the hound. A green-eyed, auburn-haired woman suddenly flew into the fray between the dog and the men, pounding one guy in the chest to get his attention off the animal. "Holster your weapon, Sully. Tubbs is playing with Micah, that's all."

"Oh, for the love of Mike." The man called Sully swept the woman behind him with a quick tug on her wrist. "You have no way of knowing what he's going to do, Bree."

"Of course I do. I'm a vet, remember?" She rolled her eyes, peeked out from under Sully's big arm, and poked his ribs with a finger. "See? His tail is wagging. The big goof is just trying to prove he's the boss. Someone get me a piece of meat and we'll end his power play."

Melena shouted from an upstairs window. "I'm on it!"

She hammered down the outside steps a few seconds later while all eyes remained glued on Micah, flattened like a pancake by what Remy surmised was a ginormous English Mastiff. Muffled swear words reached her ears, the murderous expression in Micah's dark eyes talking loud and clear.

Mel passed a rib steak to Breeana, who promptly plopped it in Remy's hands. "Here, you do it."

"What? I don't know anything about dogs, especially the killing kind." The Mastiff caught the scent of meat. He paused from glaring at his prey, staring at her through calculating eyes as if judging the distance he needed to pounce to get to the steak. An icy chill prickled her spine. Would the dog gnaw her hand off to do it? *Should I save Micah or run like hell in the opposite direction? The running part makes better sense.*

"Remy, pay attention." Breeana nudged her sideways with a jolt. "You're the person Tubbs must learn to protect and obey. Because, as you can see, these jokers don't know the first thing about dog handling, not even Rocket."

"Hold on there, Bree." The Rocket guy stepped to the fore and offered to take the slab of meat Remy clutched to her chest—hoping to hide it from you-know-who. "I've worked with a lot of dogs on search and rescue missions with Rizzo. Hell, I've even tracked down killers with them. Pass me the steak and I'll get him under control in no time flat."

"Oh, for heaven's sake. Stow it, Reece." A willowy, smoke-eyed woman with a mane of blond-streaked curls—Remy guessed this was Billie, Rocket's better half—stepped out from behind Rocket and shot Micah a wave. "Hey, Mic, how are you doing? Don't worry. Remy will have you on your feet again in a jiffy."

Micah mumbled something unintelligible. Remy guessed this was her cue to swallow her fear of the dog with the massive body and square-like head. Joe moved in beside her. "I'd wrastle the beast for ya, but I don't got my bang stick."

"No, Papa Joe. Let me handle it." Inhaling a steadying breath, she passed him the rib steak. "Have Melena put this back in the fridge. I won't reward him for bad behavior."

Setting her shoulders, she stepped forward until her foot tapped one of the big paws wrapped around Micah's head. "Bad dog! Bad, bad, bad!"

Tubbs gave a mournful cry. If she didn't know better, Remy swore she'd hurt his feelings. Scooping the leash from the ground, she gave it a snap. "Tubbs, come! Get over here. Now!"

And, he did, much to everyone's amazement, especially hers. He heaved himself off his quarry, lumbered to her side, and pivoted, assuming a sit-stay position while Micah dragged himself off the flagstone, wiping dog drool from his neck with his shirttail. "That's just great. I ask for a guard dog and this is what Rizzo sends me? And what's with the brute's ridiculous name? He's a powerhouse, man. Nowhere near a tub of lard."

"Tell me about it." Rocket cracked a grin. "Rizzoli was on a Miami Vice kick when he rescued Tubbs and Crockett from a hellhole puppy mill. Shut them down and added two Mastiffs to his training stable a couple years ago. This is Tubbs first foray into the world of guard dogging."

"Forget it, Rocket." Micah shot him a scathing look. "I need a trained mutt and fur face here doesn't measure up. He's on the next flight home."

"No can do, my friend." Rocket crossed muscled arms over his powerful chest. "You know Tubbs can't travel alone. Besides, Rizzo claims he's one hell of a guard dog. Just give him a chance. He'll work out fine, you'll see."

"He damn well better." Micah eyed the brute as if he'd like to boot him to kingdom come. "It's going to cost me a bundle just to feed him."

"Uh, there is one teensy snag." Rocket wrapped an arm around Micah's neck and pointed down to the dock. "You planning to take Tubbs on the boat anytime soon?"

Micah nodded. "That's the whole idea. He can't guard Remy when she's out and about if he's not riding with her. Why do you ask?"

Rocket backed off a few feet, then a few feet more. "Here's the thing, Mic. Rizzo didn't know about the water situation, about you being on a lake and all. And, apparently, Tubbs is scared shitless of water."

"What?" Micah advanced on Rocket with his fists clenched.

"Not to worry, pal. It's all cool." A couple more paces and Rocket was almost to the driveway. "Rizzo says if you want Tubbs to get in a boat with Remy, all you have to do is teach him how to swim. A piece of cake, right? Just give Nick a call whenever you're ready and he'll be happy to talk you through it over the phone."

"You moron!"

Oh brother. Remy watched Rocket clear the side of the house with Micah hot on his heels. The others roared with laughter, except for Billie. She chased after Micah, cursing and swearing. "You touch my man, Micah Rivera, and I'll skin you alive!"

Remy shook her head, gazing down at Tubbs licking the steak juice from her hands with his slobbery, black tongue. *Grrrp?*

"Yes, the men are making fools of themselves. Just pray Rocket makes it into the trees before Micah hauls out his gun and shoots him." She turned toward the French doors, Tubbs turning beside her like a well-trained guard dog. "Meanwhile, let's go find you some dinner."

She hadn't taken a step when a buzzing sound caught her attention. Micah's cell phone vibrated on the path where Tubbs had sent him flying. As she scooped it up, Pete Mandel's name flashed on the screen. He must have news from the Everglades.

MICAH CAUGHT UP TO Rocket, grabbed him, and tossed him through the air. It was the least he could do, given the man had brought him the guard dog from hell.

Rocket hit the lake with a satisfying splash then torpedoed straight up, swearing a blue streak. "That was uncalled for. Just because Tubbs has a few training issues is no reason to take it out on me. You should be blaming Rizzoli."

"Not when it's your fault." Hands on his hips, Micah shot him the stink eye. "And just so we're clear, you'll be teaching the mutt to swim."

"Ah, come on, Mic. Have a heart. The dog will sink his teeth into me if I bring him anywhere near the dock."

Micah flat out laughed. "If you're real lucky, I'll stand by with a first aid kit to stitch you up. Without anesthetic," he added. "You knew you were bringing Tubbs to the lake and you should have told Rizzo. What the hell good is a guard dog that hates water?"

Billie flew down the path a second later. She jumped on Micah's back and sent the two of them flying in the drink close to Rocket. She broke the surface, dragged the hair out of her eyes, and screeched at the top of her lungs. "You leave him alone!"

"Let it go, Billie." Micah pushed her in his friend's direction before she scratched his eyes out. She was all about protecting her man, a hard-as-nails cookie when the need arose. Then again, why wouldn't she be? He'd been around brave, strong women enough to know they could do anything a man could and sometimes do it better, physical limitations aside.

And yeah, he knew Remy was tough and butt-whipping capable, too. He couldn't help the pride swelling his chest as he swam toward shore, knowing how she'd turned the tables on the knife-wielding maniac in the Glades and then killed him with his own weapon. Amen to that. Too bad the other freak had gotten away.

Micah shook himself dry as best he could, climbed the stairs to the deck, and entered the house, heading across the living room to his bedroom and the shower. He stopped cold at the sight of Remy sitting cross-legged on the carpet in his bedroom, a phone pressed to her ear and tears streaming down her cheeks. He felt for the phone clipped to his belt. *Gone.* The same phone Remy now had clutched in her fingers.

And wouldn't you know? Tubbs was in full protection mode, positioned between her and the door. He looked about as welcoming as an Abrams tank. Spotting Micah, his lips peeled on a snarling display of teeth, bringing out the big guns to scare anyone off who had half a brain.

"No!" Micah edged past him, praying the beast wouldn't chomp on any of his essential body parts. He didn't, choosing to growl, shake his head, and cover him with dog drool instead.

Micah laid his wet Glock on a towel on the dresser, grabbed sweatpants off a hook in the cupboard, and ducked into the bathroom to strip down and pull them on. A minute later, he dropped to his haunches beside Remy, easing the cell phone out of her hand. His jaw tightened at the look of desperation in her eyes. Pulling her to him, he tucked her head under his chin to offer as much comfort as he dared. He felt her arms loop his waist and hold on tight.

The problem? She was the principle in an investigation, a woman under his protection. Which meant his "hands-off" policy was non-negotiable. But damn, she felt good wrapped around him, smelling too sweet for his peace of mind. Remy was off limits to him, end of story, and he'd do well to remember that.

Micah forced his attention back to the cellular and away from the scent of her soft skin. Her curves in the skinny top and yoga pants made it near impossible. Pete Mandel's name narrowed his gaze to the screen. What had the park ranger said to upset Remy?

He brushed tears from her face, felt a tremble roll through her. It was a sure bet nothing good lay at the other end of the phone line. "What's going on, Pete?"

"He can't come to the phone right now. This is Frank Renaud, Remy's oldest brother. And just so you know, Rivera, I'm going to kill you when I find you."

Micah shook his head in disbelief. *What in blazes is happening?* Remy shuddered again in his arms. He tightened his hold, her heart pounding a staccato beat against his bare chest. "This isn't a good time, Frank, so if you've got nothing more to say, let me speak to Pete."

"I can't do that." The deep tenor stalled, as if Frank was choosing his next words carefully. "Mandel was beaten to a pulp and left for dead. My brothers and I found him when we stopped by his place searching for our sister this morning."

"Jesus." Micah's gut pitched and rolled. He had no doubt who had done this. Pete was the serial killer's only link to finding Remy. Thank God, Pete hadn't told him anything because he had no idea where she was. "What's his condition?"

"He's on the critical list. A fractured skull and a shot to the leg, among other things. It doesn't look good," Frank said. "He's being treated at Jackson Memorial. The doctors have him in a medically induced coma to minimize any brain swelling. They don't know if he'll make it."

"He will." Conviction burned bright in Micah's soul. His friend was tough. He wouldn't give in without one hell of a fight. Still, he needed protection, and Micah didn't trust cops he didn't know to handle the job, even if they guarded him around the clock. Meanwhile, the Renaud brothers had just stepped into the crosshairs of a lunatic who would stalk them to find Remy.

"Listen to me, Frank." From what he'd heard from Pete, Micah knew Frank and Remy's other brothers wouldn't cave like a bunch of wimps, but they needed to get off the grid. "If you care about your sister and the rest of your family, you'll disappear. This killer is already hunting you if he's monitoring Pete's whereabouts. If he finds your wives and children, you could all end up like Pete. You're Remy's family, the only leverage he's got now to bring her out in the open to finish her off."

"Hold on." Micah heard male voices in whispered conversation—were all the brothers keeping vigil at Mandel's bedside? It made the world a safer place for Pete, but not for any of them. They needed to beat boots out of there while they still had the chance. "Okay, Rivera, you've made your point. We're on the move. I'll call you when we're so deep underground we'll be halfway to China."

"Not from Pete's cell, you won't. Memorize my number. The line is scrambled and can't be traced. Buy a burner phone to stay in contact. I've got a hunch this lunatic is tracking you through Mandel's cellular as we speak. It's what I'd do. Destroy the phone and get the hell out of there."

"We'll be in touch."

Remy dried her face on Micah's chest—which he managed to ignore, barely, and keep his focus where it belonged—as the connection died in his ear. Eyes the color of violets stared up at him. She gave him a tremulous smile, the soul-eating fear evident in her gaze. "I wish I'd killed that bastard in the swamp, instead of letting him smack me on the head with a gun."

"Trigger, there was no *letting* him involved. The animal almost killed you, and would have, if Papa Joe hadn't shot him with the bang stick."

"With a rubber bullet," she said, derision riding her voice. "Enough to knock him out and let me get away, but not enough to kill him. I should have finished him off when I had the chance."

"You're not a cop and you're not Rambo." Survivor's guilt was a terrible thing, and right now, Remy was drowning in it. He guessed the atrocities she'd seen in the swamp had broken her spirit and changed her forever. Still, harboring false confidence in her abilities might only prove deadly. "It's a goddamn miracle you escaped with your life, honey.

You're neither physically trained nor mentally equipped to take out the bad guys. It's enough you're still alive."

She inched away from him and stood with her shoulders back and fists clenched. Micah felt his blood kick when her sunburst of red hair caught the overhead lighting. Which made no sense at all, given Remy wasn't his type of woman.

"Not nearly enough, damn it! And now he's after the people I love." She leveled a look at him that was pure determination. "I'm heading back to the Everglades, Mic. It's the only way to catch the killer and keep my family and Pete safe."

Sure, like he'd let her set herself up as bait to find the guy. No dice. He sprang to his feet and stepped toward her. "Forget it. It's not happening."

In a lightning-fast move, she hauled his Glock off the dresser and pointed it in a two-fisted grip at his chest. "Don't try to stop me."

"Too late." Micah kicked Remy's feet out from under her in less than a heartbeat.

The gun went off.

ONE MINUTE REMY WAS in control, the next she was laid out flat on the floor with Micah on top of her. The gun stretched above her head beneath a muscled arm. Her neck cradled by the hand that somehow managed to break her fall.

"Jesus, woman, what the hell is the matter with you?"

Shock rolled through her in sickening waves, along with the realization she'd nearly shot the pissed off giant of a man sprawled on top of her. Micah pried the Glock from her shaking fingers while she still lay stunned. He tossed the weapon on the bed, yanked her to her feet, and pinned her against a wall.

Reality invaded her brain with horrifying clarity. She'd almost killed the warrior who protected her because she'd flat-out panicked.

The look in his eyes said it all—he thought she was insane. Never mind the fact she wholeheartedly agreed.

And Tubbs? He growled at her as if he'd gone wild and forgotten who he was supposed to be protecting. He nipped at her yoga pants and closed his jaws on her hamstrings, although he didn't puncture the skin. No, he seemed perfectly content to let Micah handle the strong-arm tactics. But how could she blame the dog? He was wicked smart, and even *he* knew she had done a horrible thing.

Heavy boots skidded to a halt in the hallway. Remy's gaze spun past Micah's shoulder to see his friends crowded in the doorway with Papa Joe, some of them pointing guns at her. Mel, Breeana, and Billie were nowhere in sight. She guessed they had taken cover when the Glock went off.

Sully stepped forward, running his eyes over her clothing as if he could search her for concealed weapons with nothing more than a calculating gaze. He seemed satisfied and leaned against the doorframe with his hands on his hips. "You need help in here, Mic? We heard a gunshot."

Micah's focus was still on her. He didn't turn around, just looked straight through her. The disappointment in his eyes shamed her. The anger in his tightly controlled body terrified her. Nostrils flaring, he wrapped a hand around her bicep when her legs gave out from the sudden crash of adrenaline. She was scared to her toes—at what she'd done, and what would be done to her. Would Micah step aside and let one of the others handle her, maybe even lock her up? God knows she deserved it.

Seconds ticked by which seemed like hours. The room so quiet Remy swore she heard a tap dripping down the hall in the kitchen. And still Micah stared at her. Looking for all the world like he wanted to wrap his hands around her throat and strangle her.

If only he would, she thought. The pain in her soul for Pete laying broken in a hospital room and her family on the run from the serial killer was more than she could stand.

Not to mention what she'd almost done to Micah. No, she couldn't face it, except to thank the heavens she hadn't hurt or killed him in her desperation to break free. Did she deserve his anger? Yes, and much, much more. She only prayed he'd be merciful.

His voice was controlled, measured, and smooth when he finally spoke. Oh, but the look in his eyes said something entirely different. "I didn't hear anything, Sully. It must have been somewhere out on the lake. You know how sound travels up here."

So, he planned to punish her himself, didn't need his buddies to back him up while he took his revenge. *Yeesh.*

"That's what we thought." Papa Joe talked around his usual unlit cigar clamped in his mouth. "Just like the stink of cordite in this here room probably floated in through the windows, and there was already a bullet hole in the wood paneling. Must be one of the neighbors shooting squirrels for dinner in this high-fallutin' neighborhood."

Joe's gaze met Remy's for an instant before he looked away, disgust playing across his features. "I'd like to help ya, girlie, but you done outdid yourself this time." He sighed, shaking his head as he turned to the other men. "Come on. Don't guess they need us gawkin' at 'em while they work this out."

Crap. Remy flinched when the door closed tight, leaving her alone with Micah. She knew she was in for it now. Nothing she could say would ever make this right. The desperation she still felt to protect her family and Pete pounded her breastbone, her head close to exploding from the turmoil flooding her brain. Mixed in with the undeniable fact she'd very nearly shot the one person who seemed to care what happened to her. Understood the trouble she was in. A man she liked, probably more than she should. Misery times a thousand and then some, because she'd betrayed his trust.

She wanted to die, wished he'd just kill her and end the agony. Then she wouldn't feel this gnawing pain at the grief she'd caused so many people. God, if she'd only listened to Pete when he'd offered to be her guide in the Glades, none of this would have happened. She wouldn't have been in the wrong place at the wrong time. But it was never her style to admit she might need a helping hand. She'd been stubborn about it, driven to stand on her own two feet rather than let Pete help her do her job.

She inhaled a shaky breath, raising her eyes to face Micah and the music. To confront the man she had wronged in the worst possible way, the same man who had sacrificed, done things that were even illegal to help her.

He studied her now like a predator about to flay its prey. Well, she had it coming in spades. Still, a shudder ran through her from her head to her feet. "You don't have to say anything, Micah. Let's just get this over with."

"What are you talking about, Remy?" He brought a hand up under her chin, resting it against her neck. "You think I'm going to hurt you?"

"Why not?" She flinched at the feel of his calloused fingers on her skin. "I almost killed you."

He inhaled hard, exhaled soft, his mouth flattening in a grim line. "Hurting women isn't my style. So what do you suggest I do instead?"

"You should make an exception in my case. Then we'll both probably feel better." Tears welled in her eyes. One fell, tipping over her bottom lashes as she blinked to hold it back. He brushed it away, watching her through those oh-so-serious dark eyes. "But, please. Let me go back to the Everglades to face this madman after you've finished with me. It's the only way I know to stop him from killing my family."

Micah slid his hand under her hair to the back of her neck, pulling her closer. "Facing him down won't do any good. If this guy was monitoring Pete's cell phone, he already knows you've spoken to your family and could have given them a description of him. No, he'll still go after them, even if he manages to kill you first."

"You can't know that for sure."

"Yeah, I can, because it's what I would do. I've dealt with monsters like him before. I know how he thinks and what he's capable of."

"Look, I have to do something. I can't just sit here and wait for him to murder someone else."

"We are doing something," Micah said as he tugged her toward the bathroom. "I'm calling Graciella to have her and her team keep eyes on Pete in the hospital. I also need her to keep her ear to the ground—I need intel on this bastard. Then I'm taking a shower."

"A shower? Be serious. Let go of me first." Remy tried to wriggle free from his grip, but he just dragged her along behind him like a ragdoll. "I'm not taking a shower with you."

"No? That's probably wise, considering your stitches. But I'm not leaving you on your own so you can shoot somebody else and steal a vehicle." A smile curved his mouth as he snagged the belt loose from a bathrobe hanging behind the bathroom door. In a lightning-fast move, he looped her wrists in the sash and tied her to the shower frame on the outside of the glass.

She wanted to kick him, would have too, if the stitches tugging at her thigh didn't burn like the devil. "You miserable son of a—"

"Don't say it or I might have to spank you. My mother, bless her heart, is sacred to me." Micah grinned at her as he made the call to Graciella in Miami to arrange protection for Pete. Then he dropped his sweatpants, sauntered past her into the shower stall, and turned on the jets.

Remy swallowed hard, telling herself she wouldn't watch. Impossible to do in a room walled with mirror tiles, especially considering the extraordinary view. Damn the man and his arrogance—and his magnificent warrior's body.

"You know, you're not showing me anything I haven't seen before. I was raised by four brothers, remember?"

"That's good to know." Micah laughed in his deep, throaty bass. "Hey, Trigger, you don't snore, do you? 'Cuz we'll be sharing my bedroom from here on out, since you can't be trusted to behave yourself. I can't cut you loose until we know what's happening in Florida."

Chapter 5

"I have to take this call." With the cell phone vibrating in his hand, Sig left the conference room full of engineers and architects and moved out to the lanai. The verandah offered him privacy as well as an excellent view of his new Hawaiian resort.

A lesser man might have shown more interest in the construction of his hotel on the shores of Hilo Bay, but Sig had another priority that took precedence. He didn't notice the idyllic scenery or the sounds of heavy machinery sinking support beams. He didn't give a rat's ass about any of it right now. The Renaud woman was still in the wind, and he needed to find her fast. *How hard can it be to find one bloody female?* Apparently near to impossible.

Christ, even he had struck out with the forest ranger. He flexed a fist and released it, noticing the healing scrapes on his knuckles. Pete Mandel must not know her location, otherwise he would have spit it out, considering the beat down he had suffered at Sig's hands. And monitoring his cell phone had been a total waste of time. The one call that went out had been scrambled, the signal impossible to trace. Then the phone had died.

But the icing on his shit storm cake? Remy Renaud's brothers had disappeared like smoke after connecting that call from Mandel's hospital room—a call to their sister, he was sure. Yeah, the bastards had scooped up their families and bugged out in a heartbeat. He had people searching for them, but so far no leads on their location.

"Talk to me. This had better be good."

"Oh, it is, Sig," the Dentist assured him. "I think we've found her."

"It's about goddamn time. Where is she?"

"She's off the grid in the mountains. Somewhere in Quebec, a place called Silver Lake. Micah Rivera's got a seasonal residence there. It's a new acquisition that only came to light when we did a second search of his holdings."

"Nice work, but how do you know she's there?"

"I'm sending you a snapshot Ice-Pick took with a telephoto lens. He flew up there as soon as we heard. Recognize anyone you know?"

Sig viewed the photo as it uploaded to his phone. He inhaled a deep breath to calm his nerves. Remy Renaud stared out at him, a hand shielding her eyes from the glare off the water. She looked as pretty as he remembered. A freaking wet dream for a man of discerning tastes like him.

"That's her." The thrill of the hunt thundered through his veins. His prey was finally within reach. He wanted her badly, couldn't wait to finish what he'd started in the Glades. "I'll fly back to Miami tonight and on to Quebec tomorrow."

"We'll be ready. Ice-Pick rented cottages on the lake under a dummy corporation." The Dentist chuckled. "Apparently, there's a regatta taking place next weekend and the area is flooding with tourists. We should blend right in with the rest of the crowd."

"I wouldn't bet our lives on it. Micah Rivera is trained by the military, which means he's neither a pussy nor a fool. He'll scope out everyone, probably even run background checks, which could work to our advantage, since we're all squeaky clean. Still, we have to play it smart until we're ready to make our move."

"Just how do you suggest we do that? Stay out of sight in the cabins?"

"No. Shut up and I'll tell you." Sig laid out his plan in finite detail, the dentist responding with monosyllabic grunts.

"Shit, I don't like it. We've always hunted alone."

"You mean we've chased down women who couldn't fight their way out of wet paper bags. But this bitch is different. She has skills...let's not forget how she killed Blade. She also has a bodyguard who is well trained. And there could be others. We need a smokescreen to cover our tracks."

"Then maybe we should wait it out," the Dentist said. "A few months from now and she'll be yesterday's news, and so will the body dump in the Everglades. Why not go after her when things calm down?"

"You're not getting it." Sig loosened his tie before he choked on his saliva. He had no patience with fools who weren't able to see the big picture. "Every law enforcement agency in the U.S. is searching for her. If they extend their search into Canada, get lucky, and find her, they'll drag her back to Florida, staking her out like a sacrificial goat to catch us."

"Exactly, Sig, which means we'd have a better chance of nabbing her."

"And what about the hundreds of cops and agents with eyes on her twenty-four/seven, waiting for us to make our move?"

"Fuck, I see your point."

"Damn right you do. Look on the bright side. Either way she's the crown jewel of challenges. But pitting our skills against Rivera and taking her out from under his nose? Think how much fun we could have. It would be one hell of a thrill ride. Make the game interesting and the prize that much sweeter. Besides, this is our best chance to succeed and get away clean."

"Still—"

"Just do what I tell you and spread the word."

"Look, man, I don't like it and neither will the rest of the crew."

"I don't give a shit. You want to avenge Blade's death and nail the bitch—this is how we do it."

Disconnecting the call, Sig sat down in a chair and lit a cigarillo. No worries. The others would fall in with his plans because they craved revenge and would enjoy the kill.

Hitting speed dial on his other phone, he dialled his pilot. He had a lot to arrange before heading to Silver Lake tomorrow. "Have the jet fuelled and standing by. We're flying back to Miami in a few hours."

Next, he called his assistant to clear his calendar for the next several days, blaming it on a family emergency. Hells bells, he had enough people working for him who could manage the day-to-day functions of his company until he returned.

He sat back in the chair and forced himself to relax, a smile curving his lips. It wouldn't be long before he came face-to-face with the woman who got away. She would pay for that, and for killing Blade.

MICAH SIPPED HIS COFFEE, staring at the mist floating off the lake. The water gently lapped against the shore, relaxing him as the sun rose with the promise of another beautiful day. Sure, except for a couple of things—Remy tearing a strip off him after he'd flex-cuffed her to the bed last night was one. And she wasn't exactly his best friend this morning.

He knew she wouldn't thaw toward him anytime soon without an incentive, and frankly, her chilly stares and wounded expression made him feel like a total jerk. What he needed was an ice breaker to get them back on the same side.

Rocket joined him on the pier, tsking into his mug. "Looks like Mel, Bree, and Billie have joined Team Remy. They're giving all of us the cold shoulder this morning. Hell, Billie even stuffed pillows between us in the bed last night and refused to kiss me. You're ruining our relationship, pal."

"As if I have a choice." Micah felt bad enough as it was. Restraining Remy wasn't his idea of a good time. "God knows what will happen to her if she shakes loose on her own. I can't take the chance."

"Then you'd better get used to eating cold cereal and peanut butter and jelly sandwiches. The ladies are on strike, or at least that's what Breeana told Sully before she stomped back to their room and locked him out. She says you're a big bully, and so are the rest of us for letting you shackle that little hellion."

"Hmm, that's a few steps up from what Remy called me. The woman knows more swear words than I do."

"Which says a lot." Rocket laughed. "I learned a few new ones myself last night after lights out. It's a wonder you got any sleep at all bunking on the floor in her room. Fool woman was screaming her head off."

"Earplugs," Micah said, cracking a grin. "Let me know if you need some tonight."

The dock vibrated with heavy footsteps. Sully joined them, handing Micah his cell phone. "I got through to Nick like you asked, but he's pissed we disturbed his beauty sleep. We forgot about the time difference—it's only five a.m. in the Rockies."

"Like I care." Micah grinned and took the phone. "Listen, Rizzo, I'm doing you a favor by teaching the mutt how to swim. The least you can do is hold up on the snark and tell me what to do."

He held the phone away from his ear while Rizzoli launched into a tirade before finally getting down to the business of dog training. Micah listened hard, not liking where this was going, but determined to give doggy swimming lessons a try.

He noticed Theo and Hunt jogging down to the water carrying deck chairs and spreading them out along the shoreline. Law and Hawke followed behind them, placing coolers beside the chairs.

Papa Joe brought up the rear carrying two trays loaded with sandwiches. "I whipped these up afore the gals booted me out of the kitchen. I had to run like the wind when Melena pulled a carving knife out of a drawer. Dang women are prickly as porcupines this morning. Go figure."

Micah handed Sully his phone back and glared at all of them. "I suppose you think this is funny and you morons are planning to enjoy the show? The fool dog will probably kill me before I even get his tootsies wet, and here you are with front row seats."

"We can but hope," Sully said, giving him the stare down. "Maybe if he does, Bree will forgive me for letting you manhandle Remy last night. I knew we should have stayed at Theo's cottage instead of protecting your ass."

"All I know is we better have some decent shut-eye tonight, or you're dead even if the dog doesn't drown you," Hunt growled.

Theo punched a fist into an open palm. "Yeah, you nixed my love life big time, Mic. Melena won't even talk to me. Remind me to break your face later."

"Relax guys. The whole point of this exercise is to make Remy laugh and feel better, right? Come on, Mic, it's obvious you don't have a chance in hell of teaching Tubbs how to swim." Hawke sank into a chair, hooking a leg over the armrest. "But, trust me. She'll feel a whole lot better after the dog kills you. And so will the rest of us."

"You're all a bunch of cream puffs and whiners—who needs you?" Micah strolled to the boats bumping the dock, leaned into the Tahoe, and hauled out the biggest life vest he could find. "Watch and learn, oh ye of little faith. Here Tubbs! Come on, boy!"

The dog pushed through the screen door and ambled down the stairs, stopping just short of the dock. He parked himself like a cement truck on the path and waited.

"Good boy." Micah walked up to him, lifted a heavy paw, and began the process of wriggling the beast into the life jacket. He managed to get it on him and secure the straps down his back, just like Rizzo had told him to do. *So far, so good.* "You're set to go, buddy. What do you say we have ourselves a nice romp in the lake?"

Tubbs peeled back his lips to display his canines. *Grrrr.*

"Or not."

Remy and the other women had congregated on the deck. She glared at Micah over the railing. "What do you think you're doing to Tubbs?"

"Teaching him how to swim and I could use your help. Could you come down here and lend a hand?"

"Why not? I need a good laugh." She sashayed down the stairs. Billie, Mel, and Bree followed. Remy came up to Tubbs and patted his big head. "Hey, baby. If you go down to the water like a good dog, I'll let you tear Micah to shreds. You can even eat him for breakfast to cut down on the food bill. What do you say?"

Tubbs angled his head as if questioning her words. *Grrrp?*

"Yes! That's right, sweetie-pie." Remy's chuckle sounded evil to Micah's ears. "Pieces of Micah coming right up. Let's do it."

Tubbs shook his jowls and sprayed the usual gallon of saliva, rose from his haunches, twitched his steel cable of a tail, then sauntered after Remy to the water's edge as pretty as you please. Micah used his secret weapon, strips of cooked bacon hidden in the pockets of his cargo shorts, feeding them to the Mastiff while he moved into the water and slowly backed away from shore. Tubbs followed, intent on the treats, and not the lake bottom, until it vanished beneath his feet. In the time it took to say *oh shit, this is a really bad idea,* Tubbs panicked, his massive paws on Micah's shoulders as he tried to heave himself out of the water by climbing on top of his head.

"Oh, Miiicaah?" He could barely hear Remy's musical lilt over all the guffaws, most of his team bent over and laughing their guts out. "I sure hope that life vest was tested for at least five hundred pounds of man and beast. Otherwise, you're going to have a big problem."

No kidding? He was eye-to-eye with Tubbs now, who looked like he wanted to kill him but was too afraid to make a move. Yeah, the whole water thing had him stymied. Thank God. "Okay, boy, it's time to quit acting like a wimp and grow some *cojones* before you embarrass yourself."

Micah dropped down and out from under Tubbs flailing back legs, his neck feeling like a pincushion where the mutt's claws had raked him. He came up ten feet away and called the panicked dog. A miracle happened. Big paws moved in his direction, Tubbs propelling himself through the water like a tugboat. When he reached Micah this time, he didn't leap into his arms, instead he swam circles around him, lapping up the water with his mile-long tongue.

A whoop went up from the crowd on the shore, Remy's voice leading the cheer. "Tubbs! Tubbs! Tubbs!"

She grinned at Micah, making victory signs with her fingers in the air. "Hot damn! I didn't think Tubbs could do it! You're amazing, Micah Rivera. I'm going to call you the dog whisperer from now on."

"Don't go crazy with the kudos yet, Trigger, at least until I try him tomorrow without the life jacket. We'll see what happens then."

Micah felt a burst of pride at the joy on Remy's face—because he'd put it there—and he felt something else, a tug on his heartstrings, which was goddamn ridiculous. Praise from her was more than he'd hoped for, so he'd leave it at that. Whatever else he might feel, he didn't want to examine too closely. It was enough if they could forget about last night's fiasco and work on trusting each other for a change.

Instinct warned him the bottom was about to fall out of Remy's world, bringing with it the worst kind of evil. He knew he was right. Couldn't explain how or why he knew, but the serial killer had found her, there was no doubt in his mind. How the hell had he tracked her?

Micah glanced at Hawke—the only man among them who had the *Woo Woo* gene going on. Facts were facts. All the guys knew Hawke had some kind of psychic ability. The guy could read people inside and out, as well as pinpoint a dangerous situation before it happened. While he never talked about it or acknowledged it, he had saved their lives more than once by giving them the heads-up in enemy territory.

Hawke met his gaze now with an almost imperceptible nod. He'd felt it too. Trouble hung in the air like a bad smell. The other men picked up on their silent exchange without missing a beat, Theo touching his sidearm. Even Papa Joe seemed to understand something was wrong, although the women seemed oblivious, still laughing at Tubbs's antics. Micah guessed it was a military thing, the hair rising on the back of the neck, the feel of an ill wind blowing through.

Joe approached as he dried himself off on the dock, the ladies fussing over Tubbs up on the sundeck. "If I'm reading this situation right, you're gonna need another pair of hands real soon. So, I figure I'll speak plain so you understand. When you unlock that gun room of yours, I'll be standing first in line to get a weapon. There ain't no need to worry, Mic. I won't let you down."

"How do you know about the gun room?"

"You yankin' my chain after the stunt Remy pulled with the Glock last night? Your team hightailed it for the kitchen with a ton of weaponry while you was settin' her straight in the bedroom." Joe scratched the stubble under his chin, cracking a grin. "Guess they didn't want her helping herself to another gun. Now, I didn't find no assault rifles in the dishwasher this mornin', so I know they stashed 'em somewhere."

Micah stared at him long and hard. The guy had murder in his eyes, and he looked tough as nails. There was no point in feeding him bullshit he wasn't inclined to swallow. He called Sully over instead and quietly gave him the rundown of their conversation.

"I hear you're a Vietnam vet," Sully said, hands on his hips.

Joe rolled on the balls of his feet, but faced Sully square on. "Yep. That's a fact."

"Micah says you can hold your own, and I'm inclined to believe him. God knows, you already saved Remy's life in the swamp."

"Ain't nothin'. Any of you would've done the same."

"Maybe so, but we could use another good man on this one." Sully held out a hand and Joe shook it. "Welcome to the team."

REMY PACED BACK AND forth on the sundeck, watching Micah on the dock in a football huddle with Sully and Papa Joe. Their body language spoke volumes. Something wasn't right. Whatever was bothering him, Micah didn't want her to know about. Otherwise, he wouldn't keep raising his head to scout her location. She'd sneak down there to eavesdrop if she thought it would do any good. But he was too smart to let her get close to them, so she walked the deck instead.

Micah. She had nearly suffered a coronary last night when he'd taken that shower in front of her. His sculpted body made it impossible for her to look away—and he'd been aroused. Difficult to hide in a room full of mirrors, and oh, so amazing. And disappointing, because he had no intention of flirting with her, or...

Instead he'd tossed her one of his oversized T-shirts after he left the shower, given her five minutes alone in the bathroom to get ready for bed, and tied her to the bedpost with flex-cuffs. A daisy chain of flex-cuffs, because he hadn't wanted her to be uncomfortable during the night with a wrist pressed tight against the headboard. So, yes, he was gentle, but that didn't make up for what he'd done.

"See something you like?" With her French-Irish temper overriding good sense, Remy had teased him by opening her legs on the mattress. *That's right. Move closer so I can kick your balls blue for ruining my escape plan.*

But Micah was nobody's fool. He had looked at her, arching an eyebrow as if she was as transparent as gossamer wings. "It's the best offer I've had in a while, Trigger, but not worth the price of admission."

For a split second, she'd seen heat glowing in his eyes, but it had burned out with a sizzle. Then he'd covered her with a quilt, tossed a bedroll on the floor, and turned out the lights, while she was left to stew and feel slighted because he hadn't wanted her, or cared enough to hold her in his arms. In fact, he'd treated her like a royal pain-in-the-ass. And she'd screamed her head off for most of the night to get even.

She regretted it now, but there was no going back or starting over, because first impressions counted. She'd fought Micah's kindness every step of the way. Almost shot him, and no doubt damaged his eardrums by using swear words that would shock the worst of sinners. It was what it was. Micah thought her a miserable, thankless witch, and it broke her heart. She flinched when he touched her. When had he climbed the stairs to the deck?

"I didn't mean to startle you." He kept his hand on her arm, soothing her skin with the pad of a thumb. "What's with the sad, puppy dog eyes? You look like you've lost your best friend."

She tried to smile. A tear betrayed her. She brushed it away, but more tears gathered, spilling over her lashes. Damn it, she never cried. "I guess I'm just tired. I was so busy yelling and making your life miserable last night, I forgot to get some sleep."

Micah didn't say anything when she turned away, feeling humiliated and hurt. She hugged her arms to her chest and gazed at the water, trying so hard to get the right words out. "I behaved badly. You were trying to help me. Keep me safe. And I acted like a queen bitch. I'm sorry, although I know it isn't enough."

"I believe you really mean that." He turned her around, tipping up her chin to catch her gaze. His breath ruffled her hair, the clean scent of him drawing her in. She felt herself sway. In an easy movement, he wrapped an arm around her waist and tucked her against his body. Then he opened the screen door. "Come inside. You definitely need a nap. You're out on your feet or you wouldn't feel the need to apologize."

The living room was empty when they walked through to the bedroom. Probably a good thing, Remy realized. Her newfound girlfriends would pitch a fit if they thought Micah was tying her to the bed again.

But he didn't. He closed the door behind them, sat her on the side of the bed, and slipped off her sandals. "Crawl under the covers and I'll pull the drapes."

She flopped on the bed, covered her face with an arm, and bawled like a baby. For the dead women in the swamp, for Pete lying in the hospital, for so many reasons, and she couldn't control it. Until Micah's weight touched down beside her. Her eyes flew open and she hiccupped, wiping her eyes with her hands. "What are you doing?"

"Easy." He kissed the top of her head and gathered her to him, tucking her into his shoulder and rubbing lazy circles down her back. In no time at all, she felt the tension ease, although her tears still dampened the soft cotton shirt pressed against her cheek. "That's it, honey. Let it all out."

Exhaustion seeped into her bones a few minutes later, the soft cadence of Micah's voice and the safety of his embrace coaxing her under.

Chapter 6

Micah cracked his eyes open to find Remy sprawled on top of him, her fiery-red curls tickling his nose. Arms wrapping his ribcage, she held him in an iron grip, squeezing as though in the throes of a bad dream. Her lips parted on a terrible whimper. With a frightened shriek, she jerked, and rolling off him, tumbled across the bed, heading for the floor.

"Remy!" Micah went with her, circling her waist and landing on his back in a tangle of limbs and sweet woman. He turned her toward him, wiping a bead of moisture off her temple. "Wake up, honey. Are you okay?"

"Micah?"

He swallowed hard at the sound of her husky voice. She was still half asleep and seductive as hell, not good for his knight-in-shining-armor routine. Save the woman and leave her untouched. That was his motto when it came to her.

Elbows jabbing his chest, she brushed at the wild mane of hair hanging in her face. They lay glued together like lovers. Still on top of him, she looked down at him, her startled gaze meeting his own. Man, she had such beautiful eyes. He could easily drown in them. Dive right in and never come up for air. But he knew when to hold the line, and this was it. There was something else in her gaze, though, that set off his alarm bells. Need.

Not good. He knew that look, recognized it for what it was. When he was deep behind enemy lines, sex on the fly was sometimes the only thing that got him through. So yeah, some mindless action with a willing partner reaffirmed life in the trenches, and he could identify. Yet, the knowledge jarred him when applied to Remy. She was living in hell, the serial killer...her Armageddon.

He knew about the dismembered bodies she'd seen in the swamp. The man she'd killed in order to save herself. Worse than that was the bastard who was still out there. He'd tortured Pete to try to get to her. He'd keep on coming, Micah had no doubt. It was only a matter of time before he made his move. She was the single witness against his crimes. He wanted her dead. And she wanted—*needed*—to forget the horror.

He couldn't let that happen. Micah knew it like he was looking at her. Physical release would banish the boogie-man for a while. But after the dust settled, she would regret acting so rashly. Hate him for taking advantage in her moment of weakness. How much he wanted her shouldn't matter.

But, Jesus.

His mind fought the pull. His fingers had other ideas, tracing the silky skin where her top ended and the waistband of her shorts began. He stilled, clenching his hands into fists. Not this woman and not this time. She deserved better than a one-time hurrah.

She lowered her eyes as if realizing her thoughts played across her face like a movie prequel. "Why are we lying on the carpet?"

How about because I'm too scared to move? I don't want to play you, and I sure as hell don't want to be played. I'm trying to do what's right here.

"You had a bad dream."

He brushed a kiss across her mouth, a mistake that shot clear to his groin. He knew better. Not only was she off limits because of the danger factor, but she drew him in and laid him open like a psychiatrist's wet dream. The pull of sexual chemistry? Sure, he could provide her with release and let her down easy, if that was all it entailed. But he didn't do feelings or relationships. And he couldn't afford to push his luck on the emotional scale by cuddling her another minute.

She touched him in ways he didn't understand, and that frightened him like nothing else could.

The temper she wielded to disguise her pain, and fear layered beneath it, made him want to hold her. Her refusal to acknowledge what killing a man had cost her made him want to cry for her. The stubborn tilt of her jaw when she took on the world, hiding the uncertainty and loneliness buried deep inside, tore him to pieces. He knew how she felt and what she wanted. But he couldn't help her through it. Be her hookup and then her best pal, maybe with benefits. Trading confidences, emails, and Christmas presents. She meant too damn much to him.

He chose his sexual partners for sex. Hot, steamy, bump and grind, that was it, that was all...just sex. Remy was different, had been since he first laid eyes on her. The stab of jealousy he'd felt when he thought she was Pete Mandel's lover had blown him away. Defied logic, as did his temporary insanity while undressing her when he'd first brought her to the cottage. Remy had been sick, feverish, and out for the count. Yet he'd wanted to crawl in bed beside her. Not to make love with her. But *hold* her and keep her safe from the world. So, no, he needed to end this before it began. Or next thing he knew, he'd be buying a gondola and singing her love ballads.

"You had a nightmare, took a tumble off the bed, and I went with you. Simple as that. I didn't want you hurting yourself when you hit the floor. Roll off me and I'll help you up."

"Hmm, not just yet." She planted a trail of kisses along the side of his neck. Then she let out a breathy sigh, snuggling into his chest again. "I don't remember the bad dream, but thanks for the soft landing. Well, maybe not so soft, considering your rock-hard muscles. And something else that's poking me in the stomach."

Way to keep things under control, asshole. Much more of this and Micah would forget the reasons why he couldn't touch her. "Move off me, Trigger."

"No. I like it here." She pouted, a hand sliding under her tummy to caress the bulge in his shorts. "And I know I'm going to love this."

Jeez, she had him in her palm before he could stop her. She tugged up his shirt with her other hand, kissing her way from his collar bone to his navel. "Remy, cut it out. We can't—"

"Ah, but we can."

"Listen, there are other people in the house." Grasping at straws, Micah didn't give a fig if the Dalai Lama was bunking in the next room, but maybe she would. "They'll know what we're doing,"

She ran her tongue over his bottom lip, still stroking him below the equator. "You mean making love?"

And they *were*. Micah tasted her tongue in his mouth, the scent of sunshine and coconut on her skin tumbling him further down the rabbit hole. He was lost, or maybe he was found. Nothing else mattered but Remy and this moment. He cursed his weakness as he flipped her onto the carpet. Ran a hand under her tee to unclasp her bra and expose her breasts. His lips closed on a budded nipple, his conscience silent as he took command.

Remy was onboard. She slid a leg over his hip, gripped his shirt, and ripped it open. "Hurry, Mic. Please!"

"Not yet." Hooking a finger in her waistband, he teased her panties and shorts off. Found her center. Hot. Wet. Tight. He held her open, touching her with his mouth, his tongue. Wanting to give her bliss. Devour her from head to toe. Learn what drove her insane.

But her honeyed taste in his mouth, the feel of her contracting around his fingers, and primal need became greater than drawing out the pleasure. Hers. His. Right or wrong. They both needed this more than their next breath.

Micah rose to his feet and stripped down while she watched him. He crossed to the bureau, pulled out a condom, and suited up. Scooping her in his arms, he landed on the bed, staying near the edge and wrapping her around him. She positioned herself, slowly sliding

down his body until he sat inside her to the hilt. A perfect fit. He was
home, emotional pitfalls be damned.

Capturing her mouth to quiet her moans, he held her perfect butt
in his hands while she rode them both to peak. Their world exploded as
if the sun and moon collided, like he knew it would with this woman
in his arms. Then he lay her down and loved her as she deserved.

It was a slow glide to heaven for both of them.

SHIELDING HER EYES with a hand against the glare off the water,
Remy watched the boats streak out of the bay in opposite directions.
"Where is everyone going?"

Micah leaned in close, his breath ruffling her hair. They both
smelled of his shower gel, reminding her of how his hands had felt
on her body. His mouth...well...she couldn't go there and not go wild.
She'd strip him naked right here on the pier. And she couldn't very well
do that with Billie and some of the others still in the house. Maybe
they should sneak back to bed or... Micah chose that moment to answer
her question. The glint in his eyes saying he knew exactly what she was
thinking.

"Melena and Theo are heading to her cabin to feed her wolf. She
can't bring him here because of Tubbs. They wouldn't see eye-to-eye, so
she goes home a couple of times a day. As for Breeana and Sully, they're
off to the boat landing to pick up supplies with Papa Joe."

"Melena has a wolf? Seriously?" Remy eyed him, dragging her
thoughts out of the bedroom. He was pulling her leg about the wolf,
right? When he shrugged and didn't say anything more, the light bulb
flipped on in her head. "Come on, spill the beans. There's something
about this wolf you're not saying."

"It's Melena's story to share, not mine. But Dood took a bullet for
her, and that's all I'm willing to say." His eyes were impossible to read

behind the aviators. Was he telling her the truth? "Ask her. Maybe she'll tell you the rest."

"Spoilsport." Remy tucked the nugget of information away for later, determined to know more. "How about Breeana then and Billie? What are their stories?"

Micah slung an arm around her neck, reeled her in, and planted a kiss at her temple. "Trigger, my lips are sealed."

Damn, these people had secrets. Not that it was a problem. She'd ask her new girlfriends over a couple bottles of wine tonight and drag it out of them. It was her experience women loved to trade confidences, especially after too much *vino*. "It's need to know, right?"

"Something like that." He chuckled, threading his fingers with hers. "Let's walk."

They followed a trail into the woods. Birds chirped, flying low through the trees. Pine needles cushioned their footfalls. The air was cooler here, the flickers of sunlight floating through foliage holding less heat. Tubbs lumbered on ahead, chasing a squirrel. Remy hooted when he treed the little guy and plowed himself into the maple's trunk, bonking his head. Grace and elegance were assets the dog didn't possess.

Walking in silence for a while, Remy's thoughts strayed back to a few hours ago. She imagined she glowed from the inside out. Micah was amazing, both in bed and out. She loved his kindness and compassion too, not only his skill as a lover, although today was the best day of her life if she was counting multiple orgasms. But sex wasn't enough. She wanted Micah in her life—hook, line and sinker. Knew in her soul if she could win his heart, she would never let him go.

The thought melted her bones. Did she stand a chance? Did Micah care for her? Could he learn to love her half as much as she thought she could love him? A stupid idea, since she knew he lived life on the edge. Maybe the last thing he'd want was her tagging along. Still...she had skills he could use. She had passion to share. And she didn't want to be left behind when this was over.

Such ridiculous thoughts. She probably needed a psychiatrist to set her straight. Micah's body was honed for violence. His mind fine-tuned to a world that had little to do with her. After all, this was the man who smuggled people out of countries without batting an eyelash. The same man who had a gun room in his home, for heaven's sake, or so Papa Joe had let slip. Would Micah kiss her goodbye, pat her on the head, and send her packing as soon as she was out of danger? *In a New York minute*, she thought.

"Okay, Trigger, I know that look." Stopping on the path, he yanked her to him, resting his hands on her shoulders. He traced his thumbs up the sides of her neck, gazing at her mouth as if he wanted to taste her. If only he would. "What's going on in that head of yours?"

"I was thinking of Papa Joe." It was a bald faced lie, considering where her thoughts had been wandering. But now was as good a time as any to set Micah straight. "He had a gun tucked at the small of his back this morning. I saw the outline under his shirt."

Micah cocked an eyebrow, didn't seem overly pleased with the topic of conversation. He also didn't appear surprised by her announcement. "Sully decided he could be an asset to the team, wants him to help keep an eye on the house."

Was that so? "And where is *my* gun, Mic? I can stand watch, same as Papa Joe."

"No, you can't." He tucked a curl behind her ear, meeting her gaze full on. "Joe was a marine. Once a marine, *always* a marine, that's just the way it is. He fought against the Viet Cong and survived guerrilla warfare, which says it all. He has skills we can use."

Remy hated being treated like a child, as if she couldn't hold her own. She pointed a thumb at her own chest. "What about *my* skills? I have martial arts training, and I carry a gun when I'm on the job at my park in Alberta."

"Honey, Russian Systema won't win you the price of a gumball with me, not with your injured leg." He lowered his hands, sliding them to her hips. "And you carry a revolver in a national park that doesn't see any action. Ever had to use it?"

"Well, no. I'm a scientist, not a forest ranger or a cop," she admitted. "But I practice at the firing range all the time."

"That's not the same as taking fire." He lowered his eyes, toeing a branch to the side of the trail. "Besides, you almost shot me last night. The firing mechanism and recoil on a Glock are totally different from the six shooter you're used to. The answer is no."

Remy tossed her head. She would win this battle and earn Micah's respect if it killed her. "Care to explain Billie to me then? I saw her sneaking in the house with Rocket this morning while you cooked breakfast. And, *she* was carrying a pump action shotgun."

"Billie is different." Micah firmed his lips, clearly wanting to drop the subject. "She was raised on a ranch. Hell, she handles firearms better than most people with military training—she's a natural with a long gun. You can ask her what it feels like to come under fire. She took a bullet, not too long ago, and almost died."

Billie had been shot? That took the wind out of Remy's sails in a hurry. She fought for a comeback. Until blood curdling screams shattered the stillness.

"Help! Help! There's a bear! Daddy, help!"

"Jesus." Micah reached for the two-way clipped to his belt. "You getting this?"

Hawke's voice came over the airwaves. "Loud and clear."

"Do you have eyes on Remy?"

"Counting the freckles on her arms as we speak."

"Pick her up and stay close." Micah pocketed the radio and pulled his sidearm. He broke for the trees. "Stay here. Wait for Hawke!"

He vanished before she could get a word out, adrenaline shaking her body as the horror-filled shrieks continued. The high-pitched voices sounded like children. *Dear God, a bear!* Would Micah reach them in time?

Something flashed in her periphery. She turned to see Hawke and Law sprint out of nowhere, their footfalls silent on moss carpeting the ground. They came in low on either side of her, spinning her forward. Hooking one of her arms around each of their necks, they locked hands at her waist. Lifting her between them, the pair plunged into the woods, following the terrified screeches and Micah.

Remy's feet didn't touch ground. They would make better time if they let her run on her own. Saving those kids was all she could think about. Somehow she could keep up. She bellowed at the top of her lungs.

"Put me down!"

MICAH RACED THROUGH shadows and sunlight, flying by tree after tree. Picking up speed on an incline, he sprinted down the other side. Loose earth and chunks of moss tumbling, his Keen's lost traction in the slide of debris. He fell and rolled to his feet again, pain biting an ankle. *Ignore it. You're good to go.* Gaze searching from right to left, he caught movement up ahead. Bright colored clothing flashed through branches.

The screams had faded to strangled cries. His heart pounded at the fear in those small voices. He leapt the last few yards, sliding to a halt between two little girls. His Glock pointed at...

Tubbs, who lay in front of them, his tail pounding the ground like a wild metronome. Whines—not growls—emanated from deep in his throat. His head cocked at a questioning angle, *what did I do?* written clear as day on his face.

"So much for the bear." Micah swore under his breath, holstering his sidearm. He turned to the children and crouched between them. Identical twins, maybe four years old, wrapped their arms around his neck and held on for dear life. Their bodies shook uncontrollably. He patted their backs, speaking in a soothing tone. "It's okay. There's nothing to be afraid of."

They were dressed in red cotton shorts, red sneakers, and turquoise sparkly blouses. Wispy, blond ponytails were tied up in red ribbons, wide blue eyes staring at him with tears on their lashes. One of them sobbed, pointing at Tubbs. "You gots'ta shoot the bear."

He cupped them both under the chin, quirking his head in the Mastiff's direction. "That isn't a bear. He's just a big, scary-looking dog, and I think you frightened him."

"We did?"

"You sure did. Would you like to meet him?" Not waiting for an answer, he motioned Tubbs into a sit-stay position beside them. The big goof lumbered forward, planting himself against Micah's side and offering a paw.

"Friends." Taking the tiny hands in his big ones, he allowed Tubbs to take a good sniff so he would remember their scent. Within seconds, the girls were hugging the mutt, although even sitting down, the guard dog towered over them like a giant redwood. "Good boy."

Footfalls sounded to their right as Remy came to a halt, compliments of Law and Hawke. Her face was ashen, probably more from fear for the children than the mad dash through the woods. "Relax, we're cool here. You guys have a nice stroll through the forest?"

"Shut it." She looked like she wanted to spit nails at him, but wouldn't with those curious young eyes watching. She shot him a murderous glare before focusing on the twins with a huge smile on her lips. "Hi girls. My name is Remy. What are your names?"

"Bethie and Jessie."

"It's nice to meet you." She held out a hand, shaking both of theirs. "Can you tell me where your mommy and daddy are?"

"Prob'ly looking for us," one of them said, hugging her sister. "We saw a bunny rabbit behind the house and we chased it. Then the bear—I mean, the doggie—founded us. We gots scared 'cuz he followed us."

"*Really, really* scared, 'cuz we thought he was a bear," the other twin said. "Then we gots lost when we ran away from him."

"Jessica! Bethany!"

"Looks like mom and dad have arrived." A glower crossed Law's face for an instant. Micah didn't blame him. The parents should have been watching their daughters, not reading the paper or whatever else they were up to inside the house. Hell, anything could have happened to these kids.

A spindly guy wearing plaid Bermudas, a white button-down shirt, knee socks, and sandals tripped ass-over-teakettle on a tree root and landed at Micah's feet. He was knobby kneed with skinny arms and legs. Peach fuzz lined his jaw—or was it a beard?—thinning brown hair framing a pasty, elongated face. The girls looked nothing like their father, a bloody miracle to Micah's way of thinking.

When the missus appeared on the horizon, he realized who they resembled, a pretty woman with a curvy body and a sense of style. He couldn't help but wonder what had drawn her to her husband in the first place. Was there more to him than he saw on the surface, or was it an arranged marriage?

"Girls! Thank God, you're all right!" The geek drew up on his knees, about to hug the girls with a paring knife in his hand.

Jeez. Had the fool planned to go up against a bear with the knife? Micah went to grab the blade before he hurt someone, most probably himself. Tubbs beat him to it, chomping on a bony wrist until the knife dropped in the dirt.

"Yeowwww!" Yep, the guy was a real prince, screaming and scaring the crap out of his kids all over again. Micah brought him to his feet and dusted him off. He also checked the wrist for damage. Not a mark on him.

"For Pete's sake, Winston." His wife came up beside them, rolling her eyes. "You're frightening the twins."

Micah waited until the family hugged and kissed each other for a few minutes before shooting out a hand to the adults. "The name's Micah Rivera. I'm your neighbor in the next bay."

"Nice to meet you. I'm Winston Templeton." He wiped his hand on his shorts before shaking in a stronger grip than Micah expected. "This is my wife, Chloe, and you've already met our daughters. I want to thank you for rescuing them from the b...dog. We could hear them screaming, but this is our first time visiting Silver Lake. We rented the cottage for regatta week and we don't know the area, especially the woods. Gawd, it's a jungle back here."

"No problem." Micah levelled a stern look at the man. "But understand, you can't leave your children alone outside again. The lake...the woods...let's just say you have to respect nature and know your limitations."

"Got it," he said, a sheepish grin on his face. "Say, why don't you come over for dinner during regatta week, so we can repay your kindness? All of you are invited."

"Micah and I would love to, wouldn't we, darling?" Remy batted her eyelashes in his direction. What was she up to? "My name is Remy, by the way. And I'm his girlfriend."

Damn it, Trigger. Micah had been about to decline the offer and she jumped right in, probably to even the score after Hawke and Law had shanghaied her in the woods. The last thing he wanted was to get friendly with the neighbors until they caught the bastard hunting her. Still, her "girlfriend" comment was a kick. If she thought she'd pissed him off with that one, she was dead wrong. In fact, he was warming to the idea.

"Great. We'll figure out a date and let you know." Winston chuckled, wrapping an arm around his wife, who looked less than pleased. Whether it was because of the physical contact or the dinner invitation, Micah had no idea. "Chloe's such a great cook. I'll fire up the barbie and we'll dine like royalty on veggie burgers and tofu salad."

"Looking forward to it." *Yeah. Sure.* He almost gagged at the thought of veggie burgers and tofu. Micah tipped a hand in Winston's general direction then turned into the trees, heading for home. He tugged Remy along beside him. She could barely stand up, she was laughing so hard. "You're gonna pay for that one, Trigger."

Hawke tapped him on the shoulder. "Bet you can't remember the last time you ate like a vegetarian. Play your cards right, and they might even have non-alcoholic beer to round out the meal."

"Yeah, I'll be sure to bring you a bottle if they do."

Damn Remy. Damn veggie burgers. Damn tofu salad.

Chapter 7

R emy was a little ahead of Micah when they left the trail through the woods. She wanted to beat him to the bathroom and lock herself in for a couple of hours. A girl needed some alone time to soak in a bubble bath and paint her toenails, especially since Micah was a wee bit cranky after she'd fed him to the wolves, or in this case, the vegan neighbors. And she'd laughed about it too, which meant he'd get even. She came out of the forest grinning like a loon, thinking about the barbeque invitation. Yep, he had no choice; he'd suffer through it because of the twins.

She was almost to the house when she noticed a crowd down by the water. Wait a second, why were Breeana and Sully, Mel and Theo, Billie and Rocket, Papa Joe, and Hunt gathered on the dock? Was there a party going on? "Hey, what did I miss?"

Melena inhaled as though startled, her eyes as round as saucers. "Go back, Remy. You shouldn't be here."

"Why not?" Her gaze fell on a small cardboard box sitting on the pier. Her name was scrawled on the label in big block letters, right above Micah's address. This made no sense at all, since she hadn't told anyone where she was. She leaned forward to see the address better. "Oh. It must be a mistake."

"Don't touch it." Grabbing her by the elbows, Micah eased her back until she stood several feet away. He scowled at Sully, clearly unhappy. "Where did you find this?"

Sully's gaze moved from the box to Micah, then back to the box. "Stella had it at the store. She said someone left it on her porch, most probably during the night. Too bad she didn't see who made the drop."

Remy tried to disentangle herself to get a closer look. Micah held her tight, not giving her an inch of wiggle room. "All I can think is it's from my brothers or Pete. Let me open it and find out."

He shook his head. "Not going to happen, Trigger."

She huffed in exasperation, and Breeana touched her arm. She nodded to the package. "Look at it carefully. See? There's no postage or even a courier waybill. And no return address."

Remy scanned it again, realizing Bree was right. "What do you think, Mic?"

"Your brothers didn't send it. They wouldn't risk jeopardizing your location like that. And they have my cell number." He rubbed the back of his neck, looking pale as he checked a recent text message. "It's from Graciella. She says Pete is still in a coma, although the doctors say he's improving and they'll bring him out of it soon."

"So he didn't send it." Remy's heart sank at the thought of Pete lying in a hospital bed. Knowing the coma was medically induced didn't change how she felt. He was injured because of her. Switching mental gears, she refocused on the package, otherwise she would burst into tears. "Then it has to be from my brothers. No one else knows I'm here, unless..."

"Unless..." Micah reached out to cup her cheek. "He's found you through me."

"Could he do that?" Resignation tightened her throat, and she felt hollow inside. Haunted. Hunted. Powerless. She turned her head away, until he tipped her chin back to face him.

"It's possible." He spoke quietly but his meaning was clear, demanding her full attention. "If he got a look at the tags on the SUV I rented in Florida. He could have traced it back to me, and put two and two together."

She nodded, feeling the blood drain from her face, in danger of emotional overload from a fear she couldn't handle. "H-how do you think he did it?"

Micah's eyes were gentle, but a muscle ticked in his jaw. "Only one of two ways. He either has powerful friends in high places, or he's in law enforcement. No one else could make the connection so easily." He glanced over his shoulder at Tubbs, who waited patiently for a command. "Come here, boy."

Rocket's eyebrows arched. "You think he'll go *en pointe* if there's Semtex or some other explosive in the box?"

"He should. Rizzo said he's been working on it with him." Micah hooked a finger under Tubbs's collar and led him over to the package. "But I doubt that's what he'll find. Too many variables for the psycho to take a chance like that."

"Whoever made the delivery has no way of knowing if or when Remy received it." Rocket raked a hand through his hair, looking grim. Remy remembered, he was an explosives expert. "He'd need to be close by to detonate it with a cell phone."

"Right," Micah said in a low tone while scanning the lake in the distance.

"I'll get my gear and have a look around." Theo moved toward the house, taking Mel with him.

Oh, God. Theo's a sniper. Has my life really come down to this? I need a sniper to protect me?

"Don't worry. He ain't out there." Papa Joe lowered the binoculars strapped around his neck. "I been keepin' watch since we got back from the store. Hell, I even had my eyes peeled in the boat to make sure we wasn't followed."

Micah shot Remy a look that enforced his next words. "He'll never get near you before I take him out. I'll kill him first."

The icy calm in his voice left her no reason to doubt. He meant what he said. She knew none of those women in the swamp had stood a chance. But they hadn't had Micah and his team on their side, or her martial arts training. And the bastard who killed them was working alone now, since his partner was dead. She liked her odds a lot better, trusting Micah and herself. "I'm not worried."

He nodded, seemingly satisfied. "Atta girl."

Tubbs finished sniffing the box and didn't make a sound. He ambled back to her side once Micah released him with a command. Remy patted his big head, glad to have him with her. If all else failed, Tubbs would be her early warning system.

Hawke's cell phone rang. He answered, listened for a second then disconnected. "Theo's in position. He says we're clear."

Micah nodded, knelt by the carton, pulling a wicked looking knife from the sheath on his belt. "I want everyone off the dock."

"I'll give you a hand." Rocket dropped to one knee beside him as the others moved away, pulling a similar knife out of his boot. "I'm ready when you are."

Billie edged closer to Remy, threading their fingers and holding on tight. "You guys be careful."

"Always, peaches," Rocket said, flashing her a grin.

Remy watched them inspect the package, her heart thumping, chills raising the hairs on the back of her neck. What if Tubbs was wrong and there were explosives inside? Micah's concentration didn't waver as he slid the tip of his knife along the top of the box, breaking the seal. He eased a flap back. Rocket did the same, both of them using their blades. She could see crinkled paper at the mouth of the carton. Micah poked the knife into it, carefully raising it a fraction.

"Shit." A quick glance at what lay beneath the paper, and he pulled a Zippo from a pocket in his cargo shorts. Lit it and dropped the lighter in the carton. Then he and Rocket backed away, waiting until the box was almost ash before he booted it in the lake.

"What was in there?" Sully wrapped an arm around Breeana. She hugged him around the waist, clearly uneasy.

Micah didn't answer right away, crossing the distance in dock-eating strides until he reached Remy's side. She could tell by the look in his eyes. He didn't want to tell her. Her first instinct was to fall to pieces. Her next was to grow a backbone. *Damn it, pull yourself together. Whatever was in there is dead. It can't hurt you.*

"A message from the Glades." Micah shifted closer, his eyes burning hot with anger. "The bastard loaded the box with spiders."

"Don't that beat all." Papa Joe stood behind her now, a hand squeezing her shoulder, trepidation ripening his voice. "What kind of spiders?"

"The venomous kind. Red Widows."

"Fuck me." Papa Joe clucked his tongue while Remy searched her memory for information on Red Widows. As a wildlife biologist, she kept up-to-date on any information crossing her desk. But no, she'd never heard of the species, guessing from Papa Joe's reaction it was better that way. "Them sons of bitches live in the Everglades. You sure you got all of 'em, Mic?"

"Relax. They're gone. They wouldn't survive once the weather cools down anyway."

"Maybe so, but they could breed here all summer long. Wouldn't that be fun? Red Widows settin' up house and crawlin' into our beds at night."

"Tell me." Remy could hear the breathlessness in her own voice, despising herself for being so weak. But spiders weren't her favorite thing. "Could they have killed me?"

"Probably not, since you're young and healthy. But more than one bite? I just don't know." Micah bent down, leveling his gaze with hers, his voice quiet. "There's nothing to worry about."

Sure, nothing except the madman who had followed her out of the Florida swamp. She bit her bottom lip. "I don't understand. Why would he tip his hand like this? It makes no sense."

"No it doesn't—not to a sane person," Micah said. "He's playing with you, Remy. It's his version of cat and mouse. And he's going to lose."

ONLY AFTER HE DOCKED the Tahoe at the boat landing did Micah notice Joe's new look. Clean white shirt and chinos, his hair tied back with a strip of leather, and the hint of expensive cologne on his skin. He looked...impressive...for lack of a better word, like the ex-marine he was, not some crazy man who lived in a swamp. Standing tall, Joe even took control of Tubbs, removing his life vest, clipping on his leash then walking him along the docks and through the parking lot.

Micah followed behind holding Remy's hand. He watched men loading or unloading their boats, most of them with families. Some headed to cottages on the lake while others carted empty beer cases and gas cans to their vehicles, most probably driving into town for supplies.

Remy whispered in his ear. "Who is that striking man pretending to be Papa Joe and what has he done with the crotchety real guy?"

"No idea, but I have a feeling we're about to find out." His pulse quickened at the scent of her skin, the navy sundress hugging her curves shooting a blast of heat south of his belt buckle. "You look pretty amazing yourself."

"As opposed to what?" The sarcasm in her voice was only outdistanced by her narrowed gaze. "Can't a girl wear a dress once in a while?"

"Yeah, and it's a nice change, given the wild woman thing you had going on earlier." Her flinty stare was as good as a stake through the heart. Micah knew he should quit while he was ahead, but what the heck? A little humor might ease the tension. "The twigs in your hair and mud on your face after Hawke and Law carried you through the bush made an impression, that's all."

She tossed her head, the fan of her hair sparking copper and red in the sunlight. "Those idiots tripped over their size fifteen feet and dropped me. I was perfectly capable of following you under my own steam, you know. So you're an idiot too, for making them carry me."

"My turf, my rules. I didn't want you getting lost." Micah diverted her attention before she could say anything more, nodding to the white clapboard building up ahead. "That's where the package was delivered."

Gas pumps and an old-fashioned telephone booth stood on the right. Summer flowers in decorative clay pots framed the front porch. They climbed the stairs, a bell jangling when they entered the store. Joe and Tubbs were already inside.

The tiny woman behind the counter glanced over as Tubbs drooled a puddle on the floor. "Joe, get that beast out of here. There's a sign in the window, or can't you read? No dogs allowed."

"Sorry, Stella, but the mutt stays." Joe shot her an apologetic grin. "Tubbs is a search and rescue dog in training." *Sure, he was.* "Where we go, he goes. Pass me some paper towels and I'll clean up the mess."

"We?" Stella's tossed him a roll of towels, her gaze cutting to Micah standing behind Joe, a smile lighting her eyes. She dashed around the chip display and came in for a landing, arms held wide open. "Mic, I'm so happy to see you. Melena told me you'd bought the Fergus place." She planted a kiss on his cheek. "One visit to Silver Lake and you were hooked, eh? And who is this pretty gal you've got on your arm?"

"Remy, say hello to Mel's aunt." Micah reeled Stella in for another hug.

She patted his biceps and slowly stepped away, saying in a quiet voice to Remy, "Are you in trouble, like my Melena was?"

Remy glanced at him for a second, her throat working before answering. While she might not know Mel's story, she was smart enough to guess it hadn't been pretty. "Yes, ma'am, I believe I am."

"Okay then." Stella tugged down the hem of her blouse as she stepped back behind the counter. "The dog stays, and so does Joe, even though he's packing a gun under his shirttail. I assume he's one of the good guys, Mic?"

"That he is."

Joe beamed a smile at Stella, waggling his eyebrows. "I'll be over in the plumbing supplies if you need me, darlin'."

"Fat chance." Stella mumbled under her breath. "Why does my winning smile and girlish figure always appeal to the nut jobs?"

Yep, Micah figured there was definitely an attraction there, at least on Joe's part. He spied Doc Finley standing halfway up the narrow aisle as Tubbs lumbered past after taking a sniff at his shoes. Doc flattened himself against the freezer section to let him squeeze by. Then he approached the cash register, a hand scratching the back of his head under his fishing hat. Laying a Styrofoam container of worms on the counter along with a bottle of water, his eyes lit up when he saw Remy.

"Hey! How's my favorite patient doing? You changing the dressings on that leg like I showed you and taking the antibiotics?"

A smile tipped her mouth as Remy planted a kiss on Doc's stubbled cheek. "Every day, like clockwork. And I'm doing fine, thanks to you."

Doc patted her back, his eyes meeting Micah's over the top of her head. "I have a feeling the big guy standing next to you may have something to do with that. Stay close to him and you'll be all right."

Remy nodded, turning to Micah, placing a hand on his arm. She might put on a brave face, but he could see the shadows under her eyes and the pallor of her skin. She was frightened and putting a positive spin on it, because that's the way she did things. Damn, she made him proud.

Doc paid Stella for his purchases. "Be sure to call if you need me, Mic."

"Trust me; you're at the top of my list." Doc had been instrumental in the ugly business with Melena a while back. He knew he could count on the man, for both his silence and his help.

"I don't like it. There are too many strangers on the lake for the damn regatta to suit me," Doc said. "Too many freaking boats and folks who don't know how to drive them. They're scaring the fish."

"Hang in there." Micah scanned the store to make sure no one was paying attention to their conversation. He noticed a family in the soft drink section. Otherwise, they appeared to be alone. "It will all be over soon. Another week and everything should be back to normal."

"From your lips to God's ear and it can't happen soon enough. Still, I ordered in extra medical supplies for the *regatta*. Never can tell who's going to hurt themselves." Doc winked. "Just do me a favor and don't send any dead bodies my way. Too much paperwork, and the local cops can be hard asses on dotting the 'Is' and crossing the 'Ts'. Too bad they don't know anything about forensic evidence."

Micah chuckled. "I heard Sergeant Dupré is dumber than a horse's rear end."

"You give him too much credit," Doc said. "The last time we had trouble, Melena had to pull a *Marilyn Monroe* and keep his eyes on her while Sully and Hawke handled the actual investigation."

"They were the right guys for the job, Doc. Hawke is a chief RCMP investigator, and Sully is a homicide lieutenant with the Montreal force."

"Yeah, and Theo being a lawyer was an added plus. Otherwise, Melena would be in jail for a murder she didn't commit. Or maybe she'd be dead."

Micah heard Remy's sharp intake of breath. He leaned lower and murmured in a soft voice. "Relax, honey. This is old news. Besides, it had a kick ass ending for Melena and Theo. They're crazy about each other."

"True enough. And on that happy note, I'll be on my way." The bell jingled again as Doc opened the door. "I'd best get home before Effie remembers my list of chores tacked to the fridge. She's liable to chain me to the house until I get those done."

Remy nudged Micah in the ribs, hissing in his ear. "When we get to the house, I want to know everything you're not telling me. The only reason I don't punch your lights out now is because Stella is watching us."

Micah planted a kiss at her temple. "Speak to Melena. She'll tell you."

After the family paid for their pretzels and soft drinks and left the store, he talked to Stella about the package. She didn't know anything about who had delivered it or when it arrived. He felt deflated, had hoped she would remember some detail that hadn't come to light when she'd talked about it with Sully earlier. No dice. Joe came back from plumbing supplies with some pipes and couplings, laying them on the counter so Stella could ring them up on the cash register. "What have you got there, Joe?"

A grin lit up the man's face. "The makings of a new bang stick, my friend. I miss my old buddy."

Remy took Tubbs's leash as Joe carried his bang stick components back to the boat. He shot down Micah's misgivings about the new weapon he intended to build. "Quit worrying, it'll work fine. I've made a few of these in my day."

"I'm sure you have." Micah glared at Joe's back while he loaded his purchases in the stern. Then he switched on the blower to clear the gas fumes before he started the engine. Cranking the key, the motor revved for a few seconds and died. He tried again. Nothing happened.

"Mic, you'd better get back here and take a look." Joe leaned over the passenger side of the stern, a scowl on his face. "You're not gonna like it."

Micah joined Joe and followed where his finger pointed. Sugar crystals sprinkled the fibreglass around the gas intake. *Fan-fucking-tastic.*

"What is it?" Remy touched his back, peering over the side.

"Someone dumped sugar in the gas tank." Micah swiped an arm across his brow to catch the sweat. "It's already turned to syrup and fouled the engine. We aren't going anywhere."

Hauling out his sat phone, he hit speed dial, waiting for someone to pick up. He watched adults and children move about on the docks, the tension in his gut building. Too many people around if all hell broke loose. The situation was a nightmare waiting to happen. Jesus God, what kind of monster staged something like this knowing innocent people would get caught in the crossfire? He already knew—only a man without a conscience—a psychopath with everything to lose if Remy identified him.

Joe knelt in the bow, his Glock out and nestled by his side. He dragged a pump action shotgun from under the bow cover, sliding it along the floor in Micah's direction. He caught it, but didn't raise it; his gaze falling on Remy's terrified face. He thought about taking her back down the pier. But there was nowhere to run and nowhere to hide. "Hit the deck between the seats and stay there, Trigger. We'll be out of here soon."

Sure, if a bullet didn't hit the gas tank first.

REMY STOOD AT THE CERAMIC island in the sunny walk-through kitchen, filling Tubbs's food dish with steak and kibble. She carried it around the corner to the sun room, placing it beside his water bowl while he licked his chops. She glanced down at her hands. They had finally stopped shaking, thank God. It was a good sign, considering the spider delivery and then the sugar in the gas tank. What would be next? Micah's reassurances earlier did nothing to calm her. As a matter of fact, he annoyed her. Why wouldn't he admit they had reason to worry? And why not give her a gun?

The men congregated in the dining room at the far end of the kitchen, murmuring in quiet undertones. She couldn't help but notice the dark oak table and sideboard contained enough weaponry to infiltrate a small country, so they had to be more worried than Micah let on. He glanced up and caught her gaze when she entered the room, his eyes dark and unreadable. "Is there something I can help you with?"

"First off, you can quit being such a dolt." Remy clenched her fists and sank into the nearest chair, fighting for control. Stubborn, pig-headed man. He owed her the truth. "I want to know what's going on. Why are you in here whispering and making plans without me?"

His mouth curved in a sardonic tilt. "We're talking about the boat, Trigger. I'd hardly call it whispering. Theo and Law just came back from transporting the Tahoe to the mechanic. It should be repaired within a day or two."

"Bullshit!" She tossed her head to clear the hair out of her eyes. "When the guys picked us up at the boat landing, they came loaded for bear. So *don't* pretend that was all you were discussing. You thought that idiot was going to shoot us."

Micah blew out a breath, shoved away from the table, and stood, towering over her like the soldier he was. Remy almost swallowed her tongue, wondering where this was going. Had she pushed him too hard? "I want to show you something. Can you ask the other ladies to join us?"

"Sure, but this had better be good, Micah Rivera. No more stall tactics." Remy flounced out of her chair and headed for the stairs, hoping no one noticed her knees shaking. No doubt about it. Micah's team was a bona fide death squad, although she knew they would never hurt her. Still, they could make her life uncomfortable if they chose.

She found Breeana, Melena, and Billie in the downstairs game room, flipping through channels on the big screen. "We're needed upstairs. And I'd suggest you get ready to run. I may have rattled a cage or two up there."

"Aw, they're all a bunch of pussycats," Breeana said, taking a sip of her coffee. "There's not a mean one in the bunch."

"Yes, don't sweat it, Remy." Melena uncurled herself from the sofa, stretching her arms over her head. "Theo's like a cuddly teddy bear when he's not chasing bad guys. He wouldn't hurt a fly."

Oh, brother. "I hope you're right."

"Relax, honey." Billie came out of a comfy chair to wrap an arm around her. "It's about time the big, brawny men realized they can't live without us."

When they reached the dining room, Micah walked to a recessed panel near the Irish Waterford woodstove and punched in a code.

"Better stand back a little." He took Remy's hand and drew her deeper into the dining room. A wall in the kitchen began to move. The entire section of ivory cabinetry containing chrome stacked ovens and a double-door refrigerator rolled out across the hardwood floor.

Micah urged everyone closer once the wall had stopped moving. "Ladies, welcome to the gun safe."

"Holy Hannah!" Remy stood dumbstruck, unable to believe her eyes. "Did this come with the house?"

"Ah, no." Micah touched the nape beneath her hair, pulling her into the room behind the wall. His hand felt warm and strong on her skin, causing a round of goose bumps that had little to do with the hidden space. "I have my own security company. My people built this to my specifications."

"Hot damn, that wall slid out as smooth as hair on a frog." Papa Joe eyed Micah with a satisfied smirk. "I knew you weren't stashing them guns in the dishwasher."

It was a small room, not more than ten by twelve feet. Guns of all shapes and sizes were secured to peg boards on the far wall, ammunition stacked neatly in see-through bins beneath. A narrow, stainless steel prep table lay in the center of the room. Remy couldn't help but shiver when she noticed a lethal display of knives and other sharp objects on a half wall on their right, some of them shaped like stars. What were they used for?

A laptop computer sat on a small metal shelf to their left. Four flatscreen monitors—built into the wall above it—flashed on areas of the house, the boathouse, garage, and the entire outdoor property. *Holy crap!*

"The gun safe doubles as a panic room, so I want all of you to memorize the code. Once you're inside, you punch the red button by the door to retract the wall back to its normal position. It slides back fast, so don't stand in its way." Micah drew her deeper inside the small space, his breath fanning the top of her head. The men on his team stayed outside. They obviously knew about the gun safe and didn't need an explanation.

"This room is impenetrable. I'll show you how to work the monitors later on, so you can view the rest of the house and see who's out there." Micah walked to the back of the room near the knife display. "Step back here ladies."

"Consider me one of the gals." Papa Joe fell into step behind them. "I ain't missing out on the grand tour."

Remy agreed, watching in disbelief as Micah took a set of keys off a hook on the wall and descended a small staircase. Unlocking the door at the bottom, he ushered them through. They stepped into a narrow cement tunnel, recessed track lights shining along the corridor. The air smelled fresh, not dank, the walls painted a creamy white. "We'll go this way."

After walking a hundred feet or so, they came to another set of stairs. Micah unbolted a trap door at the top and pushed it open. They climbed through to the garage. "The keys to the SUV are always in the ignition and the garage remote is clipped on the sun visor."

"Handy for a quick getaway," Billie surmised.

Breeana cocked her head back to the stairwell. "Where does the other end of the corridor lead?"

"It brings you out in the woods at the far side of the boathouse. There's a little runabout in there you won't need a key to start. I'll show you how it works in the morning."

"Don't bother." Melena flashed him a big smile. "I know all about boats since I inherited my cottage. And I know how to drive them."

"About that, Mel." Micah looked as if he'd rather choke than get out his next sentence. "I've seen you drive, and so have the rest of the guys. The fact is you could use a few more lessons."

"That's not fair, Mic. Just because I hit a few docks and a rock or two, Theo won't let me drive the Bayliner anymore. But I'm sure I could handle a little runabout."

"We'll see." Micah escorted them out of the garage, across the gravel road and down to the house. As the others filed through the doors, he held Remy back. "No more secrets, Trigger. I promise. You're in this thing deep, and from now on, we'll work things out together. Before we run out of time."

Chapter 8

S ig sat in the bar at *Charlie's*, a watering hole nestled in acres of woodland near Silver Lake. He ignored the western decor, focusing instead on the bourbon in front of him. Downing the whiskey, he held it up for another round, a hundred-dollar bill flashing between his fingers. The bartender pocketed the c-note and left the bottle, happy with his tip and probably sensing Sig's black mood.

He sighed, shaking his head. Killing women was a pleasure, and his conscience hadn't pricked when he'd beaten the snot out of the forest ranger. But offing a fellow member of his club? A necessary evil, but not easy to do. Goddamn Spider and his bullshit. How he stalked prey on his own turf was his business. But disobeying a direct order and placing them all at risk? Stupid fucker.

He'd crossed the line, brought it on himself by pulling that dumbass stunt and sending spiders from the Everglades to the bitch. As if Rivera wouldn't figure it out in about five seconds flat and cover the woman like a bulletproof vest. Hell, Spider might as well have hung a sign around Sig's neck announcing the Swamp Killer had arrived, because Rivera sure as shit knew he was there, thanks to Spider's special delivery.

Sig heard a car spitting up gravel as it spun into the parking lot. As the black sedan zoomed past the windows, he glanced at his watch. Spider—at least the limey was punctual. Nodding to the bartender, Sig edged off his stool and headed for the door. "Keep an eye on my bottle. I'm going out for a smoke."

"Hey man!" Spider climbed from his ride and strode in Sig's direction with a smile from ear-to-ear. "How long has it been? Nearly a year?"

"That long? It's good to see you, buddy." Spider laughed when they tapped knuckles and back slapped. Sig angled his head toward the woods, lowering his voice while encouraging Spider into the trees. "Let's walk. I have a job for you and I don't want to be overheard."

Spider grinned. "Sure. Anything for the big dog."

"Glad to see you're still kissing ass." Sig squeezed his buddy's nape as they went deep into the forest. "Listen, since I'm the guy in charge, maybe you can answer one question for me. Why didn't you mention the package you sent to Remy Renaud? Not to me, and not to any of the others. What the hell was that about?"

"Listen, I only did it for a laugh." Spider's smile slipped a notch when he noticed the look in Sig's eyes. His face paled. "Come on, you know it's my signature. I couldn't resist!"

Sig felt his blood pressure spike. Could the selfish jerk really be that stupid? "Your signature move blew our chance to grab her at the marina today, shithead. I sugared their gas tank, planning to offer them a ride, all nice and innocent. A fisherman doing a good deed—some of the other guys lying in wait in a secluded area in the next bay."

"Bollocks! I didn't know that's what you'd planned. I wasn't even at the docks today." Spider scratched the back of his neck, a muscle twitching his jaw. "What's this got to do with me anyhow?"

"*Everything*, you dumb fuck!" Sig fought hard to control his anger, a losing battle. "I followed them to the store after souring their gas. And there was Rivera, firing questions at the sales clerk about your spider delivery. You sent *Florida* spiders, you stupid son of a bitch. Now he knows I'm here and he's geared up for trouble."

Sig pulled the Walther P99 from under his jacket, the silencer already threaded to the barrel. Not his weapon of choice, but he wasn't on his home turf, and Ice-Pick had made the purchase out of the trunk of a car.

"Come on, Sig!" Spider whined, backing up a few paces until he smacked against a tree. "I screwed up, I admit it. But give me a chance to make this right. For Christ's sake—"

Sig shook his head as he aimed the weapon, feeling the power in his grip. "Are your spidey senses tingling yet? Because this is the end of the road for you."

Firing point blank, a hole appeared in Spider's forehead. He sank to the ground, blowback slicking the tree trunk behind him. *Goddamn!* Sig quickly dragged the body into the bushes, frantic to clean up the mess. He pulled on the rubber gloves he had tucked in his pocket, scooping up brain and skull fragments and dumping them with the body. He used leaves and chunks of moss to mop up the blood. When he was satisfied, he emptied Spider's pockets.

Not that he gave a crap if the cops identified him—he just didn't want him traced back to the group. Didn't want him found until after they got their hands on the bitch. Until they faded back into their rich, respectable lives.

Still angry, Sig drew the gun again and fired a couple more rounds into Spider's face. Then he rolled him into the hole he'd dug earlier, covering him up with dirt and heavy branches. Using Spider's burner phone, he dialed Keyhole. "Did you get rid of the car?"

"An easy break-in and I didn't waste any time. I dumped it in the rapids on the Rouge River."

"Excellent. They'll be searching for his body for weeks." Sig disconnected and retraced his steps to the bar. The parking lot was quiet, no one in sight. He dumped his jacket, the gun, gloves, and the contents of Spider's pockets into the back of his SUV under a tarp. After carefully checking his wig and stage makeup in a side mirror, he strolled back into *Charlie's*. His bottle was exactly where he'd left it, and he wanted the bartender to remember the big tipper who had bought it.

MICAH STOOD IN THE shadows of the boathouse, watching Remy and the other women up by the fire pit. He searched her body language for clues—the tilt of her head, the set of her shoulders, the way her hands gripped the arms of the chair—any hint that would tell him how she felt. What she was thinking. But as the wine flowed, the nonverbal cues lessened, making it tough for him to reach any conclusions.

To all outward appearances, Remy was experiencing a *Kumbaya* breakthrough with Mel, Billie, and Breeana. They had even sung a song or two, Christmas carols of all things. Then they'd laughed. And cried. Tubbs didn't appear to be the least bit concerned with their odd behavior. He stretched out by the fire near Remy's feet, content with the chatter, handholding, and emotional ebb and flow of conversation.

But Micah was worried, and so were the rest of his team. It would be much safer for her to be inside. But female intuition apparently trumped logic, at least it had tonight. Remy believed the spider delivery and sugar in the gas tank weren't good enough reasons to justify a lockdown. And Micah had caved.

Rocket stood beside him, mumbling in his ear. "This is a first. I can't believe Billie told me to get lost."

"No shit?" Sully let out a disgusted sigh behind them. "I never thought I'd hear Bree slurring her words this way. She's totally hammered."

"Better brace yourselves boys." Hawke's voice came through their headsets. "We've got incoming. That boat you hear heading into the bay is Stella with wine reinforcements. I can see her through the night vision on my scope."

"Can anyone say shitfaced?" Joe's crackly baritone sounded over the airwaves around the cigar he no doubt had locked between his teeth. "When I told Melena we'd run out of booze—which was a bald-faced lie—she got on the horn to good ole Aunt Stella. The party's just begun as far as the gals are concerned. Almost makes a man proud, don't it?"

"Guess I'll go play welcome wagon." Theo talked into his mic as he reached the pier. The engine cut. Stella's boat bumped against the wharf. Micah heard the sound of ropes being anchored to cleats. "Damn, I've never seen Mel drunk before. Never heard her get so emotional about the shit storm she survived when she first came to the lake. I thought we'd moved past all that."

"Spoken like a man with a *kill or be killed* mentality, Theo." Stella's voice came through Micah's ear bud. He turned out of the boathouse and joined them on the dock. A big bloody mistake.

She poked him in the sternum while Theo hauled a carton of wine out of her two-seater. "You men compartmentalize violence, so why would you expect women to handle it any different? You really believe once the dust settles, these gals can just go on with their lives as if nothing bad has ever darkened their doorstep. Well more fool you."

"Stella, that's not what I meant," Theo argued, walking up beside them. "But it damn well hurts to see Melena miserable and frightened again. Talking it out with the other ladies, she seems to be reliving it in her head."

"Which is good for her, Theo. If you love her, you'll be there for her afterward. And that includes expressing your feelings and letting her do the same."

"Help us out here, Stella." Micah felt Theo's frustration, and Melena's aunt wasn't even his almost-relative. "We were there for all of it, remember? We know what happened in the past and what's still going on, but we're not exactly gifted when it comes to female psychology. So, how do we handle the emotional stuff and get them over this hurdle?"

"Oh, for pity's sake!" Stella raised her eyes heavenward as if asking for guidance from The Man, Himself. "You don't, Micah. There is no magical cure. These gals have gone through hell in the past month or so. And Remy is still living it. They're always putting on a brave face, pretending the creak of a door or a window slamming in the wind doesn't make them jump out of their skin."

Stella took a deep breath then relaxed her stance. "You really want to do something? Let them get drunk as skunks if it helps them to share their nightmares and ease their fears. And listen to what they're trying to tell you. Don't make them keep on their game faces all the time."

"But, we never asked that of any of them." God, Micah felt sick to think this was going through these women's heads.

"I know that, Mic." Stella gentled her voice. "The sad truth is none of you had to ask. These gals set high standards for themselves and they are trying to live up to their own expectations. They see how all of you react to violence and horror...they figure they should be able to do the same."

"That's ridiculous. It's what we've been trained for." Sully's frustration reached through the headset, loud and clear.

Rocket turned the corner out of the boathouse. "Jesus. I never saw this coming."

Theo swore under his breath. "I thought as long as I was with her, Mel wouldn't be frightened anymore."

Micah shook his head. "How could we be so blind?"

"Work it out, boys. Feelings, remember? Try sharing some of yours and show your human side," Stella said. "All the rest is gravy, you'll see."

With Stella and Theo off to the fire pit, Micah brought up the rear. Theo uncorked a couple of bottles and filled the wine goblets. Stella grabbed a lawn chair and settled in beside her niece, while Micah stoked the fire after instructing Papa Joe to kill the floodlights from the house. No point in making them targets if anyone was watching.

Stella gave both men the eye to make themselves scarce. Yeah, like Micah wanted to leave. What he needed was to gather Remy up and hold her. Tell her it was all right to be scared. Say how sorry he was he hadn't really understood the terror she must feel at this hellish situation.

But Stella was right. Remy needed to talk to the other women and get things out in the open. He bent and kissed the top of her head. She gave him a lopsided grin. *Pretty as sin,* he thought, *even with her eyes crossed.* She whispered at the top of her lungs. "I'm getting the ladies dwunk and they're telling me their stowies, Mickey. Just like you said. But it's so sad to hear what happened."

"I know. But believe it or not, you're helping them deal with it, Trigger. And I'll be here if you need me." Micah kissed her again before fading back into the shadows.

Theo squeezed Melena's shoulder as he walked by her chair. "See you later, sugar."

"Okay, Sparky, but don't wait up," Melena giggled.

Micah watched Remy sway to her feet, looking as if she wanted to make a toast. He saw her squint into the darkness, probably to make sure he and Theo were long gone. They weren't going anywhere by unspoken agreement. Theo was ten feet away from him, the two of them making like statues crouched on the slope leading down to the water. Remy's voice, a little unsteady, carried to Micah on the evening breeze. "Ladies, here's to the first meeting of our Survivor's Club!"

"Yippee!" Melena wrapped an arm around her aunt, almost knocking her chair over when they stood up. "Aunt Stella, you're one of us, since you helped save my life...and you're a woman."

"Gee thanks honey-girl. It's a real honor to be a member of the group." Stella raised her glass. "Salut!"

They tossed back their wine and threw the glasses in the bonfire pit. Then they sank back in their chairs, each of them reaching for a full bottle.

"Well, hell." Hunt laughed into his mic. "Something look familiar?"

"I'll say," Law snorted. "They look like us at the end of an op."

Joe agreed. "My personal doctrine since going to 'Nam—who needs a glass when the bottle is handy."

Aw, jeez, Micah's heart broke when he looked at Remy again.

She swiped at her eyes, her tears flowing. "I *looove* you ladies. I just pray I'll still be alive for the next meeting."

That's enough. Micah was on the move to comfort her when Hawke's voice boomed through his ear bud. "Hold up. Doc's heading in, full throttle. If he doesn't slow down, he's going to ram the dock!"

Micah raced for the fire pit, scooping Remy up on the fly. He had her through the downstairs entry before he heard Doc's boat smash the metal edging on the wharf.

"Micah? What's happening?" Voice trembling, she held onto his neck like a lifeline.

"Doc did a bit of a crash landing at our pier." He kissed her cheek and set her down as soon as Rocket and Theo brought the other women into the house. "I want you to stay inside while I go check on him. Okay?"

"As long as you come right back." She grabbed his wrist and held on for a second. "You won't be long?"

"I promise." Micah kissed her full on the mouth, tasting the wine on her lips, hating that she was frightened again.

Joe nodded at him over her shoulder. "Come on, girlies. We'll continue this gabfest in the game room. Make yourselves comfy and I'll get you some chips and dip from the kitchen."

"Let us know if Doc needs anything," Stella murmured as he hustled for the door.

Micah double-timed it back to the water. Doc stood on the pier talking to Sully and Hawke. He appeared to be fine. "Are you suffering from night blindness, Doc? Or did you plan to park on my wharf?"

"Sorry, Mic." Doc scooped to pick up his medical bag. "I was in a rush to get to a crime scene and needed to borrow a car. Didn't notice my GPS wasn't working right on the lake."

Micah felt his antennae twitch. "What crime scene?"

"Some hiker's dog found a dead body in the woods behind *Charlie's*. Sergeant Dupré called me in, since the regular medical examiner is on vacation."

Micah felt his blood turn to ice. *Please tell me this isn't a woman's body, and it hasn't been hacked to pieces.* "Is it a man or a woman?"

"I won't know that until I view the body." Doc knew what Remy was up against and understood Micah's concern. "I'll call you as soon as I have more information."

Micah nodded, glancing at Sully. "Are you planning to work the scene?"

"Yeah. Hawke, too." Sully dug in a pocket to pull out his car keys. Hawke grabbed them and headed for the SUV, taking Doc with him. "We'll have no problem with Sergeant Dupré, since we worked together on Melena's case. The guy might be a jerk, but he knows his limitations. And he doesn't have crime scene techs. I've already requested a unit from Montreal."

Micah relaxed a little, knowing the investigation would be handled properly. "Let me know when you have something."

Sully started to move, then hesitated. "You'll be two men short on watch tonight. Be careful."

"Count on it." Micah watched his CO slide behind the wheel and hit the bar lights. As the SUV careened around the first bend in the road, a terrifying thought rose in his mind. How close was Remy to ending up like the corpse behind *Charlie's*?

REMY EASED INTO THE kitchen, thanking the coffee gods the carafe was full. The sun was barely up, her hands were shaking, her knees were weak, and she had a headache. Could she possibly feel any worse? At least she'd tossed her cookies before passing out last night, and now she vaguely remembered drinking a big bottle of water with an ibuprofen chaser, thanks to Micah. So, yes, she could be feeling a lot worse. While she might be one of the hangover wounded, she would survive.

Pouring a mug of java, she moved into the sunroom to suffer in private, in case whoever had made the coffee came back for a refill. She really couldn't handle any jokes from the guys until after she was wide awake and felt better. She looked outside, surprised to see Tubbs on the deck. Then she heard voices—Micah's and some of the others'. Were the men back from the crime scene? Slipping on sunglasses and tightening the sash on her robe, she pushed the screen door open to join them. "Good morning."

"Hey, Trigger." Micah's questioning gaze didn't escape her. He took her in from head to toe, no doubt wondering how she could stand on her own two feet after last night's wine fest. He nudged a chair out from under the table with a foot. "Come and join us."

She made her way to the far end of the deck and sank into the black wicker, breathing in the fresh air. The sun was a brilliant, orange ball rising through the trees. Mist burned off the water and birds began to chirp welcoming the new day. Hawke, Sully, and Doc were sitting with Micah, looking at photos, none of them smiling. They probably hadn't been to bed yet, but they didn't look tired. They seemed keyed up about something. "What do you have there?"

"It's a snapshot of the victim's ring." Micah flipped the other prints facedown, sliding only one to her across the glass tabletop. "Do you recognize it?"

Remy studied the picture. The ring was gold, heavy and thick, a man's band carved in an intricate web pattern. At the top of the ring sat an arachnid, its legs clinging to the sides of the filigree. A large diamond was nestled in the spider's body. She shook her head, feeling her stomach roll. "It's ugly, but I've never seen it before. I would remember something like this. Does it belong to the man who murdered the women in Florida?"

"No," Sully said. "But it may belong to the one who sent you the spiders."

"What did you say? You're telling me it's not the same person?" Tubbs laid his head on her knee as if sensing her confusion. Were there still *two* men chasing her, even though she'd killed the guy's partner in the swamp? "How do you know the dead body isn't the man I got away from in the Glades?"

"Because the owner of this ring was British." Micah tipped his chin at Hawke. "You might as well tell her what you found out."

Hawke cleared his throat, clearly not happy to give her the bad news. "We traced the gemstone in the ring—a diamond of this quality contains a serial number—back to a jewellery designer in London. The ring was one of a kind, a special order, and the jeweller kept a record of the sale. The name of the buyer popped up when we ran him through immigration. He flew into Montreal a few days ago. Now we're checking the rentals to see if he was staying in a cottage at the lake."

"There...there must be some mistake," Remy tugged her hair behind an ear, fighting for control. What did a ring belonging to a man from England have to do with a serial killer in Florida? And why would the Brit send her spiders? *Breathe in, breathe out. This will all make sense in a few minutes.*

"We don't exactly have a face to make a comparison—he was that badly damaged—but the musculature, weight, and height of our dead body are the same as the guy with the British passport." Doc reached for a thermos jug on the table and poured himself more coffee. "I'm convinced our DB is James Broderick. But I won't make an official ID until after I review his dental records. I won't have those for another day or two."

"Here's the thing," Micah said, obviously tuned in to Remy's confusion. He touched her hand, a light brush of his fingers over her knuckles. She thought it amazing how he helped steady her, how his touch could calm her nerves. "Broderick hasn't visited the U.S. for the better part of three years. And this was his first trip to Canada."

"So you're saying he couldn't have killed the women in the Everglades because he wasn't in the country at the time?" When Micah nodded, she pushed to her feet. She needed a clearer head to understand the facts. "I'm going for a quick swim, but I'll be back. Don't move."

"Not a good idea," Micah said. "Take a shower instead. Tubbs will go with you."

"Okay. I won't be long." She called the dog and walked through the house. Micah was right; there was no point in making herself a target by swimming in the lake. But, damn, would her life ever return to normal? Although truth be told, she felt much better today. Knowing what Melena, Billie, and Breeana had gone through—and how Micah's team had protected them—made all the difference. She wasn't as scared, finally realizing she wasn't in this alone. The others cared about her, especially Micah. And Lord knew she cared about him. Maybe too much.

Dressing quickly after her shower in shorts and a T-shirt, and after brushing her teeth, she made her way out to the deck again, just in time to see Doc's boat shooting across the bay for home. She also noticed Stella's two-seater was gone. Remy glanced at her watch, didn't envy the woman opening the store at this early hour. Of course, Mel's aunt hadn't consumed as much alcohol as she had, so she was probably well rested and able to take her day in stride.

Sully's phone rang just as she reached the table again. He walked away to take the call.

Micah kissed her cheek when she sat down, heat shining in those bottomless, brown eyes of his. "We'll get through this, Trigger. Together."

"I know we will, Mic. I'm not worried when you're with me." It was the truth. This man she hardly knew settled her as no one else could. She started to touch his knee, only realizing at the last second the tabletop was glass and everyone would notice. Micah winked at her, no doubt reading her mind.

"That was ballistics." Sully sank back in his chair, tucking his phone in a pocket. "I sent the 9mm slugs we found and put a rush on them. It turns out there were several hits in the database. The gun was used in other crimes over the past few years. Some robberies and a gang related shooting in Montreal. And none of those have a connection to our case."

Micah arched an eyebrow. "You're saying the gun was a rental? These guys must do more business than Walmart."

"Yep, cash and carry. Hell, they even deliver." Sully scowled. "We'll never put the weapon in our killer's hands."

Remy reached for the coffee jug, draining the last of it into her cup when Hawke's cell phone pinged. He scrolled down the screen while she added cream to the dark brew. "Jesus, you're not going to believe this."

"Spill it," Micah said.

"It's from my contact in Scotland Yard. Chief Inspector Gauld is the one who traced the diamond to the jewellery designer on Carnaby Street." Hawke continued to read through the text message. "He says there's been a serial killer on the loose in London. Three deaths in six months. Prior to that, he thinks the killer was operating in Southern Ireland, and before that, in Wales. Always three kills using the same signature. Then the guy vanishes and pops up somewhere else."

"I don't get it." Micah ran his hands through his hair, thumping his elbows back on the table. "What does this have to do with the Brit lying dead in our morgue?"

Hawke tossed his phone on the table, leaning forward. "Gauld says the spider ring may have provided him with his first solid lead on their perp. Get this, the bodies of the murdered women were sealed in wooden caskets. Their remains were covered in spiders, and in some cases snakes, as well."

"Cut to the punch line, Hawke." Micah stared at him as if he wanted to shake the information out of him. "Can he place our dead man at the crime scenes in his jurisdiction?"

"Maybe. Broderick's passport confirms he was in Southern Ireland when the women were murdered in Dublin." Hawke leaned back in his chair, crossing a foot over the opposite knee. "Meanwhile, Alistair Gauld is working another angle to connect him to the homicides in Wales."

"Spit it out, pal. What does he have?" Sully had flipped open his iPad, keying in the information as quickly as Hawke spoke.

"He's convinced the earliest victim of this monster managed to escape. She hid for hours under a parked car until a unit rolled by making its nightly rounds."

"Smart woman," Remy said, shuddering. "She must have been scared to death and injured. It's a miracle she managed to save herself."

"Some miracle. She spent a week in the hospital recovering from her wounds." Disgust filled Hawke's voice as he continued, "Gauld just got off the phone with her after reading the incident report again. She remembered something that wasn't written in the original report. Her assailant wore a spider ring. A gold one, with a diamond in the spider's back."

Chapter 9

Micah upended another log on the chopping block, hefting the axe over his head and following through with a grunt. The blade split the maple like butter, both halves tumbling to the ground near his feet. He eyed the growing pile of firewood, relieved his shoulder injury wasn't giving him trouble. Not a twinge of pain or falter in his swing. Hoo-rah. He wiped the sweat from his brow with the back of a hand, the air so muggy he could cut it with a knife. A storm was brewing and it was going to be a thunder banger.

"If you tell me where the lawnmower is, I'll get started on the grass before it starts to rain." Remy's restless energy was palpable, her feet scuffing tracks in the dirt as she watched him make like a lumberjack. Tubbs lay nearby in a hole he'd dug in the shade of a tamarack tree. He slept like a snoring, drooling baby.

Micah pulled Remy toward him to kiss the top of her head. "Trigger, I don't have a lawn, so there's nothing to cut. Just trees, rock formations, and paths leading around the property."

"You're right, you don't have a blade of grass on this place." She swatted at the deerfly intent on taking a chunk out of her leg. "Just those pretty driftwood sculptures near the paths with field flowers tucked in around them. I can't believe I forgot. I need something to keep me busy, Mic, before my mind melts into a puddle of mush."

"Well, we can't have that." Micah nodded to the lean-to behind him. "How about getting the wheelbarrow and stacking the wood I'm splitting in the woodshed?"

"I can do that." She looked around them. "I'll need work gloves and some citronella. The damn bugs are driving me crazy."

"You'll find both in the mudroom. Pull on a ball cap too. It deters the flies." Micah watched her sprint for the side door. Man, she was poetry in motion, the sway of her hips and shape of her butt in the shorts grinding his gears. He thought about following her into the house and dragging her to the bedroom. He glanced at his watch. Nah, ten in the morning was a bit early to take a nap. He didn't want to raise any eyebrows with the rest of the team and embarrass the hell out of her.

They worked side by side for the next hour. Saying little as the stack of logs in the woodshed grew. Still, the physical labor didn't lessen Micah's urge to throw Remy over his shoulder and carry her inside. A Neanderthal move by any standards, but what could he say? She brought it out in him. The desire to head to the man cave. Protect her. Love her.

All this emotion for a woman who wasn't even his type. Micah cursed under his breath. He had always been attracted to dark hair and caramel skin until now, to women incapable of stacking wood and more concerned about breaking a nail or having a hair out of place. Yeah, his kind of lady worked out in a gym and didn't fend for herself. She might need a man to open her car door and look good on her arm, but knew her away around the finest restaurants and nightclubs without blinking an eye.

No, Remy was nothing like his usual woman. She was a far cry from helpless—a carrot-topped firebrand who sported pale skin and freckles to boot. Pretty and feisty, not mysterious and seductive. And the bigger puzzle? How she affected him. What was it about her that drew him in?

Micah always traveled light, loved 'em and left 'em as the saying went. He flirted, enjoyed the benefits of hookups without the down side of relationships. Then he vamoosed, telling himself his dangerous lifestyle prevented him from having a steady woman in his life. So why associate the word *permanent* with Remy whenever he thought of her, which was at least a hundred times a day when he wasn't looking straight at her.

Tubbs jumped to his feet, breaking into Micah's thoughts. He frowned as the hackles rose on the dog's back, making the fur from neck to tail stand on end. Body tense, a low growl in his throat, the mastiff pointed his nose toward the woods behind the house. *What now?*

Remy touched Micah's shoulder. "What is Tubbs growling at?"

"Maybe nothing." But he didn't believe it, not for a second. He remembered hearing Hank and McGee sound the alarm at the rodeo in Hereford—Rizzo's highly trained dogs had been there to protect Billie. He knew what the sound meant. A shitload of trouble.

Micah dropped the axe and grabbed his Glock off the ledge in the lean-to. "Rocket! I need the dog's working lead."

That was the signal that set the rest of his team in motion, because the working lead meant Tubbs had caught the scent of someone who could be a threat. Rocket shouted for Law as he jogged over with the leash, snapping it on Tubbs's collar. "Get Billie out of the boathouse. She's tinkering with the runabout in there."

Sully appeared on the deck with Joe, both of them watching Hawke as he herded Breeana and Mel off the dock. Bree's book fluttered into the lake as they hustled to the house.

Hunt appeared at Micah's side with Theo, both of them armed. "Leave Remy with us if you're heading into the bush."

"No!" Remy slipped her fingers through his, her hand trembling as she held on tight. "I'm going with Mic."

Crazy woman. With no time to argue, Micah nodded to Rocket to take the point with Tubbs. Theo and Hunt watched their backs as they entered the trees. The terrain led uphill, Tubbs moving like a locomotive, sniffing the air and staying on course. They crossed a ravine, climbing down one side and up the other, all of them listening and watching for anything out of place. Whatever had cranked Tubbs into attack mode, it was still ahead of them, the dog barreling forward as fast as Rocket allowed.

Nothing moved around them, not the flutter of birds in the trees, and not so much as a field mouse skittering in the undergrowth. Something had scared them off. Remy stayed glued to Micah's side, tethered by his hand clamped around her wrist, exactly where he wanted her if all hell broke loose. She didn't say a word, her heavy breathing the only indication she struggled to keep up with his long strides.

Thunder rolled in the distance, the sky taking on a yellowish tinge as dark clouds formed above the treetops. Tubbs plodded on, leading them halfway up the side of a bluff. Then he stopped dead, his muscles gathering beneath him, his body shaking with the urge to attack. Rocket silenced his growl with a hand signal, commanding him to sit. The dog obeyed and waited.

Micah nodded to Hunt who came forward to protect Remy. She wasn't real happy with his decision, but she didn't say a word. He moved out with Theo, the two of them with their guns raised. Whatever waited for them up there, it could be deadly. Micah hit the rise, the ground shaking with another rumble of thunder. Heat lightning flashed overhead. And he saw a body. A woman lay on the open ground, unmoving, a small plastic bucket beside her. Blood trickled from a wound in her scalp, staining her blond hair. *Is she dead?*

Theo stayed back as Micah approached her, on the lookout for anyone who might be hiding up there. Micah gently rolled the woman over. She moaned when he touched her, and opened her blue eyes. The same eyes as Jessie's and Bethie's, the twins he'd rescued in the woods a few days ago. Fear and confusion clouded Chloe Templeton's gaze. "Easy. You're safe now."

He carefully ran his hands over her body, looking for other injuries. She brushed them away, eyeing him suspiciously. "What are you doing here?"

"The dog was growling down by the house and took off in this direction. He must have heard something the rest of us didn't." Micah didn't like the pallor of her skin. For all he knew, she had a serious head injury. "You should lie still for a while and get your bearings."

"Maybe for a minute or two." She seemed satisfied with his explanation, realizing he wasn't the person who had knocked her out. "But I feel fine, other than the bump on my head."

Remy joined them as soon as Theo gave her the signal to move forward. "Chloe, can you tell us what happened?" Helping the woman to a sitting position, Remy wrapped her arms around her for support.

"I d-don't know," Chloe said, brushing the hair out of her eyes. "I was gathering blueberries to make a pie for dinner, and I heard something behind me. Th-that's all I remember."

Micah noticed the berries spilling from the pail and the plants clinging to the edges of the bluff. He studied her head wound as he applied gauze and tape from the small first aid kit he carried in his cargo shorts. The edges of the gash were jagged, as if she'd been struck with something fairly sharp, like the edge of a rock. She also sported one hell of a goose egg. He wondered who would want to hit her, other than her husband. Was Templeton a wife beater? "Where's Winston, Chloe?"

"H-he's with the girls. He took them to the marina to register for the swim races at the regatta on Saturday. And I went berry picking."

Not the husband, Micah realized, as he helped her to her feet. "Come on. We're taking you to a clinic to have your head stitched, and you might need an X-ray of some kind. We'll call Winston to meet us there."

Theo and Hunt tucked Chloe between them and eased her down the side of the bluff. It was when Micah turned and raised his gaze to the view in the distance that his blood ran cold. The ledge overlooked the back of his house, a half kilometer away as the crow flies. The perfect location for someone wanting to keep eyes on Remy.

HUNT DROVE THE WINDING road from the lake to the highway with Theo riding beside him. Remy sat in the back with Chloe and Micah. She squeezed Chloe's hand. "Are you doing okay?"

"I'm fine. Just a little annoyed about conking myself on the head." She grimaced, lightly touching the bandage where Micah had covered the wound." I guess I lost my footing, although I don't remember."

Remy frowned when Micah said nothing. She was sure he thought someone had hit Chloe. But why? She couldn't very well ask him with the woman sitting there. Turning left at the intersection, Hunt gunned the SUV for the center of town. They passed a gardening supply store, the local grocery, a gas station, and a white clapboard church before pulling up to the rambling, one-story clinic. Sided in cedar with a green tin roof, it was a modular design with a country feel.

Theo ducked inside and brought out a wheelchair. Once Chloe was settled, Remy pushed her through the electronic doors to the reception area. After the triage nurse examined her wound and took her blood pressure in a small room off to the side, an attendant whisked her down a corridor to radiology.

With nothing more to do, Remy took a seat in the waiting room, watching CNN on a flatscreen bolted to the wall. Winston would arrive soon to take over and stay with his wife, but until then, she and the others would remain. Micah and Theo stood near the entrance, their arms crossed like bouncers at a nightclub. Hunt had stayed with their vehicle parked across the street. Remy tried to see the humor in the situation, but failed miserably. She felt ridiculous with all this security, and yet she knew there was no other choice. So, she kept to herself and watched television, worried someone might realize the guys were there to protect her.

Breaking news flashed on the monitor, one story after another, until the footage from Florida nearly knocked her off her chair. She gazed in disbelief, afraid to move and unable to breathe. Her own photo stared back from the widescreen. The sound muted, the caption read *"Witness to Everglades Serial Killings Still Missing...the Swamp Killer is still at large"*.

Panic ensued. Scooting down in her seat, Remy pulled the cap low on her forehead and slipped on dark glasses. Should she flee or stay where she was? And where the heck was Micah? Oh, right, he was across the room. No, he was at the receptionist's desk. He must have seen the clip. He whispered something in the older woman's ear. She patted his hand then flipped the remote to a baseball game on a sports channel. "Now that we have satellite hookup, I only watch CNN 'cuz I like to keep up with international events. But I'll make an exception, since you bet on the game. I hope you win!"

"Thanks." A killer smile on his face, Micah turned to the coffee machine, dispensing coins in the slot as if he hadn't a care in the world. Meanwhile, Remy was close to hyperventilating, wishing she could breathe into a paper bag to relieve the pressure. Micah walked over and handed her a cup, blocking her view of the other occupants in the room.

"Relax, Trigger, you worry too much."

"Are you insane?" she hissed. "I was just on a freaking news bulletin!"

"Tuck the hair under your hat, take off the sunglasses, and you'll do fine." He winked, speaking in a soft tone. "Anyone who saw that clip isn't expecting to find you in the local clinic, not when you disappeared from a location a few thousand miles away."

"You're out of your mind." Remy took a sip of coffee, partially hiding her face behind the cup. "How could they not recognize me, unless they're totally blind?"

"It's human nature. People see what they expect to see. And you look like a country girl who's been stacking wood and running around in the woods. Not anything like the woman on the screen wearing makeup and a fancy hairstyle. Your name didn't appear on the tickertape and the sound was off, so no worries."

While Micah's big body continued to block her from view, she scrunched her hair up and pulled off the shades, her eyes shooting daggers at him from below the brim of her ball cap. "Damn it, Mic. Why didn't we take Chloe to Doc instead of coming here?"

"It wasn't an option. Doc's performing an autopsy at the ME's office this afternoon."

"Right." Remy tried to appear calm as her world fell apart at the seams. Her hands shook, a headache pounded her temples, and the scent of antiseptic made her stomach queasy. "You mean the murdered man who was wearing the spider ring."

Micah nodded. "That's the one...James Broderick, although he won't be positively identified until Doc compares his dental work with the records coming from Scotland Yard."

"But—"

"Heads up." Theo approached them while disconnecting a call on his cell phone. "Hunt says Templeton just pulled into the parking lot."

Winston charged through the door with Bethany and Jessica. He motioned the twins over to the kiddy corner, which was set up with colorful chairs, books, and toys. Once they were settled, he crossed to the reception desk and inquired about Chloe.

The receptionist spoke into a phone for a few seconds before hanging up. "Your wife will be out as soon as the doctor finishes stitching her up. You can be with her if you'd like."

"Thank you, but I'd better stay here with my daughters." Winston gave Micah a wave and walked toward them. "Man, it's a good thing you found Chloe when you did. I had no idea she was out in the woods by herself."

"She didn't tell you she was going berry picking?" Micah arched an eyebrow as if he didn't believe him.

"Well, she may have," Winston admitted. "I wanted to register the twins for some swim events at the regatta and Chloe didn't want to come. But if she mentioned berry picking, I guess I wasn't paying attention."

He sat down, balancing his elbows on knobby knees. Remy noticed he wore a pink polo shirt, dark baggy shorts, knee socks, and sandals. In some ways, she could almost understand his nerdy appeal. Obviously, Chloe found him attractive, and he seemed to be a good father.

"You'd best be watching out for your family from now on," Micah said, a scowl on his face. "Otherwise, take them back to the city where they'll be safe."

"I'll just go check on the little ones." Remy stood up and hustled to the kiddy corner. She didn't want to hear Micah give Winston a dressing down, although he deserved it and seemed to live with his head in the clouds. First, the girls wandered off on their own, and now, his wife had taken a tumble. Still, it was better if the men spoke in private. "Bethie, Jessie, how are you?"

"We're fine," One of them said. Remy couldn't tell them apart and didn't want to ask who was who. "Is Mama going to be okay?"

"She sure is. Just a little bump on her head, that's all. There's nothing to worry about."

"Oh good." Satisfied, the twins went back to piecing a puzzle together, the two of them dressed in identical green shorts and striped green and white tops.

Thunder boomed, shaking the building. Remy glanced out the window as a steady rain pounded the roof. Finally, they'd get some relief from the muggy temperatures. She watched as a rusty-brown pickup squealed up to the entrance, its muffler rumbling as it braked to a stop. The passenger window rolled down, and Remy felt the blood drain from her face.

She was staring at the Swamp Killer, with nothing but a pane of glass between them. He grinned at her, an ugly, slashing leer. Then he raised a gun.

Remy spun away. She pulled the twins to the carpet. Covering them with her body, she screamed. "Micah!"

REMY'S SHRIEK HIT MICAH like an RPG. He jumped over chairs to reach her. Saw the pickup outside, an arm extended, a Walther aimed at her through the window. *Jesus Lord!* Micah pulled the gun from under his shirttail. Taking aim, he fired high. Just enough to have the asshole drop his weapon and take off before someone got killed. The last thing he wanted to do was shoot him in front of Winston's kids. The glass shattered. People dropped to the floor screaming. He heard Theo shout at Hunt on his cell phone to cut the truck off. The receptionist called 9-1-1. Winston ran to protect his daughters. Micah wrapped an arm around Remy's waist and charged for the door. "Come on!"

Too late to stop the pickup, Hunt screeched to a halt at the curb. Theo threw open the doors and they piled inside. Hunt stomped the gas pedal. Theo checked his magazine clip beside him. Micah did the same, glancing over at Remy who lay sprawled on the floor. He wrapped a hand around her wrist and pulled her up. "Secure your seatbelt and stay low."

"How did he find me?" Her eyes were wild, her hands shaking. She clutched his arm after snapping the belt in place. "What's happening? Talk to me, Mic!"

He goddamn wanted to, but what could he say when he didn't have a freaking clue? "You know what's going on. I'm assuming that's the Swamp Killer up there. And right now I need you to hold it together so we can catch his ass."

"Mic—"

"Later." Hunt was almost on top of the pickup now—the SUV had a lot more horses under the hood. A few more loop-de-loops in the road and Micah rolled down his window. He leaned out, rain pelting his face. Theo did the same on the opposite side. "Hold her steady, Hunt."

"Look out!" Remy screamed. She dragged Micah inside by his belt. A good thing too, since a Hum-Vee shot straight at them out of a side road.

Jesus, we're about to be T-boned. We're going to die.

Or maybe not. Hunt goosed the gas. He rammed the stick into Overdrive. The engine kicked like a mule then leapt like a gazelle. Micah watched the grille near his side window begin to move off. Their vehicle almost clear until the fucker rammed the back quarter panel.

The SUV spun. The Hummer circled behind it and took off. Another three-sixty spin and the pickup ahead rounded a bend of highway and vanished. But the third revolution was the game changer. Their ride roared over an embankment. Sailed into a ditch and shuddered to a stop. The rear axle collapsed. A back wheel fell off. They were toast.

Breathing hard, his heart pounding, Micah felt pain radiate from his head where he'd smashed it into the door frame. He ignored it, preferring a healthy dose of pissed off to get him moving. He glanced at Remy. "You okay, Trigger?"

"Yes, but you're not." She unsnapped her seatbelt, touching the side of his face with trembling fingers. "You're bleeding, and your wrist looks strange. I think it's broken."

"Nah, it's just a sprain." He nudged his chin at Theo and Hunt who seemed to be out cold. "Check on those guys while I see what's happening up top."

"No need." Hunt keyed off the ignition with a grunt and punched the inflated air bag to flatten it. "I'm alive. Just got the wind knocked out of me. And Theo's coming around. Lucky SOB, considering he wasn't wearing a seat belt. He could have put his fool head through the windshield instead of just grazing it."

"Yeah, tell me about it." Micah opened the door, using it for support while he got his sea legs under him. Sweat beaded his forehead, or was that rain? Not that it mattered. Either way his left hand hung by his side, out of commission and throbbing like a bitch. He sucked up the pain, held the gun in his right while staggering uphill to the highway. He reached the asphalt and looked around. He was pretty sure he was seeing double, but even if he was, there wasn't a car in sight. The Swamp Killer and whoever had helped him were long gone. He shoved the Glock in the front of his belt, dragged out his cell phone, and called Sully. "We have a problem."

"On my way." Yeah, Sully was like that. He didn't sweat the details, knew the guys would tell him what he needed to know. "Where are you?"

"No idea. You'll have to track us by GPS. Oh, and bring Breeana and a first aid kit while you're at it." Micah dropped the phone while his CO shouted in his ear. Man, he didn't have the energy to respond.

Swaying on his feet, he toppled back down the slope into the gully, crash landed beside the SUV, and passed out.

Chapter 10

Sig watched the Rouge River flow by below the clubhouse bar with a smile. White water spouted and gushed over rocks and through crevices, the steady roar ringing in his ears. The rain had stopped but the decking was wet and the golf links were closed, which was why Sig and his associates sat on the terrace by themselves. His gaze travelled around the table with pride. These were the remaining lieutenants of the group—now that Blade and Spider were gone—from the old days at the boarding school in the Alps. And each of them had his own special gifts.

The Dentist was known for his skill with drills, chisels, and pliers. Women couldn't be identified from dental records once he worked his magic. He was a true master of his craft.

Ice-Pick's talent was with sharp instruments. He could pierce a woman's body multiple times and take days to kill her, drawing out his pleasure until he lost interest and moved on.

Keyhole had never met a security system he couldn't breach, and he loved the women who hid behind them. Young, old, it didn't matter to him, as long as their alarm systems gave him a challenge.

The British press had dubbed Snake the Prince of Venom. He would wait until his victims were almost dead before injecting them with the anti-venom of whichever slithering creature he had used. Then he would revive his prey and begin again.

Sig raised his glass, proud of his friends and what they had all accomplished in their lives. "To a job well done."

The Dentist laughed, tapping his tumbler with Sig's. "Rivera and his crew never saw it coming. One minute they were chasing the pickup, the next they were headed for a gully."

"Thanks to Ice-Pick." Keyhole grinned and elbowed his buddy. "He nailed them at the crossroads, just like we planned."

"Not quite." Sig took another sip of bourbon. "You were supposed to T-bone the SUV."

"Yeah, I would have accelerated sooner if I'd known the piece of shit Hum-Vee was short on guts." Ice-Pick shrugged his shoulders. "Still, major damage was done."

"And don't forget, we're all out of our comfort zone here, Sig." The other men nodded agreement with the Dentist. "We're used to trapping women, not the men protecting them. This was a first."

"Which may have worked to our advantage," Sig admitted, reaching for a cigarillo and lighting it. "I didn't anticipate the Renaud woman would be inside the SUV with them. And I don't want her killed...at least, not that way."

Ice-Pick chugged from his pilsner glass before setting it back on the table. He wiped his mouth with the back of a hand. "Shit, it's too bad I didn't have time to stop after they crashed and stab Rivera through the heart."

"I'm glad you didn't. Now he's mine to kill." Sig leaned forward, rolling the ash from his smoke in the ashtray. "Did you ditch the Hummer?"

"Sure, not that it really matters, since Keyhole stole it." Ice-Pick motioned through the window to the waiter inside the bar to bring them another round. "I torched it in a farmer's field when the Dentist showed up to give me a ride."

"What about the pickup?" Sig glanced at Snake, who had arrived from Ireland that morning.

"It's done. Sunk at the bottom of the river, a couple of miles south of Spider's rental," Snake said. "Keyhole showed me the spot. I ran it over the ledge and caught a lift back with him."

"Excellent." Sig sat back in his chair, tuning the others out as the waiter brought their drink orders. The sun broke through the clouds, a breeze off the river spiraling wet leaves to the deck. The air smelled fresh, the storm long gone. Life couldn't be better, at least until the timing was right, until he had the woman exactly where and how he wanted her.

"I'm giving you fair warning." Snake pointed a finger at him, a chilly glint in his blue-eyed gaze. "I'm not pleased to hear aboot my hunting partner's death. Spider and I go back a long ways."

Black Irish bastard, Sig thought, as he stared at the dark haired man with the lilt in his voice. "It needed to be done before he brought all of us down."

"Maybe." Snake clamped a hand on his shoulder. "But I'm telling you now. I'll be on your arse if there's any more fook ups."

Sig shook off his grip, resisting the urge to cap the guy where he sat. He fought for calm, not happy Snake dared to question his motives. "I lost a partner too, remember? Blade died in the Everglades, murdered by that bitch. Or have you forgotten that's the reason we're here?"

"I haven't. But we didn't kill one of our own when Blade died." Snake tipped his glass, his gaze unreadable over the rim. "I trust it won't happen again."

"There's no reason it should." Fuck the Irishman. Sig was in charge, not this smooth-talking, poetry-spouting devil from across the Atlantic. Yeah, that was Snake's MO. The ladies loved his gentle ways, his corduroy jackets with the suede patches on the elbows, his tenure as a professor at a college in Belfast. Little did they know the kind of monster he was, until it was too late. Sig had to admit, though, Spider and Snake had done good work. Arachnids and reptiles, torture and sex culminating in grotesque deaths and perfect crimes. Still, it wasn't his problem if Snake had to work alone for a while, especially when he had to do the same.

Sig's focus moved back to where it belonged. On his quarry, on the end game with Blade's killer, on the woman who occupied his every thought. Because seeing her terror today, the sweat on her skin, hearing her screams only made him anticipate their time together more, caused his body to throb with need. If he were honest, he'd admit he wanted her for more than killing Blade. She was his type of woman, after all, a ball buster if he gave her half a chance. Oh, she would fight, but he would win. Break her. Have her as many times and in as many ways as he wanted. Torture her with the other guys. He would kill her, of course, but only when he was good and ready.

And he would make Micah Rivera watch.

THE POLICE STATION in the little town resembled a small alpine lodge, a wooden structure with lots of glass overlooking the town square. The morgue behind it wasn't quite as appealing, an ugly gray cinderblock box. And, Sweet Lord, this was the last place Remy wanted to be.

She helped support Micah's weight as Hawke pulled him from Sully's SUV. Micah shook Hawke off once his boots hit the ground, but he kept an arm around her shoulders. She wondered, was he protecting her or did he need her help to stay upright? They made their way to the entrance, Breeana standing behind them with Hunt and Theo. As Remy pushed the buzzer and waited for someone to usher them in, she noticed Sully and Hawke heading around the corner to the police station.

Her legs wobbled when the security guard led them down a quiet hallway. The ceilings were low and she felt the walls closing in. She focused on the yellow stripe painted on the cement floor that led to the far end of the corridor.

"You'll find Doctor Finley in there." The guard pointed to a set of metal swinging doors then retraced his steps in the opposite direction.

Remy whispered under her breath. "You want to tell me why we're here, Mic? I don't like this place."

"I don't blame you, but we need Doc's services and this is where we'll find him." He wrapped his good hand around hers as they entered a cold, cavernous room. She shuddered as Doc greeted them, introducing them to his assistant, Sam.

Casting a wary glance around the arctic-chilled space, Remy hoped she wouldn't see anything to add to her nightmares. The gleaming autopsy table Micah eased himself onto was enough, never mind the nearby cart containing what she assumed were pathologist instruments—forceps, saws, scalpels, syringes, and other tools she couldn't identify. A weight scale hung from the ceiling near the stainless steel sinks. She had watched enough forensic shows to know what it was used for. Body parts, like the ones she had seen in the Glades. Her mind whirled back to that god-awful night. The knot in her belly tightened. The smell of antiseptic cleaner filled her senses. She fought for breath, determined not to play the fool by hurling her stomach contents into the nearest garbage pail.

Micah's gaze zeroed in on her in an instant. She imagined her face was pale and she looked like death. She gave him a sick smile, hoping he wouldn't catch on. The last thing he needed was to worry about her when he was the one with the injuries. God, he looked terrible, and blood still dripped down the side of his face. He slid off the table as soon as Sam had X-rayed his skull and wrist. Pulling her against him, he held her tight so she wouldn't fall apart. "Someone take Remy into Doc's office. She doesn't need to be here."

"This *is* my office, Mic, and it's the only space that's...available." Doc pointed to the far side of the room where Micah's digital X-rays already appeared on the computer screen on a small desk in the corner. "Remy, you can grab a seat over there while Bree and I tend to the others."

"It's okay, Doc." Determined to do her share, she pushed her nausea and fear aside and focused on what needed to be done. This wasn't the body dump in the swamp. There was nothing here that could hurt her. Through sheer force of will, she managed to bring herself under control. "Tell me what I can do to help."

Doc handed her some gauze pads and a bottle of alcohol. "You can clean Hunt up while Bree tends to Mic's head injury." He moved to the desk to study Micah's X-rays. "You're lucky. It's only a mild concussion."

Micah scowled. "Do I look like a cream puff to you, Doc? Toss me a compression bandage for my wrist, a Band-Aid for my head wound, a couple of aspirins, and I'll be out of your hair."

"Not so fast." Remy angled her chin at him. "You're not going anywhere until you've been patched up."

"Look, we're wasting time. I need you locked down at the house so we can find these scumbags before they come after you again."

Remy was sure Micah would have hauled her out of the room in an instant but Breeana blocked him, backing him up. She held a wicked looking needle in a rubber-gloved hand. She had forgotten Bree was a veterinarian and knew how to cope with medical emergencies.

"Relax, Mic." Breeana stood her ground, looking ready to stab him if he so much as moved an inch. "You don't have any transportation until Sully and Hawke come back, so you might as well hop up on the table again."

"What's in the syringe, Bree?" Micah quirked an eyebrow as if he didn't trust her. "Don't even try to sedate me. I need to stay alert."

"It may surprise you to know, Mic, but you aren't a flippin' superhero!" Remy shook her head in frustration. "I swear if Theo and Hunt weren't so wrecked themselves, I'd have them tie you down so Breeana could stitch your head in peace."

"We're up for it." Theo sat on another autopsy table grinning through his split lips, his nose bleeding and slightly off kilter. "What do you say, Hunt? Should we hogtie him?"

"You really want to go there?" Micah cranked his good hand into a fist. "The way you guys look, I could KO both of you with one good punch."

"Don't count on it." Hunt winked at Remy as she dabbed at his cuts, a glint of mischief in his eyes. "We'll take you on if it means you'll shut your trap. Quit acting like a whiny little girl."

"Bring it on, jerk face." Micah set his stance on the balls of his feet. "Let's get this over with so I can take a victory lap."

"Will you relax, Mic? It's only lidocaine in the syringe." Breeana handed him the drug ampoule. "See? This is the same anesthetic dentists use and it's topical. It deadens the nerve endings in the skin. I just want to freeze the area to put in those stitches."

"Bree does real nice needlework, Mic. Go ahead and let her do it." Doc slipped by them and headed for the hallway. "I have to take care of something for a client in the next room. I'll be back in a few. Then I'll remove those stitches in Remy's thigh. They look ready to come out."

Yeesh, a client in the next room? Is it the spider ring guy? Remy didn't want to think about it.

"You know, you're lucky Doc carries a fully stocked medical bag, because I doubt the morgue keeps anesthetic on the shelves for its patients." Breeana approached Micah again with the needle. "Now, can we please get this over with, so I can make Theo's face pretty again for Melena?"

"I'm all yours, but without the lidocaine."

Breeana shrugged her shoulders. "Suit yourself, big man."

Remy almost laughed, watching Micah glare at Bree with every painful push and tug of the needle through his scalp. Nine sutures, and if she didn't know better, she might think Breeana was prolonging the agony because of Micah's snarly mood.

Doc came back while Breeana added a bandage to her handiwork. He removed Remy's sutures, and minutes later, Micah had him huffing and puffing over repairing his wrist fracture.

"I asked you to splint it." Micah nudged Doc away when he saw the wet strip in his hands. "I didn't ask for a cast."

"Listen, this is a serious fracture and it needs a full cast." When Micah continued to balk, Doc changed tacks. "Well, how about this? I'll give you half a fibreglass cast instead, on the underside of the wrist for support. It's lightweight, waterproof, and can easily be removed."

Micah huffed. "Is that the best you can do?"

"Honestly. Give Doc a break." Remy was about ready to knock Micah unconscious herself. "If it wasn't for him, you'd be sitting at the clinic waiting your turn *and* being interrogated by the police, since they are probably looking for us."

Sully heard her comment as he cleared the doorway with Hawke, shaking his head. "It seems Micah dodged that bullet. Have I mentioned he's got horseshoes up his...boxers?"

Remy couldn't believe it. He had shot off a round in the treatment centre. Wasn't that serious? After all, he wasn't a cop.

"Sergeant Dupré wants you to stop by his office to fill out an incident report, Mic." Sully paused to give Breeana a kiss on the lips. "But you're in the clear for firing your Glock, and he knows you're licensed to carry concealed."

"You are one lucky s.o.b., my friend." Hawke nudged Micah's shoulder, nearly knocking him off the table. "Would you believe the folks at the clinic called you a hero? There were plenty of witnesses who saw the creep pull his gun before you took a bead on him. And you fired high, not to hit him. Otherwise, you might be cooling your jets in a jail cell for a while."

"It wouldn't be the first time," Micah scoffed. "Still, it's easier to keep Trigger safe if I'm not behind bars."

Remy asked, "Do I have to go to the police station and fill out a report too?"

"No." Sully said. "I slipped Dupré the bad news that you are a protected witness in an ongoing investigation. He didn't want to hear any more about it, not even your name."

"Of course, we may have led him to believe it was a joint RCMP and Montreal Homicide operation," Hawke added.

"In other words, you lied your asses off," Micah said. "And he bought it."

"Yep, and we didn't even have Melena handy to flirt with him." Theo growled at that remark, while Sully rocked back on his heels. "The bottom line is...Dupré doesn't want to get involved."

Micah shot Doc a look as he finished off the cast, wrapping it with a pressure bandage. "Do you have an ID yet on the dead man with the spider ring?"

Doc nodded. "I confirmed it a few minutes ago. His dentals are an exact match to the ones Chief Inspector Gauld sent us from Scotland Yard. James Broderick is our victim."

Hunt rested a hand on the holster riding his hip. "We'll need a window for his time of death."

Doc glanced at the overhead clock. "About twenty-four hours ago, give or take a couple hours. That's as close as I can narrow it down, given the condition of the body when it was discovered."

"Good enough." Micah slid off the table, wincing as he tested his fractured wrist. "We need to head over to *Charlie's* to question the day staff. Broderick was probably drinking there before someone walked him out back and shot him in the woods."

"We'll do it tomorrow. They'll be going off shift soon." Sully glanced around the room at his three injured teammates. "The only place you guys are going is back to the cottage. You look like crap and you'll scare the bejesus out of the bar patrons."

Remy asked, although dreading the answer, "Do you have a suspect in Broderick's murder?"

"The same guy who's after you." Sully's expression was as serious as a heart attack, causing shivers to dance up her spine. "One serial killer offing another, it's the only theory that makes any sense. The Swamp Killer didn't want spider guy beating him to his prize."

Damn, she knew who the prize was. Remy's heartbeat sped up and her hands began to tremble. She shoved them into her back pockets. "How could Broderick know about me when I've never laid eyes on him?"

"That's easy." Micah stared at her, a muscle ticking his jaw. "They were working together. Until Broderick crossed the line."

"What in God's name are you talking about? I don't understand any of this."

"Trigger, I—"

Remy held her ground, levelling him with a glare. "Just spit it out. We agreed. No more secrets, remember?"

Micah sighed, the pain etched clearly on his face. "Broderick taunted you with a gift—the box of spiders. It's his signature, which means he was stalking you. The fact he sent you Red Widows, arachnids that are only indigenous to Florida, suggests he was setting up the Swamp Killer to take the fall...after Broderick killed you himself."

MICAH STARED OUT THE window toward the water. The rain had stopped, clouds scudding away, the moon bathing the lake in silver ripples. He opened the slider and inhaled cool mountain air. He needed Remy's scent out of his head. She was getting to him.

He turned slightly to watch her sleep—an angel tangled up in his sheets. The woman who owned his heart and had no idea the power she held over him. Her smile and trusting ways a few hours ago had reeled him in. She'd laid him bare. Her passion, her seduction when she took them both to heaven left him empty. He needed more. Always more. Because she made him want things he'd never had, which was absurd.

Sex had always been enough, not thoughts of building a life together and raising a family. Damn, he half believed he was in love with her. And if that was true, they were both lost. The time for loving was later, when he could think straight, when killers weren't hiding in the shadows and stalking his woman.

The time for battle was now.

Micah took in the night again, still breathing the forest air, loosening his jaw before he ground his teeth to dust. Remy was his to protect, his to die for. But love? No. Not now, and maybe never, unless he got her out of this alive.

A soft tap sounded at the door. Micah closed the slider, locked it, and moved around the bed. Remy stirred in her sleep while he pulled on sweatpants. He shook his head. She took up a lot of real estate, didn't exactly keep to her side of the bed, and had the habit of crawling on top of him during the night. Too bad he loved every damn turn and tumble she took.

Tubbs's ears perked up, a soft growl in his throat as he stared at the door. Micah patted his head and turned the knob. "Easy."

Papa Joe stood out in the hall. He checked Micah over and holstered his Glock. Without saying a word, he turned, walking through the living room and outside to the deck. A laptop lay open on the tabletop and Joe sank into the chair facing it.

"What's up?" Micah asked, following him out and taking a seat while Joe brought up a schematic on the screen.

Joe shrugged, gazing at the computer. "An alarm went off in your bedroom. I wanted to be sure it was you who tripped it, and not some unfriendly who'd gained access."

Micah ran a hand through his hair and sighed. "Yeah, it was me. I couldn't sleep and I opened a slider. Sorry, I forgot it was armed."

"What's the matter? Your owies giving you trouble?" Joe levelled a glance his way. "Or maybe it's the little gal you've got warming your bed."

"Remy is off-limits, Joe." Micah felt his good hand curl into a fist. "Better shut your mouth or I'll close it for you."

Joe laughed, took a cigar between his teeth, and lit a match, its tip puffing like smoke signals. "Might as well enjoy this here Cuban cigar then, while I still gots my teeth. 'Cuz you're about to hear an earful and you ain't gonna like it."

"You can cut the hillbilly shtick, too. I pulled your file and I know you've got a Master's Degree in political science from Harvard." Micah pulled a saucer off the bottom of a potted plant and handed it to him to use as an ashtray. "Did you really think we wouldn't check you out?"

"Never gave it much thought, one way or the other. I've gotten in the habit of talking like I'm damn near stupid. That way, people don't expect much, and I hold all the cards." Joe eyed him between puffs on the cigar. "Funny how you saw through me, and yet, you're completely blind when it comes to your feelings for Remy."

"Fuck you." Micah squirmed in his chair, wishing he could pound on Joe like he would on one of his buddies. Too bad the guy was closer to sixty than thirty. Still, he had no business sticking his nose in where it didn't belong. "What I feel or don't feel is none of your business."

"Not true." Joe tapped the cherry off his cigar. "I'm not much for telling another man how to run his life, Mic. It's not as if I've done a bang up job with my own. But I'm making an exception in your case, because your brain is so far up your arse you can't see daylight."

Micah clenched his jaw, clamping his good hand on the armrest of the chair to keep from taking a swing. "I don't want to hear it."

"Tough shit." Joe pulled a beer out of the cooler beside him and slid it over. He cracked the cap off one for himself and took a long pull. "You've got to get your head in the game, son. Quit ignoring the love you feel for her. You have to accept it. Take it and use it. Hone it like any other weapon in your arsenal."

"You're talking bull crap." Micah blew out a breath, not sure where this conversation was headed. "Love and combat don't mix, or haven't you heard?"

"That's where you're wrong." Joe had his attention now, leaning forward in his chair, a hand closing on Micah's shoulder. "It's true...a man with nothing to lose is formidable and dangerous in battle. But a man with *everything* to lose? Now *that* man is lethal. He's a stone cold killer."

"Maybe." Man, could it be that simple? Micah had never thought about it in those terms. But, then again, Sully, Theo, and Rocket had been in love when they'd protected their women. Each of them had fought the pull and lost, while at the same time being kick-ass vicious when bringing down the enemy. Hell, he'd seen it for himself, had been there when Breeana, Melena, and Billie had come under fire.

Damn his eyes, why hadn't he recognized it for what it was?

"Figure it out," Joe said. "Do whatever you have to do. But be *that* man...for Remy."

Chapter 11

T he next afternoon Remy sat in the game room, sandwiched between Billie and Breeana on the couch while she watched the hidden camera feed from *Charlie's*. Micah had wired Sully for live transmission before he and Hawke had left to interview the day staff at the bar. A lapel pin on his jacket supplied her window to the action. While she might not understand how it worked, she had to admit the electronic gizmos Micah kept in his bag of tricks were top of the line impressive. Whether it was because of his spec ops assignments or his security company, she wasn't sure. But he'd nixed her idea of going to the RestoBar to sit in on the interviews, and although she wasn't happy about it, at least he'd given her a front row seat.

Now she watched in comfort from the cottage, in spite of feeling like a powerless wimp with no control over her life. Eating popcorn with the others crowded around the flat screen while she hoped she wouldn't choke on it. It was a good thing Micah had agreed to stay home with her or she would have knocked him unconscious.

She watched as Sully and Hawke parked in the lot at *Charlie's*. She heard the crunch of their boots on gravel as they stepped from the SUV. The screen door swung open with a squeak and they were inside. Taylor Swift sang *Mean* on the jukebox. The low rumble of conversations could be heard over the music.

Hawke approached the barmaid, flashing his RCMP credentials. Sully stood off to the side, the woman filling the screen. A bottled-blond in her late forties, she had big hair and a bigger chest straining the front of her tee. Ample hips swayed in tight jeans as she circled around Hawke to fill a drink order.

"I have questions about the day a man was killed in the woods behind this club," Hawke said. "Did you see anything that could help us with the investigation?"

Blondie shrugged her shoulders, intent on pouring Tequila and adding a dish of limes and a salt shaker to her tray. "It was nothing special. Just an ordinary afternoon."

"I'd hardly call it ordinary when someone was murdered in close proximity to where you work." Hawke clamped a hand on her shoulder when she punched up the sale on a computer terminal and hefted the tray. "We can talk here or down at the police station. It's up to you."

She glanced at his hand and then flicked her gaze to the far end of the polished oak bar. A man wearing a T-shirt matching hers stood pouring drafts for a couple of guys wearing John Deere caps. Remy could hear their discussion about tractors and backhoes—the audio reception was amazing. "Speak to my husband. I remember the place was dead that afternoon, if you'll excuse the pun. He served the drinks while I stocked beer fridges and helped out in the kitchen. Maybe he can help you."

And maybe he can't. Remy nibbled on her bottom lip, fear blooming in her belly. Was it possible no one saw anything that day? Was Broderick's killer invisible? Able to strike and run without being seen? If that was true, her chances of survival were slim to none, even with Micah's help. Crap, they were all in trouble if this guy could pop up out of nowhere, but after the wild car chase yesterday, she knew he had help.

Blondie whistled for her husband, who moved away from his customers to shake hands with Hawke and Sully. He studied their ID badges while Sully asked him questions about the day of the killing.

"Yeah, there was a new face sitting at the bar that day. All the rest were regulars. I remember him because the joint was quiet. He came in early, before Happy Hour, and paid a hundred bucks for a bottle of bourbon. But he left it on the bar when he went out back for a smoke. Come to think of it he was gone a really long time."

"How long would you say?" Sully asked.

"At least forty minutes, maybe longer." The barman ran a hand along the back of his neck. "I mean, why buy the bottle, considering he'd barely touched it before he went outside? He told me to keep an eye on it while he was gone, and that's why I noticed the timeframe."

Hawke picked up on Sully's line of questioning. "Can you tell us what happened after he came back inside?"

The bartender shrugged. "There's nothing much to tell. He looked the same, no blood on his clothes or anything. The squirrel poured himself another shot, knocked it back, and then he left. And not only did he take the bottle with him, but he also took his glass."

"I'm not surprised. It's the only way he could eliminate his fingerprints," Sully explained. "Can you give us a physical description of the guy?"

"Sure. He was swarthy looking, maybe Italian or Latino. A skinny guy dressed in a tight silk shirt, tighter flared pants, and pointy-toed shoes. Not exactly country, if you know what I mean."

Remy almost dropped the popcorn. She slid the bowl to the table before it tumbled out of her hands. Micah was right. There was no mistake, no matter how badly she wanted there to be. *He's describing the Swamp Killer.*

Hawke leaned his elbows on the bar, speaking in a low voice. "Was there anything about him that didn't seem right? Maybe something about him didn't ring true?"

"You mean besides the flashy gold jewellery?" The bartender laughed. "Hell, nothing about him was on the up and up. It's as if he was acting the part, you know?"

"No, we don't, which is why we're asking you." The camera angle moved in as Sully settled at the bar. All Remy could see was the white

Charlie's logo printed across the front of the barman's black shirt. "Give us a clue here, pal."

"Look, I know this sounds crazy, but I think the creep was wearing makeup and a wig. His poufy, slicked back hair went out of style in the seventies, and the tan on his face didn't match the backs of his hands. Not to mention the strut in his step, like he was dancing to music in his head when he walked back in the bar after his smoke. The dude was off-the-charts weird by my take on things, but what the hell do I know?"

"You think you could describe him to a police sketch artist?" Remy recognized Hawke's voice.

"Are you kidding me? Just let me know when and where."

"Sergeant Dupré will set something up and he'll be in touch. We're the lead investigators on the case, but he's in charge since it happened in his jurisdiction."

Micah shut down the feed as soon as Hawke and Sully left the bar.

Remy shot off the couch, blocking his path when he would have walked out of the room. Damn, the guy chasing her was slick. If the bartender was right, he could change his appearance as easy as changing his underwear. She couldn't depend on anyone recognizing him before he got to her. "That settles it, Mic. I want a gun!"

"Oh, jeez!" Papa Joe was out of his chair and charging for the stairs. "I gotta take over for Rocket on sentry duty."

Theo headed for the French doors. "I need to check on Law and Hunt. They're doing a security sweep in the west sector of the woods."

"And we have to get dinner ready, don't we, ladies?" Billie hustled out of there with Breeana and Melena on her tail. A minute later, Remy could hear pots and pans banging in the kitchen.

"Trigger, I'll give you this, you sure know how to clear a room." Hands on his hips, the corners of Micah's mouth twitched as he shook his head. "And the answer hasn't changed. It's still no on having a firearm."

"Come on, Mic!" Remy threw her hands in the air, leading with a healthy dose of frustration and the urge to take him down. If she wasn't still nursing her leg wound, she would do it—just to wipe the grin of the big, stubborn oaf's face. "I need protection!"

"You already *have* protection, and that would be me and my crew." He wrapped an arm around her waist with his good hand and reeled her in for a kiss. Not fair. His lips singed hers, her thoughts spiralling in an entirely different direction. *No.* She convinced herself she was only playing along. Just because she allowed the physical contact didn't mean anything had changed. She wanted that gun and she would get it.

"I'm not about to hand you a weapon after you almost shot me."

"That's old news. Besides, I already promised not to shoot at you again." She pressed her body against him, kissing her way down his neck. Felt the answering heat in his response. *Two can play at this game, buddy.* She feigned a yawn. "Why don't we continue this in the bedroom?"

"Great idea." Micah nuzzled her ear, sending electrical shocks down her spine to other, more intimate places. His hands moved to her backside, cradling her between his thighs. "I'd like nothing better, but I'm giving you fair warning. The answer will still be no when we're done."

"It doesn't matter. I know you're right." Remy took his hand, sighing her sexiest sigh and leading him up the stairs. After all, sex with Micah *and* a firearm? What more could a girl ask for? *And I know just where to shop for that gun, big guy, with or without your blessing. You won't stop me.*

REMY FELT THE MATTRESS shift when Micah sank into it for the second time that night. Her eyes flew open, the clock on her nightstand reading three a.m. He'd been on guard duty again. His hand squeezed her hip as he dozed off. One thing she'd learned from sleeping with him—besides his amazing sexual prowess—was military guys could conk out at the drop of a hat. *It must be a requirement*, she decided.

She relaxed, pretending to sleep, and waited for her chance. Ten minutes later, he was out for the count and breathing deep. She eased out from under his hand, pulled his sweatshirt over her head, and padded out the door.

The click of Tubbs's nails on hardwood followed her across the living room. Damn, he was right behind her, breath snuffling like a pig. Not a good thing when she wanted to go unnoticed. But luck was on her side. Remy made it to the kitchen without being spotted, opened the fridge, and pulled out a juicy steak. Punching in the access code on the control panel, she tiptoed to the far corner of the dining room and laid the steak down. As the wall in the kitchen opened, revealing the gun room, she slipped inside just as she heard Tubbs scarf down his snack. The door shut behind her. Heart racing, she pumped a fist in the air. She'd done it.

Welcome to gun heaven. She would choose her weapon and be out of there in a flash. Micah would never know. She'd let him keep his peace of mind while she took hers and secured the extra protection she needed. It was a win-win situation by all accounts. All she had to do was shop, and she was *very* good at that. The room was as she remembered with recessed overhead lighting, pale-cream walls, and black rubber flooring. Guns of all shapes and sizes hung on the back wall, the ammunition in see-through bins beneath. A stainless steel prep table occupied the center space, with knives and other sharp objects on the wall to the right. The door that led to the tunnel was past the knife display. The computer and flat screen monitors were on her left.

Oh, this was way better than the *Cabela's* catalogue. She could touch each firearm. Feel the weight of it, run her hands over the design, and decide which one was right for her. Nothing too big, of course, she could hardly hide a sniper rifle down her pant leg. No, she'd settle for a handgun and there were lots of those.

She hummed as she searched, opening each drawer beneath the pegboards to check what was inside, surprised to see they held more than ammo. Surveillance cameras, rifle scopes, two-way radios, GPS tracking systems, night vision goggles, headlamps were all included—what more could a girl ask for? Remy blinked, not quite sure, but she thought she recognized hand grenades and flash bangs.

She pulled out the last drawer and found something she didn't expect—packets of unlubricated condoms. She read the handwritten instruction sheet, thinking this was someone's idea of a joke. But no, they were an integral part of field kits. Condoms kept debris out of rifle barrels, were used as emergency water containers, and also as sterile wound dressings in emergency situations. There were a number of other uses, as well.

Okay, this was taking too long. She had to stop reading and touching things that weren't gun related. *In and out, remember*? Otherwise, she'd still be there when everyone else was having breakfast. She forced herself to concentrate on the guns. This should be easy.

TUBBS SOUNDED THE ALARM in the wee hours of the morning, howling like a banshee. Micah awoke with a start. Rolled to the side of the bed and flipped on a lamp. He was alone. Remy was AWOL. He called Hunt on the two-way radio to make sure the house and perimeter were locked down tight. They were. So whatever Tubbs was baying at, it wasn't the bad guys. Besides, Micah knew the difference in the dog's voice. He wasn't in attack mode.

No, something else was at play, and Micah was pretty damn sure its name was Remy Renaud. Small bloody wonder Pete had called her a pain in his ass. Make that a pain in *everyone's* ass. Pulling on jeans, Micah cursed the fact he was crazy in love with her. Of all the women he'd met in his life, why fall for the one who gave him ulcers? The one who had nearly shot him? The one who teased him, calling him "pieces of Micah" while he'd taught the vicious guard dog to swim? The way he figured it, he'd put up with a lot of guff from her. Whatever she was up to and he had the feeling he already knew. It ended now.

"This time, she's gone too far."

Grabbing his Glock off the nightstand, he thundered through the living room and headed for the kitchen. Tubbs had already gotten inside the refrigerator, knocking food off the shelves while trying to dig through the back wall. No damn wonder, considering his job was to protect Remy and she'd left him behind. "Get out of the fridge. You're making a mess. And quit the howling before you wake everyone up."

"It's a little late for that. We're already up." A scowl on his face, Sully poked his head around the corner from the dining room. "I'm guessing our principal went shopping for weapons of mass destruction and forgot to take her sidekick along?"

Law moved to the alarm panel for the gun safe and punched in a code. "Yep, she's already been in there five minutes."

"Dang, I can't seem to help myself, but Remy makes me so proud." The grin on Joe's face slipped a notch with his next thought. "Except I don't want to deal with the fallout when we drag her out of there. Maybe I should make myself scarce."

"Jesus H. Christ." Hunt shot Micah the evil eye, shaking his head. "The last time you pissed Remy off, none of us got a wink of sleep."

"You've got that right," Theo growled, leaning back and balancing his chair on two legs with his feet planted on another. "I say we use the failsafe and keep her locked in there until morning. My ears won't survive going another round with her temper. Not to mention the other ladies will think we're abusing her again. Then we'll all be up shit creek."

"Son of a bitch, the other women will kill us if she makes a scene." Hawke scrubbed a hand over his jaw. "They'll lock up the kitchen again and go on strike. We'll be eating army rations out of our go bags until this op is over."

"Not to mention Billie will pound the crap out of me. Again." Hands on his hips, Rocket stared at the ceiling and cursed a blue streak. "Theo's right. Let's keep Remy in the gun room for tonight. It's soundproof, and she can't shoot us. She's got a wicked temper...almost as bad as Billie's."

"Forget it. She knows where the key is to the tunnel. If she exits through the garage or the boathouse, she could get hurt. We can't take the chance." Micah sighed, pulling the Glock from his waistband and handing it to Sully. "Better take this...in case I'm tempted."

"Jumping Jehoshaphat! That's a mighty big leap of faith going in there unarmed, Mic." Joe stared at him with a gleam in his eye. "She's sitting on a whole bunch of firepower, not to mention the knives. Hell, Remy's liable to shoot first, filet you later, and serve you up for breakfast along with them pan-fries and eggs. We'd never know a blessed thing until we got heartburn."

"Thanks for the touching concern, but you're all a bunch of whiny bitches. I can't believe you're scared shitless of this woman." Micah was a tad edgy himself about bearding the lioness in her armed-to-the-teeth den, but it couldn't be helped. Someone had to corral her before she came out of there packing an M16 for "protection" as she called it, with enough rounds to overtake a small nation.

Micah glared at the lot of them. "Walk the perimeter with Tubbs, Joe. I want it real quiet in here when I breach the door. The rest of you get back to whatever you were doing. It's 'Go' time."

After they made themselves scarce and the room went silent, Micah punched in the code for the gun safe. He padded to the entrance on bare feet and waited. It didn't take long for the stove and refrigerator unit to roll forward. He slipped into the room behind it, the wall sliding back in place at the touch of a button.

Remy didn't notice him. She was too busy singing a show tune and admiring the inventory—namely his artillery stash. While she ran her hands over weapons and *oohed* and *aahed*, he had a pretty good fantasy of his own. She wore one of his sweatshirts, the one that fell off her shoulders and barely skimmed her thighs. *Oh yeah, another place, another time, Trigger. But not right now.*

It took a while before she zeroed in on the Smith & Wesson 642 Airweight. Micah's .38 Special with an internal hammer and a five round capacity. Not the lightest weapon for her to handle, but by far, the smallest in his arsenal. It fit nicely in her palm and in the leather ankle holster she had pulled off a shelf. *Hokay*, the woman had taste and knew what she wanted. But it didn't change a thing. She wasn't keeping the gun.

Micah bided his time. Waited until she found the right ammo drawer and focused on loading the weapon. Then he moved. He came up behind her. Grabbed her by the scruff of the sweatshirt and shouted in her ear. "Face the wall! Eat it!"

HOLY HELL! I'M GOING to die! "Micah, I—"

"I said face the wall!" He shoved her forward, looping flex cuffs around her wrists and pulling them tight. "You want to act like a criminal? I'll damn well treat you like one."

A leg between her thighs, his body pressed into her back as he frisked her under the sweatshirt, his touch cold and impersonal. Where were the hands that knew her intimately? The ones that held her, chased away her night terrors? *God, oh God!* This wasn't the man who made love to her. Fear rode her hard. It dug deep, sinking its tentacles into her soul. Her heart hammered. Her knees shaking so badly she thought she'd collapse.

"Wha-what are you doing?"

He spun her around, his words bitter, his gaze furious. "I'm searching you for weapons. Like maybe something to rip out my heart."

"Micah stop! Please...you're scaring me!"

He picked her up and set her on the table. Chilled steel smacked against her bottom. She tried to slide away. His arms shot out, fists slamming the metal on both sides of her, locking her in. Her lips trembled and tears spilled. She refused to look at him.

Please, let this be over soon.

"Jesus, enough." Micah exhaled on a long breath. He cut her loose and pocketed the blade. "I can't do this." Remy watched him walk away. His hands raked through his hair, his gaze on the floor as he shook his head. "I'm sorry if I hurt you. I shouldn't have lost my temper."

As much as he'd frightened her, she knew it was her fault, and it was eating him up inside. "I'm the one who's sorry, Micah. If I could take it back, I would."

"Don't say something you don't mean." He turned to her. When he touched her hair, she stopped breathing. He bent down and kissed her, his hand curving her cheek as he delved deep inside her mouth. His lips were soft and warm in contrast to the scrape of his stubbled jaw and his anger from moments ago. His tongue danced with hers, searching and stroking until her mind and body held only one thought. She wanted him.

"I mean it, Micah. I'm sorry." Her hands slid up his biceps and held on. He smelled of hot male and tasted like sin. Fire raged inside her as he took the kiss deeper. She was light-headed and dizzy, didn't want him to stop, needing his kiss to go on forever. To heal the rift between them. To make everything right.

He brought her to the edge of the table. Spreading her thighs, he stood between them. She hooked her legs on the outside of his hips, her breasts swelling, buds peaking against the hard wall of his chest. And still their tongues met and danced.

"I want you," he said against her mouth.

"Make love to me." Her shaking fingers unsnapped his jeans but he pushed them away.

"Wait."

He moved to a drawer under the pegboard. She heard a foil packet rip, and then he was back. He palmed and lifted her bottom, plunging deep inside her, pulling back and thrusting again. She gasped, trying to accommodate him. He wasn't gentle. He was on fire. Body sweating, his pulse-pounding passion demanded and took. All she could do was cling to him and give back. Hands clutching his arms, legs clamped around his waist, Remy couldn't think. Couldn't breathe, could only feel. Lifting her off the table, he pressed her against him. His need climbed, but hers climbed higher, outdistancing his. Fast and hot, stroke after stroke until she begged for release.

Frantic now, she increased her rhythm. Micah stilled, refusing to give her what she craved. When she thought she would die of want, he began again. Thrusting slow, plunging to the hilt, grinding his hips to better angle and tease. His mouth closed on her breast. She arched, giving him better access. He drew back his head, blowing warm air across her nipple. Remy whimpered. "Now."

"Not yet." He watched her as he pulled out of her, placed her back on the table and lay her down near the edge. When she reached for him, he shoved her wrists across her waist and clamped them with one of his hands. "Easy."

His other hand cupped her, his fingers caressing the nub beneath her curls. Circling, rubbing, he lowered his head, his mouth arousing her until her body bowed and she whimpered for mercy.

He looked up and studied her, his gaze unrelenting. "Your taste belongs to me, and only to me. I'll never get enough of you. Do you like it when I kiss you here?"

"Micah..." She writhed, but struggling was useless. His hand still pinned her wrists. She couldn't touch him to push him over the edge. "Please..."

"Not until you answer my question." His mouth touched her again, his tongue caressing, his teeth scraping gently, his lips suckling until her insides quaked. Again, he stopped. "Your scent blows my mind, Trigger, so I'll ask you again. Do you like me kissing you here?"

"Yes!" Her legs wrapped around him, her body taut, every inch of her begging for his attention. Time stood still, her thoughts and desires lost in the moment. "Love me."

"I do. I love you with all my heart."

Before she had time to think about his words, he was inside her again, scooping her up in his arms and riding them both to heaven. She exploded, her body pulsing around him, tears streaming her cheeks with pent up emotion. When they were done, he brushed them away with a pad of a thumb. He sighed, tucking a curl behind her ear and touching his forehead to hers. "I meant what I said, Remy. I'm in love with you."

"Don't say that. Love is too great a risk." Pushing him away, she hopped off the table, smoothed the sweatshirt down her thighs, and began to pace. "Take it back. It's a mistake."

He grabbed her arm and drew her in. Tipping her chin with a finger, he caught her gaze. "What are you talking about? You love me, too. I can feel it."

"No, no, I don't! My family is hiding because I endangered them. Pete is still in the hospital and that's *my* fault too." She shoved him and backed away. "And if that's not enough? The Swamp Killer still wants to murder me. He'll kill you, too, if you stand in his way. I just can't take anymore!"

"Honey, settle down." Micah tried to grab her, but she circled to the other side of the table. "Let's talk about this."

"No. I don't want to love you. Bad things happen to people I care about." She broke for the door to the kitchen, pounding on the button release. "Leave me the hell alone."

Chapter 12

Remy loaded the dishwasher while Breeana and Billie busied themselves wiping countertops and returning food to the fridge. A dark cloud hung over Remy's head. The others knew she'd tried to take the handgun. Even Melena looked at her with troubled eyes. And the men? They'd grabbed their plates of bacon and eggs and were out on the deck with Micah. Everyone was polite, but no idle chitchat.

Even she hadn't spoken a word since being with Micah. What could she say in her defense? That she'd thought a gun of her own would help her feel safe? Or should she tell them the *real* reason she was halfway out of her mind? Micah loved her, and loving her would get him killed.

She couldn't explain because they wouldn't agree and would try to convince her otherwise. Did they think he was invincible? Damn it, he was flesh and bone, not some plastic action figure. She knew loving her placed him at far greater risk than the others guarding her.

She shook her head, hoping to clear it, trying to decide what to do to protect him. She might as well face it. Being secreted away from the FBI limited her options. She couldn't very well turn herself in. Not without getting him in hot water for smuggling her into Canada. Still, staying here with him put everyone in danger. Especially Micah. She couldn't bear it. She loved him to the depths of her soul and beyond. He was her world. She needed him to disappear before he got hurt.

It was only a matter of time before more men came for her, namely the Swamp Killer and his pals. She'd known it since they rammed the SUV, sending them spiralling into the ditch. How could Micah protect her from so much evil and survive himself? His love for her would blind him to the danger.

She jumped when his hand touched her elbow, his voice as soft as velvet-covered steel. "We need to talk. This is getting us nowhere."

She turned to challenge him, wishing she could hate him. He was so strong of mind and body, better looking than a man had a right to be, and so caring he sliced her heart with a glance. His eyes held sadness and confusion. He didn't understand the change in her, why she refused to accept his love. And she didn't want him to. "No, I need to take a walk. I have a lot to think about, and I can't do it with you hovering over me."

He held her gaze, irritation in the press of his lips and the determined stance of his body. He rocked back on his heels. "I can't let you go. It's not safe."

"Then *make* it safe!" She hated playing the bitch, could see the pain she inflicted with every callous word. But she couldn't think clearly when he was within reach. All she wanted to do was bawl like a baby and fall into his arms. What would it accomplish? Dead was dead. Better to end it now. Kill Micah's love. Piss him off and keep him out of the line of fire.

"I can't let you traipse around out there by yourself." Muscles bunched in his arm as he rapped the side of a fist on the doorframe. "Walk the treadmill or run laps around the basement, I don't give a damn. But you're staying inside, unless I go with you."

"Surely, the woods are safe. You and your men spend enough time out there. I can't imagine trouble lurking when you people patrol every freaking hour of the day and night." A shaky thought unsettled her. No one else would go to the same extremes as him to protect her, would they? She hoped not, because she cared about all of them. "I mean it, Mic. I need to walk to clear my head. So unless you plan to lock me up, I'm leaving as soon as I put on my ball cap."

"You'll wait until I have men watching you." When she opened her mouth to argue, he silenced her with a finger to her lips. "Listen, Trigger, I don't care if you stay five feet in front of them to do your *thinking*, but you're not wandering off without an armed escort."

He was a man of his word. He walked her and Tubbs as far as the flagstone path where Theo waited with Melena and Papa Joe. Theo nodded to Micah. "We'll be back in good time."

"Stay safe." Micah squeezed Remy's arm. "I'll see you later."

She felt his eyes drilling holes in her back until she rounded the corner of the cottage. Knowing how much he worried made it hard to walk away, but not impossible. She wanted him out of her life, sooner rather than later. She hoped he'd fall for her feigned disinterest and take the hint. She owed him the chance to move on with a clear conscience.

Theo and Papa Joe motioned for her and Melena to walk ahead of them as they picked up a trail into the woods. Micah wasn't kidding when he said the men would be armed. Theo carried an assault rifle as well as his Glock and a tactical knife on his belt. Remy knew he had other toys, his utility belt loaded with a lot of paraphernalia. Micah kept a second gun in an ankle holster and she suspected Theo did the same. He wore long pants when it was hot as Hades out. Papa Joe carried his newly designed bang stick, a handgun at his waist, and a utility belt about the same weight as Theo's. Melena seemed to be weaponless as she walked along beside her, but who knew for sure? Still, the thought of Melena packing heat, a tiny little pixie like her? Remy couldn't see it.

The men stayed about ten paces behind them, probably relieved not to have to put up with any girl talk, although little was being said. Melena seemed willing to let Remy carry the conversation, and she wasn't ready yet, if at all. Instead, she contented herself watching Tubbs amble along in front of her as they went deep into the forest. She listened for the men bringing up the rear but like always, they didn't make a sound.

About a half mile later, Tubbs stumbled and collapsed in the dirt. Remy hurried to his side, worried he might have broken a leg. The dog didn't move. He seemed to be breathing, but he was almost out for the count. *What's the matter with him?*

She heard Theo's voice somewhere behind her. He seemed to be struggling for breath. His voice was weak. She turned, but couldn't see him or Papa Joe. Where were they? "Get out...of...here! Mel, Remy...go!"

"Oh my Lord! Run!" Melena grabbed her hand, hauled her to her feet, and took off between the trees.

"Wait!" Remy struggled to stay where she was. Melena was stronger than she looked and caught her off balance, dragging her away. "What are you doing?"

"Theo and Joe went down like Tubbs. They're barely moving in the brush over there. We have to get help!"

"Crap." Remy jerked the two-way radio from her shorts pocket, pressed the mic button, and screamed for someone to answer. Micah's voice came on the line, calm and reassuring. "Settle, honey. Tell me what's happening."

"I think someone's chasing us! Papa Joe and Theo are in trouble...and Tubbs!" She gasped for breath, ducking branches, weaving between rocks and praying for a miracle. Melena lengthened her stride. For a small woman, she could race like the wind. A twig slapped Remy's face, blinding her for a couple of seconds. She snagged a tree root with a toe and stumbled, dragging Melena down with her. *Thwack.* Something hit the tree above their heads. "It's a dart! Someone's shooting darts at us! It hit the tree!"

"Oh, shit!" Melena flattened herself against the ground, her cobalt eyes alive with fear. "What do we do? Run or hide?"

Micah cut through on the two-way. "We need the dart. See if you can pull it out, but be careful."

Remy tossed her water bottle to Melena. "Quick, empty it."

Working the dart free of tree bark, Remy dropped it inside the water bottle and screwed the lid on tight. She hooked the bottle back on her belt. "Got it."

"Great. Now move. Run like hell."

Remy heaved to her feet. She broke into a full sprint. Melena kept pace, the two of them leaping over a log and sliding down an embankment. Melena tripped and rolled. She hit the bottom with a thunk and groaned.

"Oh Lord," Remy sobbed.

"Talk to me." She had trouble hearing him, the roar of an engine overriding Micah's voice. "What's going on?"

"Mel just took a fall in a ditch. She's not moving."

"Okay. Get down there and give her a hand."

"Mel!" Remy slid on her butt the rest of the way. She turned Melena over, checking for injuries. Thank heavens, no blood.

"I'm good." Sure, like hell she was. Remy could see the pain etched on her face. "I just turned an ankle."

"How bad?" *Jesus*. Melena was small, but Remy doubted she could carry her.

"Not bad enough to lie here and wait for someone to shoot a dart in my ass. Let's go."

Remy pulled her friend to her feet and wrapped an arm around her waist, helping Melena claw her way up the other side. Remy lost a shoe and managed to grab it, skinned her knees, and didn't dare look back. Twigs cracked. Was someone behind them?

Micah came back over the radio. "We're tracking you and you're doing great. You're almost at the water. Keep moving as fast as you can. We're coming."

Micah must be close. He *had* to be.

The lake rippled in the distance between the trees. She focused on that. Thunder rolled overhead. A boat roared into view. Theo's Bayliner. Men leapt off the bow and charged in their direction. Just a few more feet to clear the woods, they was almost there. Melena staggered and they fell in a heap.

Micah and Sully were first to reach them. They scooped them up and raced for the boat.

MICAH KEYED THE BAYLINER'S ignition. The engine roared to life as thunder rumbled in the distance. His eyes scanning the shoreline, he watched Sully disappear into the woods with Law and Hunt. He gunned the throttle. Remy huddled beside him in the shotgun seat while Melena stayed low in the stern next to Hawke. The boat shot forward, waves rolling from its wake. It should be a short ride to the cottage under safe conditions, but not when another boat engine fired nearby. Shit.

The cruiser blasted out from a feeder stream. Micah flew by it and swivelled in his chair as Hawke sized up the passengers through binoculars. Once he gave him the "all clear," Micah relaxed his hands at the controls.

Normal.

He'd forgotten the meaning of the word since this had begun. A few months ago, he would have said his average day was flirting with danger and pretty women. Violence had rarely left a mark on him except for the adrenaline rush of serving his country. Get the job done and get out in one piece was his mantra. Trusting in God and his Spec Ops team was his religion. His anchors had been his security company in Ottawa and his family in Miami. But it had all changed with Melena, Breeana, and Billie when Theo, Sully, and Rocket had asked the team to surround and protect their women from brutal enemies.

Then along came Remy—the woman who blew his *normal* to hell and back—the woman sitting beside him whom he was afraid to touch in case she fell apart. The woman he wanted to love but needed to keep his distance from in order to protect her. Sweet Jesus, Micah couldn't imagine life without her anymore. But she had to stay alive for them to work out their differences. One thing was crystal clear in his new *normal*. Whether Remy chose to love him or not, she would damn well survive to make the choice.

Micah kept away from shore, roaring down the middle of the lake until he cut across the bay to his dock. As he shut down the engine and bumped the pier, Rocket broke from the house with Billie and Breeana close behind. Micah approved his choice of hardware—a Benelli M4 Tactical shotgun. In Rocket's hands, the semi-auto 12-gauge wasn't a weapon for the faint of heart. It was deadly.

Billie backed her man up with a Glock 26 in a two-handed grip. Nicknamed the "Baby Glock" due to its size, it was capable of unleashing ten rounds of lethal at the squeeze of the trigger. Micah relaxed a fraction knowing Billie and Rocket had their protection covered while they stood in the open.

He leapt to the dock, focused on lifting Melena out of the Bayliner while Hawke held it steady. Breeana took Mel's weight against her when he passed her off and turned for Remy. She curled into him until her feet landed on the pier. "You doing okay?"

"I don't know." She gazed up at him, her lower lip trembling as she whispered in his ear. "Do you think the others are dead?"

"No." He squeezed her arm before releasing it, smelling her fear, seeing it in her eyes. He could identify. Right now, he was scared more than he'd ever been in his life, because the danger centered on her. All he could do was spout a load of crap to hopefully ease her guilt. "A hit from a dart is sissy stuff."

The throb of the boat engine distracted him as Hawke reversed thrust and lit out across the bay again. Micah knew he'd join in the search for Joe and Theo. *The sooner the better, and please God, bring them home.* He tossed Rocket the water bottle with the dart inside before lifting Melena in his arms. "Take this to Doc at the morgue. Tell him we need the chemical breakdown of whatever's inside, and we need it sooner than yesterday. Then bring him back here to give us a hand." *In case, by some miracle, Joe and Theo are still alive.*

Grim faced, Rocket kissed Billie on the mouth, handing her his headset. "Keep out of sight, peaches. Back Micah up, but from a safe distance."

"Don't worry, I will." Billie attached the receiver to her ear, holstered her Glock, and took the Benelli from him. She moved off toward the boathouse as if the shotgun weighed less than a feather, tossing a determined glance over her shoulder at Micah. "Shout if you need me."

He nodded, eating up the distance to the cottage with long strides. When Remy tugged on his belt to keep up, he cursed under his breath and slowed a bit. There was so much he wanted to say to her, with no time to say it. Any chance of a private conversation was off the table. All he could do was hope she kept it together.

He stopped for an instant to watch Rocket gun the SUV, gravel spraying from the tires as his friend took off down the road. Satisfied, he carried Melena inside to the game room. Setting her on a couch, he dropped down beside her. "How bad is it?"

She shook her head, her blond cap of hair tangled with leaves and bits of bark. "It's nothing, probably just a sprain. It's Theo and Joe I'm worried about."

"Sully will find them, Mel." Sure he would. He wouldn't leave anyone behind, especially his brother. But would it be in time to reverse the effects of whatever was in the darts? *Goddamn*, Micah's team had seen action all over the globe and hadn't lost a man yet, although there had been injuries. Still, the thought something like this could happen on his home turf, that he could lose a brother-in-arms because of his own stupidity, tore him apart. The blame lay squarely on his shoulders, because he'd underestimated the men hunting Remy.

Remy hobbled down the stairs with a bag of ice and a load of towels in her hands. Her knees were scraped raw and bleeding, a welt on her cheek swelling. The urge to take her in his arms almost overpowered him, but now wasn't the time. Seeing she was still in one piece and holding her own had to be enough.

He wouldn't be caught off guard if the bastards showed up at the house to try to take her again. He knew it could happen and he had to be ready. That realization trumped everything else that needed saying or doing. "I'll be outside."

"We'll handle things here," she said, not meeting his gaze. "I'll lock up behind you."

She might look done in, but he noticed she was still strong, her hands steady. Still, he figured she blamed herself for what had gone down and that was the bigger problem. "Trigger—

"Please, Mic, you need to go. I can't deal with this right now."

"Break it up you two. Remy, I need a basin of warm water to clean Mel's cuts." Breeana pushed between them to kneel on the floor beside Melena. She opened a first aid kit. "Let me take a look at that ankle."

Micah shook his head to clear it, grabbing his iPad. A couple of keystrokes on the tablet assured him the alarm system hadn't been breached. So far, so good, but he couldn't count on it staying that way. He had to do better. Billie stood guard on her own, a dangerous position for anyone to be in. Pulling the assault rifle from his shoulder, he checked the load and stepped outside.

He walked the perimeter of the cottage, listening and watching for anything out of place. With his weapon raised and a fire in his belly to destroy the Swamp Killer and his crew, his vision sharpened with hate. Had the freaks killed Theo, Joe, and the dog to get to Remy? Only God knew what was in those darts. A 20cc dose could pack a lot of ominous shit.

It could be anything from Grizzly tranquilizers to poison, most of which a man wouldn't survive. Tranqs for large game were too strong for the human respiratory system. Lungs and hearts would shut down within a short period of time. He stared at the acres of forest, knowing a dart rifle had an accuracy of up to seventy meters. His brain screamed he was a sitting duck if someone was out there aiming at him. If they put him down, they'd have a straight run at Remy and the others. Jesus. No way could he let that happen.

Micah activated his mic. "Billie, get inside the house. Run!"

REMY UNLOCKED THE DOOR, stepping back as Micah urged Billie into the game room in front of him. Something was wrong. She had seen Billie sprint up the hill from the boathouse and Micah fall in behind her, looming over her as if to protect her. "What's happened?"

"Nothing." Micah locked the door and reset the alarm. He bristled with energy, his voice clipped, his gaze searching the trees down by the water.

"Tell me the truth." She touched his arm. As scared as she was, now wasn't the time for him to lie to her. Not when she felt responsible for the danger they were in since insisting on taking that damn stroll in the woods. Couldn't he see she needed to be involved? Not protected like some empty-headed china doll. "What's going on?"

"Don't worry about it. I'm being careful, that's all."

"Look, I'm not a complete fool. You and Billie came rushing in here like the house was on fire."

"I think Remy has a point." Breeana set a tray of coffee and fruit down on an end table, tipping her chin in Micah's direction. "Quit treating us like we're going to freak out at the first signs of trouble." She clucked her tongue. "I don't know what it is with you alpha males. You know we can take the heat, and yet, you still try to protect us."

"Spill it, Mic." Billie tossed her head, her eyes shooting daggers in his direction. Remy knew Rocket sometimes called her Billie the Hammer because of her temper. Right now, the nickname suited her to a T. "You told me to run for the house and I did. But I think you owe me an explanation. Why are we in here instead of outside guarding against bad guys?"

"Better cough it up," Melena said, pouring a mug of coffee from the carafe. "The news can't get much worse, so tell us what it is and maybe we can help."

"Man, you're a tough audience." Micah grimaced, the hint of a chuckle in his voice. "Okay, here's the deal. The guys were shot with a dart rifle that has long range capability. And that's bad for us."

"How do you know?" Remy asked. "It could have been some nut ball hiding up a tree with a handgun."

"'Fraid not. Theo or Joe would have spotted anyone close enough to use a pistol, and Tubbs would have caught their scent." He glanced at them over his shoulder. "We're inside because if the bastards have eyes on the cottage, I don't want to give them another target."

His sharp gaze landed on Billie. "Get upstairs and keep watch out the back windows. And stay out of sight."

She nodded, shouldering the shotgun as she took the stairs. Then Micah did something Remy didn't expect. He tugged up a pant leg and unsnapped his ankle holster, offering her the Smith & Wesson she'd tried to steal from the gun room. "Here, take it."

Once she had it in her palm, he returned his focus to the other side of the glass. Remy breathed deep and let the air out slowly to keep from losing her cool. The situation must be serious if Micah was giving her the weapon. It meant he didn't think he'd be around long enough to protect her. Touching his back, she felt the knot of muscles beneath her hand. "I don't want it."

"You've earned it, Trigger. You kept it together this morning and got Melena out of there." He tapped the handgun, his expression a blank mask. "Don't hesitate to use this if you find yourself in a jam. Shoot to kill."

"I won't need it." She touched his face, standing on her tiptoes to kiss his mouth. He kissed her back, stirring the blood in her veins.

Sanity sparked. She stepped to the side, but it was too late. Micah knew she loved him no matter how many times she denied it. Like recognized like and wouldn't be denied. She whispered, "I don't need a gun because you're here for me."

"I'll do my best." He leaned in to sample her lips again before turning his gaze back to the window. "We'll continue this later, honey. Now's not the time."

"Tell me one thing first." She managed to squeeze between him and the windowpane. His eyes focused on the landscape but he knew she was there. She placed a hand on his chest to stop the sway of her body against his. His heart sped up beneath her fingertips and she almost sighed. Animal magnetism was an invisible natural force and their combustible reality. She had never experienced it with anyone before Micah. But, God, how he drew her in. "How did you find me in the woods?"

"Ah, that. Would you believe I slipped a GPS chip in the sole of one of your Nikes the day I brought you here?" He bumped his chin on the top of her head. "I won't apologize for it. I wanted to tuck transmitters into every article of clothing you own. I was pretty sure you'd balk at the idea, so I settled for the shoe."

She dropped her hand from his chest before she wrapped her arms around his neck and held on for dear life. "I'm glad you did."

"Then do us both a favor and keep wearing those shoes." His gaze shifted to Melena on the couch, her ankle propped on cushions with ice bags packed around it. "How are you doing, Mel?"

"I'm fine," she insisted, but her eyes said different. Remy knew she was scared to death for her man, and who could blame her? "Any word from the others yet?"

Micah shook his dark head, a look of frustration in his eyes. "We'll hear something soon."

Sweet Jesus, Remy couldn't face Melena after the pain she'd caused her. She had to keep busy or she'd lose her mind from the guilt. Tucking the gun at her waistband, she raided a closet for extra pillows and blankets and walked back to Micah. "I'll make up the other couches. Bree thinks Papa Joe and Theo might be in shock when they arrive. We have to keep them warm until a medevac helicopter can transport them to the hospital."

"Good idea." Micah's phone vibrated in a pocket. Pulling it out, he hit speaker, tucking her into his side. "It's Doc."

She dropped the linens to wrap her arms around his waist, dreading what Doc would say. Breeana took Mel's hand and sat down beside her, waiting to hear the news—good or bad. If Theo and Papa Joe died... Remy couldn't finish the thought. It was too heartbreaking.

Micah gave her a reassuring squeeze. "Talk to me, Doc. What did you find in the dart?"

"It's ketamine, Mic. Not poison."

"Thank God!" Melena collapsed in Breeana's arms, the two of them in tears.

Remy's knees gave out, her body slumping against Micah's strength. He held her up, brushing a quick kiss across her forehead. "Good job, Doc. That was fast work."

"The scent was the giveaway." The drone of tires on asphalt rumbled in the background. Remy guessed Doc was riding in the SUV with Rocket. "Liquid ketamine smells like dish soap. Once I took a whiff, I had Sam run it on the mass spectrometer. The result was positive."

Micah cleared his throat. "What about the dose?"

"Since the men and Tubbs are all well over two hundred pounds, it won't kill them. Now, if Remy or Mel had been hit? We'd be planning a funeral."

Wasn't that a cheery thought? Remy's ears picked up at the sound of a boat cutting across the bay toward the house. Micah heard it, too. He swivelled, peering down to the water. "Gotta go. The others are back with Theo and Joe."

"We're pulling in the driveway now." Doc disconnected.

"Keep everyone inside," Micah murmured as he disarmed the door and made tracks for the Bayliner.

Sully was the first to cross the threshold. "Mel, you're feeding him too much. My bro weighs a damn ton."

Melena hid her tears, struggling to stand when Sully approached her with Theo in a fireman's carry. Remy liked seeing Sully's softer side. He grabbed a pillow off the floor and tucked it beneath Theo's head after he laid him on a leather sofa. Then he wrapped Melena in a bear hug. "You sure you're up to babysitting Prince Charming while he gets his beauty sleep? I can toss him in the broom closet if you want to rest that ankle."

"Let me think about it." Melena laughed as she covered Theo with a blanket, threaded her fingers through his and cuddled up beside him. "Let's hold off unless he starts snoring."

"Better face it, Mel," Law said, carrying Tubbs past her to the doggie bed in the corner and setting him down. "Theo can sleep for years but he'll never be beautiful. He's almost as ugly as the mutt here, and probably snores just as loud."

"Be nice to my patient." Breeana gave Law a stern look and a good natured shove. "Or I'll tell Tubbs what you said about him. He'll be chomping on your buns when he wakes up."

"And what great buns they are." Law slapped his backside and grinned. "I need to find a woman who'll appreciate them."

"Forget it." Billie came down the stairs straight into Rocket's arms. "The butt might be prime real estate, but what gal with half a brain would put up with the rest of you?"

Remy poured Hunter a coffee, since his hands were full of sports bags. "I'll dump these in the gun room and take the first shift at the back of the house." He made for the stairs. "I might hurl if I hear any more talk about Law's fat ass."

Hawke helped Micah deposit Papa Joe on the last vacant couch. Doc dropped his medical bag on the floor and began to examine his patient. "For the love of Mike, didn't any of you goofballs think to remove the stogie from Joe's mouth? He's still chomping on the blasted thing."

Micah shrugged his shoulders, winking at Remy. "He looks normal to me."

That set the tone for the rest of the afternoon and evening. A lot of laughing and good natured camaraderie filled the cottage. It seemed the only way for everyone to decompress. Remy and Billie tossed together a simple meal of sandwiches, salads, and coffeecake. They served it on the pool table in the game room. The men took turns guarding the house and checking the alarm system. Breeana and Doc saw to the needs of their groggy patients. Melena and Sully rode herd on Theo, who wanted to take a shift at guard duty, although he could barely stand.

Remy divided her time between Tubbs and Papa Joe. Tubbs was the easier of the two. He seemed content to snooze off the after-effects of the ketamine, occasionally opening his eyes to lick her hand. Papa Joe was the difficult one. She finally broke down and brought him a beer before he crawled up the stairs to the kitchen to get one himself.

"That's better. Now if you'd be kind enough to light my stogie, I'd say we're even." He clamped the cigar between his teeth and waggled his eyebrows. "After all I've been through, it's the least you can do."

Remy was sure she saw the inside of her head when she performed one of her better eye rolls. Papa Joe had no shame, although she was glad to see him morph back into his cantankerous self. "Stuff it. If you want to smoke, move outside and risk another round with the dart rifle."

"That ain't no way to talk to your elders, missy. I've got half a mind to—"

Kaboom!

An explosion rocked the house. The lights went out.

Chapter 13

Micah watched the woods at the back of the house. A muzzle flashed. He ducked, taking cover behind the wall supporting the windows. A split second more and an incendiary round hit the propane tank outside. *Holy fuck!* He hit the floor as the hydrocarbon gas blew. A ball of fire punched the house with the force of a missile. Glass imploded. Flames licked inward while wood blistered and sizzled. Smoke swirled as he army-crawled out the bedroom into the hallway.

He shot to his feet and raced for the stairs. "Remy!"

"Got her!" Sully met him at the top of the staircase, shoving her and Melena forward before charging back down again. Micah heard Rocket shout for Billie below him. He saw Joe hug the handrail, crawling past Sully toward the upper floor.

Micah grabbed him by the shirt collar and hauled him the rest of the way. He pushed him through the kitchen with Remy and Melena, the three of them staggering, barely able to stay on their feet. Soot thickened, curls of flame licking through an outside wall. The breeze from shattered windows spread the burn.

Micah tapped in the code on the solar panel and released the door for the panic room. He hustled them inside. Clean air filtered around them, the room fireproof, solar lights shining down from the walls. "Stay here until I get back."

"Micah?" Remy clutched his hand, gulping in air, her other arm tight around Melena's waist. "Be careful."

"Always."

"Step aside." Micah spun as Rocket carried Billie across the threshold and set her down on the table. She coughed, trying to catch her breath. "Easy, peaches."

Micah reached around them, pulled a small oxygen tank from a drawer, and handed it to Remy. "Take care of her."

She nodded and opened the valve, placing the mask over Billie's nose and mouth. Reassured by the sight, Micah hustled from the room with Rocket and heard the door lock behind him. "Who's left downstairs?"

"Sully was dragging Bree away from Tubbs. And Law's trying to get Theo's ass in gear. The drug hit him harder than it did Joe and he started to hallucinate." Rocket unsnapped the flashlight from the charger in the kitchen and turned into the hallway. "Hawke and Hunt were patrolling when the explosion hit. As far as I know, they're still outside."

Micah shot down the stairs with his Maglite. He crouched at the bottom, staying below the worst of the smoke. "What about Doc?"

Rocket raised his voice above the hiss of flames. "He cut out an hour ago in the Bayliner."

"Shit. That only leaves the runabout in the boathouse." Micah made out Law's bulky shape dragging Theo across the floor. He probably didn't have a choice and KO'd him. He nudged Rocket. "Give Law a hand. I'll find Sully and Bree."

The air thicker than slime, Micah stayed low, close to the stone floor in order to breathe. He crawled toward the dog bed, wondering how long they had before the house burned to the ground around them. At least the panic room would remain standing. It was steel-reinforced concrete, the supports drilled into bedrock twenty feet below the cottage foundation. It wasn't going anywhere.

He reached the dog bed. *Empty.*

"Sully! Where are you?"

"The storage room!"

Micah felt for the door on his left and rolled through. "What the hell?"

Breeana's voice came through the haze. "Help!"

A few more seconds and Micah saw Sully. "Are you crazy? Get Bree out of here!"

"Can't!" Sully coughed. "Tubbs crawled behind the freezer and I can't budge it. Bree won't leave without him."

"Yeah, she will." Micah knew what he had to do. No choice. He wrapped his arm around Breeana's neck from the back. When his elbow was under her chin, he applied pressure. Four seconds and she was unconscious.

"Motherfuck!"

"You'll thank me later." Micah pointed toward the game room. "Get her out! Do it!"

Sully scooped up Breeana and hustled for the door. "You asshole. I'm going to make you pay for that!"

Micah searched the tools beside his workbench. Grabbed the crowbar and wedged it between the wall and freezer. He used it as a fulcrum, putting his strength behind it. The freezer inched across the cement enough for him to get behind it. The dog was down. He dragged Tubbs out and hefted him over his shoulders, holding onto his paws.

Standing upright and breathing wasn't happening, but somehow he held his breath and made it up the stairs. Jesus, the kitchen was lit up like the 4th of July. He ignored the flames licking his boots and almost plowed into Sully's back to reach the panic room. The door slid open, thank Christ.

Rocket took Tubbs from him while Micah counted heads. "I need a status report on Hawke and Hunt."

"They're taking gunfire outside." Joe scanned the monitors, the feed running on solar. He also talked into a headset. "Hawke thinks he nailed one of 'em."

"We need to get out there." Law threw the go bags up on the table, breaking out hardware while shrugging into his Kevlar vest.

"Hold on." Sully crouched on the floor between Theo and Breeana. Both were just starting to come around. "I can't leave them like this."

"No need." Micah pulled extra ammo clips for Sully's Glock from a bin. He tossed them to him. "Stay inside until it's safe to bring them out."

"That's the plan?" Man, Sully's head wasn't in the game or he wouldn't relinquish his command.

Micah dressed for battle, adding a gun to an ankle and a knife to his belt. "The bastards should scatter like vermin once the fire department arrives. We'll let you know when it's clear."

"What about the rest of us?" Remy touched his arm, fear shining in her eyes. "Please, Mic. I want to go with you."

"Why not take her to my place? I could stay with her." Melena glanced at Theo who moaned on the floor. "Theo's fine with Sully, and Remy would be safer there."

"She has a point, Mic." Rocket added a taser to his utility belt. "If you can sneak Remy out of here in a boat, without the bastards knowing and get ahead of them, they won't be able to navigate the Narrows at night. They'll never find you. Hell, even I can't drive that stretch in the dark...too many rocks beneath the surface. That section must be a graveyard of boat skeletons."

"Tell me about it." Melena shuddered. "That's where I crashed and almost drowned. If it hadn't been for Dood—"

"Where is your wolf, Mel?" Micah remembered that god-awful night and the wolf. He also knew Dood had taken a bullet for her when she'd been attacked. Yeah, the wolf would definitely be a plus if push came to shove.

"We leave him loose on the island when we aren't there. He won't let anyone out of their boat if he doesn't know them."

"Sully? What's your take on this?" Micah thought the idea a good one, but he wanted his CO's opinion.

"I think the Swamp Killer torched your house for a reason, to flush Remy out. And he expects you to move her by car." Sully took Breeana's hand and helped her to sit up beside him. "I'd lay odds his goons are waiting along the road somewhere to grab her."

"Listen, if you're taking Remy to Mel's, I'm coming." Billie studied the gun rack, removing the Benelli shotgun she'd used earlier. "You might need an extra pair of hands."

"Make that two pairs," Joe said, reaching for his bang stick and a sidearm. "Remy ain't goin' nowhere without me."

Micah packed up his go bag and tossed it to Joe. Then he removed the half cast on his wrist for better freedom of movement. He winced a little, grabbed an assault rifle, and motioned to Sully. "Watch the monitors until we clear the boathouse."

"Yeah, and thanks for earlier." Sully shot him a two-fingered salute.

"No need. You would have done the same for me."

Micah opened the door to the tunnel. Law and Rocket turned right for the garage and started to run, talking through their headsets to Hawke and Hunt. A plan was in the works and Micah hoped it was enough. The other guys would lay down cover once he gave the signal, allowing him to get the women in the boat without being spotted. Only four guys against how many? He smiled, knowing they'd kick ass no matter the odds because that's what they did.

Micah walked through the tunnel with Joe and the women toward the boathouse. Melena's sprained ankle didn't allow them to increase the pace. He was in front when he noticed water running through fissures in the ceiling. Sure it had stormed off and on all day, but the tunnel was built to withstand the elements. He talked into his mic. "Rocket, you're the engineer—there's water leaking into the tunnel here. Do you see anything on your side?"

"Yeah, and it doesn't look good. The explosion damaged the structure. Propane gas sinks into the ground when it leaks, which means we could be due for another explosion if it finds a depression. We're in the garage now, so we're clear. Better haul ass, Mic. Get everyone out of there."

Earth started to pour through the cracks, knocking chunks of plaster to the ground. Micah shouted. "Run! Get to the end of the tunnel and get out!"

The women picked up speed, Remy and Billie hoisting Melena between them. But Joe tripped and went down. He groaned, blood coating the side of his face where he scraped the wall. "Goddamn, I think I knocked my brain loose."

Micah hefted Joe, the go bag, the assault rifle, and broke into a sprint. The last thing he saw before the ceiling caved was Remy squeezing through the outer door.

REMY FROZE AS THE CEILING of the tunnel collapsed, earth and rocks pushing toward her across the floor. Billie dragged her out by the belt and slammed the door behind her. "What are you doing? Micah and Papa Joe are still in there!"

"Shh or someone might hear us." Billie pressed a finger to her lips. "There's nothing we can do for them. We need to stick to the plan or we'll die."

"We have to leave *now*." Melena took her wrist and tugged her to a ladder bolted on the wall behind the door. She pleaded with her eyes. "Look, Mic will get out of there without our help. And he'll get Joe out too. Those men have nine lives, but we don't."

"Maybe they're dead," Remy whispered, choking back sobs.

Billie gave her a shake that rattled her bones. "Then there's nothing you can do but save yourself. It's what Micah wants you to do."

"He'd *want* me to get him out of there."

"No, you're wrong." Melena took both her hands and held on. Remy heard the sadness in her voice. She saw it in her eyes. "Rocket and I believe Micah loves you. He'll move heaven and earth if it means keeping you alive. Remy, please."

God, she wanted to dig Micah and Joe out with her bare hands. She couldn't, because the Swamp Killer might be hiding in the woods on top of them. And if he heard or saw them...

There had already been too much violence, so many good people hurt because of her. She had no choice but to move in order to save Melena and Billie. But, sweet Lord, it took every ounce of her control to leave Micah behind. "Let's go."

They crawled up the ladder, slid open the slide bolt, and out the trap door, laying it back in place and covering it with dirt. Remy scanned the shadows and listened. They were at the edge of the forest down by the water, vulnerable without the rest of Micah's team. Crouching in the dark, they huddled together, mosquitoes buzzing around them and waves lapping the shore.

Remy listened to the night. She heard nothing but the raging inferno up the hill. Her eyes followed the sound. Timbers cracked and smouldered. Spot fires burned. Trees caught the flames in a hail of sparks and the night sky glowed orange against the backdrop of mountains. It was mass destruction on an evil scale. Not just Micah's house, but perhaps the entire forest. The Swamp Killer wanted her dead, she got that. But didn't he care who or what he destroyed to do it? A stupid question since he was a heinous monster. She would enjoy watching him die and took solace in it. The law would sentence him to death in Florida, or he could eat a bullet here. It didn't matter to her. Either way, she would have a front row seat.

The boathouse creaked in the darkness, about fifteen feet off shore. Untouched by the blaze, it was close enough to bring comfort. Far enough away to get them killed. Remy began to inch forward when Billie clamped a hand on her calf. "Not yet. I'll go first."

"What are you waiting for?"

"Ground cover." Guns fired as she spoke, breaking the silence. Billie leapt to her feet and charged for the dock. She pressed her back against the boathouse wall when she got there, aiming the shotgun toward the cottage. "Now!"

Remy got Melena up and running. She wrapped an arm around her waist to take most of her weight and leapt for the pier. Billie held up a hand when they reached her and edged through a doorway. She came back out. "It's clear. No one's inside."

The doublewide doors stood open in the opposite wall, moonlight shining on a small metal boat.

"Crap, this isn't good." Melena glanced around and scowled. "The Bayliner is gone. And Micah's Tahoe is still out for repairs."

"Guess we're planning the great escape in this little gem then." Billie nudged the prow with a foot. "Anyhow, this is more your speed, Mel. It's easier to handle, right?"

"It's Micah's frigging fishing boat. It'll take us forever to get to my place in this thing."

"There's no use complaining about it." Remy thought any boat was better than no boat. They could still get away. As more shots echoed from the cottage, she silently thanked the Spec Ops guys for giving them this chance. "Let's get moving."

Easing into the stern, Melena checked the gauge on the gas tank with a penlight. "Okay, hop in."

Pulling the bow line from a steel cleat bolted to the dock, Remy tossed it in the boat, waiting as Billie did the same at the stern. Billie took the middle seat and laid the shotgun across her feet. "Push us off while I get the oars out."

Remy nodded, running down the planking beside the boat while shoving against the bow. She jumped in at the last second as they floated clear of the boathouse. Billie swung them around using the oars and rowed like a madwoman. She whispered to Melena. "Pull up the engine for now. It's hard enough to steer this tub."

"So says the girl who's never rowed a boat in her life." Melena hauled up the motor. "Bet you don't get out on the water much on your ranch in the Rockies."

"You'd be surprised. We have lakes there just like everywhere else."

Sirens sounded on shore. Remy glanced up and saw lights flashing through the trees. A fire truck, ambulance, police vehicles, and several other cars careened to a stop on the road. Men raced down to the water with what she thought were fire pumps. A few more seconds and motors revved. Water churned through hoses, firemen dousing the house and trees. Others wielded shovels and axes further out from the cottage. They seemed to be digging trenches and downing burned limbs. Her tears overflowed for what was lost. What would never be again. But while Micah's house couldn't be saved, maybe the forest could.

Boats roared into the bay now, at least a dozen or more. The volunteer fire department's tom-toms must be working their magic. Remy knew the lake encompassed over forty kilometers of shoreline. That meant a lot of hands working on the fire brigade if everyone pitched in. Meanwhile, she did nothing to help, their little runabout hugging the shoreline well past Micah's dock. It went unnoticed, bobbing in the waves with its lights out.

"There's Theo's Bayliner," Melena murmured. "Doc's driving, and that's his wife, Effie, beside him."

Remy watched as Doc tied up and stepped to the pier, helping his wife out. They ran up the hill together carrying medical bags, and Remy remembered Micah saying Effie was a nurse practitioner. According to him, she was almost as skilled as her husband and routinely patched up patients when Doc wasn't available. Remy smiled at that because she knew how much Doc loved his fishing. She imagined he made himself scarce as much as possible. Still, she felt relieved for the first time since the explosion. At least Doc and Effie were there if anyone needed them. If Micah needed them. If he was alive.

She ached for him, was desperate to see him. To know he was safe. "Surely there are enough people here now. We could go back."

"Remy, we can't. You're not thinking straight." Billie stopped rowing. She stared at her as if she'd lost her mind. "What if the Swamp Killer and his buddies are with the others, dressed as firemen or first responders? Or maybe they hid their weapons and walked out of the forest to join the volunteers? It's way too risky."

Remy sighed. "You really believe that?"

"Of course she does. And so do I." Melena moved past Billie to crouch in front of her, a hand touching her knee. "Honey, I live here and even *I* don't recognize a lot of faces, especially since the regatta attracted so many tourists. And did you forget what Sully said? He thinks the Swamp Killer expects you to leave by car now that they've burned Micah out. This is your chance to get away without him knowing."

She sighed and wanted to cry, because they were right. She couldn't find fault in their logic, no matter what her heart wanted her to do. "Okay. We keep going."

They rounded a bend into the next bay, the funeral pyre of the cottage swallowed up by the trees. Billie stopped rowing, securing the oars. "Okay, Mel. Put the engine back in the water and start her up."

Melena gave them the thumbs up and dropped the motor, locking it in place. She pulled out a knob—Remy thought it was the throttle—rotated the sleeve on the tiller handle and pulled on the starter cable. The outboard purred to life. Gunning the throttle, the boat picked up speed. "Keep your eyes open. I'll have to flip on the running lights if another boat comes close to us."

Hearing tales of Melena's boating mishaps from the Spec Ops guys, Remy wondered if any of them should be believed. As far as she could tell, Melena handled the boat well. Hugging the shoreline while avoiding rocks and floating debris couldn't be easy. And risking her life to help a friend made her a superhero in Remy's book.

Melena slowed them to a crawl about ten minutes later. "Okay, ladies. Hold on tight 'cuz we're approaching the Narrows. I have to hit the lights or we'll pile up on the rocks."

"Go for it," Billie said, clutching the gunnels.

Remy turned in her seat to see what was in front of them. Her stomach churned, remembering Rocket's words. He wouldn't drive through the Narrows at night because it was too risky.

"Pull the lifejackets from the bow and pass us a couple." Melena shot her a half grin. "Not that I'm expecting to crash or anything."

Right. Remy slipped on a vest and gave two to Billie, who handed one back. Melena idled the boat while she buckled into hers.

"Oh, no!" Billie stared ahead to their right.

Remy's gaze snapped in that direction, her pulse pounding at the sight of a boat idling in the mouth of the waterway. It was a double hull with all the bells and whistles, and a couple of guys pointing rifles at them. The only good thing was they hadn't opened fire.

Billie grabbed the shotgun off the floor, stating the obvious. "We've got company!"

"Try the devil himself!" Remy called to Melena. "Can you go around them?"

"I'll try. If I can squeeze by we might be able to lose them up ahead." Melena goosed the throttle. "Hold on!"

Billie pumped the shotgun and steadied it, ready to fire. "I'll give them something to worry about if they try to stop us!"

It was then Remy remembered the handgun strapped to her ankle. Would she use it? Hell, yes, and Micah had told her to shoot to kill. She unsnapped the Velcro holster, palming the grip on the S&W as her finger touched the trigger. She scoped out the men on the boat, trying to identify the Swamp Killer. He would die for trying to destroy her, for almost killing her friend, Pete. For shooting Theo and Papa Joe full of ketamine. And for burning Micah's house down. But not because Micah was dead—her heart believed he was still alive and coming for her.

She tried to take aim as the boat dipped and rolled over the waves. A floodlight blazed from the powerboat, blinding her. She raised a hand to shield her eyes, couldn't see anything. A powerful motor roared toward them. How close were they? She fired at the spotlight and nailed it, blinking to clear her vision. Billie stood to fire the shotgun.

Wham! They slammed into a boulder. Billie pitched over the side and disappeared.

Melena screamed. "God, she's gone under the boat!"

Metal buckled and rivets sheared. Remy and Melena bailed out and swam for shore. Billie popped out of the current further down and clung to a rock. The other boat reversed then pulled alongside them. As Remy groped for a handhold on the slimy rock face in front of her, someone called to her—the Swamp Killer's voice. She didn't need to turn around to recognize it, or the sound of him racking the slide on his Sig Sauer. She'd heard and seen both before in the Everglades.

"Welcome to my world, Remy Rose. I've been waiting for you."

SIG'S BINOCULARS SHARPENED on the carcass of the house as they cruised by the mouth of the bay. Lots of frantic activity, he mused with a grin. Klieg lights burned as busy bees worked trying to save the surrounding forest. He caught the sweet scent of victory on the breeze—the stench of smoke and the beginnings of a broken man. Micah Rivera had lost everything tonight, his home and his woman, although he might not know about the woman yet. And he was about to lose more.

Sig knew his type. Watching her die and knowing there was nothing he could do to stop it would break him. And Sig couldn't wait for the long, precious hours he'd spend with Remy. For the rounds he'd fire into Rivera's kneecaps to keep him as helpless as a caged tiger.

"That's quite the haul, Sig. Three bitches for the price of one." Keyhole handled the boat controls, steering for the landing a couple kilometers away. "And here I thought I'd have to stand in line to wait for my time with the main target."

"Shit, man, we scored the mother lode." Ice-Pick kicked one of the women lying at his feet. Sig suspected Ice-Pick's libido tweaked up a notch when he heard her painful intake of breath. "I'm calling first dibs on the babe wearing the cowboy boots. She needs an attitude adjustment. The feel of my spurs digging in should calm that filly right down. Hear that, darlin'? We're gonna have ourselves a roundup."

"I bet the Dentist has the perfect bit to fit between her teeth." Keyhole laughed as he took the curve into the last bay. "Now me, I'm planning to introduce the little one to some fun water sports. I'll start with waterboarding as foreplay and see how things progress. I can always tag team with Snake, throw a water moccasin in the hot tub with her if she doesn't behave herself. What about you, Sig?"

"There's only one woman who interests me, but I'll be counting on all of you for your creative input. And, of course, you'll have time with her as well, since she's Blade's killer." Floodlights at the landing guided them into the boathouse. Keyhole turned off the engine and tied off the boat. Sig nodded to Ice-Pick. "Check outside for the others. They can help with the cargo."

Within minutes, the women were loaded in back of a van. Ankles and wrists flex cuffed. Duct tape across their mouths under the black hoods. Sig recognized Remy's shoes and the Dentist's hand on her thigh. He glared at him to back off. Now wasn't the time. "How did it go at Rivera's?"

"Smooth as glass for the most part." The Dentist removed his hand, no doubt sensing Sig's displeasure. "They never knew what hit them. It's just too bad we didn't get the chance to take some of them out.

We watched the doors, but no one exited. And the two already outside vanished in the woods."

"Maybe the others burned in the fire." Or maybe not. Sig knew enough about Rivera and his team to expect the unexpected. "You sure you didn't see anyone?"

"Might not have seen 'em, but I sure as hell felt one of 'em." Snake let out a growl, raising a bloody, bandaged hand. "The prick almost shot off all me fingers. It's damn lucky the rifle caught most of the load or I'd have nothing left but a stump. As it is, I lost a pinkie."

Sig shook his head. "That's the price of having fun, Snake."

"I'll tell ya one thing." Snake's gaze fell on the bodies on the floor. "I'll be exacting punishment from those three."

"How about this?" Ice-Pick shot Sig a glance. "We can snip a digit off each of them to send to Rivera."

"No. I'd rather do it in front of him," Sig said, watching the road. "There's the turn up ahead."

"Why are we here again?" The Dentist tapped his shoulder from the back seat.

"To shift Rivera's focus." Sig swivelled to face him. "With any luck, he'll hunt down the transients and druggies who use this place. Give us a chance to set the stage, so to speak."

"Then why toss the women's cell phones in the lake? He'd have the ability to track them through his police connections. The signals would lead him straight here."

Sig shook his head. "He won't buy it if we make it easy for him. It's better if the cops find this place and show him the evidence."

The van pulled into the drive of a boarded up gas station. Keyhole killed the engine and the lights. Sig stepped out as the Dentist opened the side panel door. He slipped on latex gloves. "Bring our guests inside."

Sig unclipped the flashlight from his belt. The place was filthy, filled with empty beer cans, drug paraphernalia, used condoms, and cigarette butts. It reeked of oil and stale sex. The small office was open, a stained mattress on the floor. A rat routed through candy wrappers in a far corner. Sig aimed his weapon and fired. One less rodent in the world, goddamn things were full of disease.

Ice-Pick and Keyhole dragged the women into the garage bay. Sig walked toward them. "Get rid of the hoods, and cut them loose."

His men surrounded them, boxing them in. He expected to see fear on the women's faces. What he saw instead was loathing. And anger, especially from Remy Rose. He focused on her. "Take off your clothes."

Hatred flared in her gaze. Not to worry. Those clear violet eyes would soon be clouded over with pain. He almost laughed when she spit in his face, her fists raised in a fighter's stance.

"Not if you were the last man on earth." She tossed her head, her red hair a blaze of glory in the flashlight beams. "I'd rather die."

Sig pulled a handkerchief out of a pocket and wiped his cheek. He nodded to Ice-Pick. "Show the ladies what happens when they don't obey."

Ice-Pick grabbed Remy from behind. Twisting her hair tight in a fist, he pulled out his trademark weapon. The stab to her shoulder was quick and agonizing. Remy gasped, buckling at the knees. Ice-Pick didn't loosen his grip.

Glancing at the other women, Sig smiled in satisfaction, the two of them already undressing. He loomed over Remy. "This is the last time I'm going to say it. Strip! Or your friends will pay the price."

Chapter 14

Micah clawed his way out of the dirt.

Looking up, he could see trees above him. The jagged hole in the ceiling looked wide enough for a man to fit through. But, first things first, he needed to find Joe and his gear. Brushing off his watch, he saw how much time had passed. Too much to help Remy; she should be long gone by now. He prayed the women had gotten away safe.

A hand popped through the earth beside him. Micah latched onto the wrist and heaved. Joe came to the surface, spitting out gravel. "If I'd wanted a mud bath, I'd have gone to a spa." He shook the worst of it out of his hair, wiping his eyes. "Where are the girls?"

"They're not here." Micah felt around for his go bag, found a handle, and tugged. Black leather torpedoed up in a swirl of dust. It appeared to be undamaged. The strap over his shoulder told him he hadn't lost the C15 sniper rifle. Good thing he'd covered the end with a condom to keep out debris. "They made it to the door before the tunnel caved in."

"Better get a move on then." Joe pulled out his other hand clutching the bang stick. "I'm ready when you are. You gonna give me a boost?"

"We need people out there to haul us up." He tapped his mic and talked into it. "Anyone getting this?"

"Yo, Mic." Hawke's voice rumbled in his ear. "You've been off our radar for quite a while. Where the hell are you?"

"Up to my armpits in dirt, man. The tunnel collapsed between the panic room and the boathouse." Micah glanced at Joe who was still wiggling his body free. "We need a couple guys up top to pull us out."

"On our way," Hawke said. "It might take us a while to find you."

"Hey, we don't have time, so do it fast. The women made it out and my guess is they're headed to Mel's by themselves."

"We already know." Hawke grunted. Then Micah heard him in surround sound, the end of a rope hitting the ground in front of him. "Grab on."

He looked up to see Hawke and Hunt, tied the rope under Joe's armpits, and signalled for them to pull him up. A couple more minutes and he and Joe were both free. "I need a boat."

"You can take your pick," Hunt said. "The cavalry's arrived from all over the lake as well as by road."

"Hold up," Hawke said. "Use your cell and call Rocket or Theo first. Theo's finally out from under his ketamine cloud. The two of them roared out of here ten minutes ago in the Bayliner. They had no way of knowing if you were with the girls when you didn't answer your mic or cell phone."

Micah dialed and waited. One ring. Two. Theo answered on the third. "Mic? It's bad news here."

Micah's heart almost stopped. "How bad?"

"It looks like Mel plowed the runabout into the rocks at the Narrows. There's no sign of them, but we see lots of wreckage. We need people out here to search."

"Wait a minute." Micah tapped the app on his cell phone to check on the GPS tracker he'd imbedded in Remy's shoe. The screen lit up, taking him in a whole other direction, and shaking him down to his boots. "You won't find them in the Narrows. Get to the boat landing and grab a vehicle. Steal one if you have to."

"What the hell?" Theo repeated his words to Rocket. Micah heard the roar of the boat engine as Theo took him at his word. "What do you know that we don't?"

Jesus, God. He knew plenty and none of it good. "Remy's GPS is pinging. She's off the lake on the outskirts of town. Take the highway and head north."

"We're on our way." Rocket's voice filled his ear. Theo must have passed him the phone. Micah recognized his tone, didn't have to guess the guy had murder on his mind. "It's the Swamp Killer, right? He's got them."

"That's my guess." Micah was running now, through the trees to the front of the house. Correction, to where his house had stood a few hours ago. What he saw was smoking ash and a bunch of people trying to save the land around it. "We'll meet you on the road. I'll get back to you."

He disconnected, saw Sully crawl down a ladder from what was left of the panic room. He carted Tubbs under an arm. Bree was already on the ground, standing beside Doc and Effie. Sully dropped the dog beside her and raced toward him. He'd obviously heard the conversation over his headset. He shouted to Bree. "You and Tubbs stay with Doc. When he leaves, you go with him!"

Damn, Micah needed wheels. He saw Sergeant Dupré in the crowd and yelled, "I need a car. Now!"

Dupré immediately caught the urgency of the situation. Smart man, considering Micah and Sully were packing heat. He shouted to his men. The road leading to the house was a parking lot. The cops scrambled to move vehicles out of the way. The ambulance was at the front of the line now. Micah sprinted for it, opened the door, and tossed out the driver. "Sorry, man."

Sully grabbed the passenger side and did the same, the EMTs backing off into the ditch. The rear doors opened. Boots scraped metal flooring and the doors slammed.

"Let's go!" Hawke appeared between the seats. "We're all here. Joe too."

"How's Joe's head?" Micah wasn't sure bringing him along was a good idea.

"I didn't ask. The guy's tough, and he'll take no prisoners."

Micah hit the bar lights and siren, his foot to the floor. A couple kilometers of hellish ruts bounced under the chassis until they reached asphalt. Sirens wailed behind them. Micah counted three police cruisers in the side mirror. He punched the tracker app and tossed Sully his cell phone. The GPS signal flashed blue on the screen. "Where's Remy?"

"She's not moving. Go straight." Sully pulled out his own cell. "I'll call Dupré and fill him in."

"Tell him to hang back when we get there, Sully." Micah knew the cops would compromise the takedown when his own team went in hot. They lacked any tactical experience. "And tell him to kill those sirens."

After a short conversation, Sully disconnected and redialed. "I'll give Theo and Rocket the location. They can't be far from us."

"We'll meet them up ahead on the road." *Damn.* Micah didn't want to wait, but they needed a full team. Some of them to kill and others to protect the hostages. Yeah, he had no choice but to think of the women in those terms. Otherwise, he wouldn't be able to function. Only a couple more bends in the road to their destination, he turned off the siren. He knew how far sound carried in the mountains.

"It's on our right." Sully pointed to a structure between the trees. The shell of a broken down garage with rusted gas pumps out front. "Is everyone hearing this on your headsets? Check in."

Micah heard the replies through his own. "Rocket and Theo must be close."

"Try almost on top of us," Sully said. "Otherwise they couldn't confirm through their mics."

"I have a visual." Micah saw a pickup pull in after the cruisers.

The back doors of the ambulance opened as his team hit the ground, silent as death. Even the cops knew better than to make any noise. Theo and Rocket joined their ranks.

Dupré approached as Micah checked his gear. "Where do you want us?"

"We'll do the takedown, Dupré. But we need your men outside in case any of them get past us. Surround the building, but stay back."

The sergeant nodded and moved to join his own team.

"Like that's gonna happen," Theo whispered into his mic. "Those bastards aren't walking out of there."

"No shit. They're dead, all of them." Rocket's words this time. "Their bodies are just waiting to hit the ground."

"Yeah, this ends now." Micah was beyond taking prisoners and so were the others. No choice. Otherwise, the women would never be safe.

Sully nudged him. "You're taking point on this. Where do you want us?"

Micah appreciated it. By rights, he, Rocket, and Theo should stand down. They were too close to the situation and had everything to lose. But with Remy's life on the line, he needed to be the primary. Knew the Swamp Killer would finish her first as soon as he sensed trouble. No fucking way. "Rocket, you have any C-4 in your bag of tricks?"

"I like where you're going with this," Rocket said. "Where do you want it?"

"The side wall by the bays should work. I'm guessing it's too risky to blow the garage doors."

"Affirmative. They could blow inward," Rocket agreed. "But a nicely shaped charge on the outside wall will get their attention."

"Do it."

Rocket moved off to do what he did best while Micah gathered the others around him.

"Theo, you're second inside. Rocket's next. The rest of you fall in behind. As soon as Rocket detonates the charge, we go in hot. The door on the far side is our best point of entry."

A couple more minutes and they were in position. Micah had no idea what they would find, but he couldn't dwell on it. All he could do was pray for Remy, Melena, and Billie. With God's help and his team as backup, they would all make it out alive.

He signalled Rocket to set off the remote. As soon as he heard the concussion of the blast, Micah kicked down the door. "Go!"

Where are you, you fucker? Micah was desperate; he couldn't see anyone, other than his team, through the smoke with his flashlight. *Where in hell are they hiding?*

"It's clear in the bays," Hunt said.

"No one in the office," Law responded.

Hawke clicked his mic. "Looks like we're all clear."

Damn it. Micah checked his cell phone, the GPS signal still pulsing right on top of him.

"Mic, take a look at this." Sully shone his light on a pile of fabric in the corner.

"Jesus," Theo said. "Those are Melena's clothes."

Rocket glanced down and swore. "And Billie's. There's her cowboy boots."

Oh, man, Micah wanted to fall to his knees and scream. He sucked it up instead. "These are Remy's, along with her tennis shoes with the GPS tracker. And there's blood on the floor."

Theo looked like he was about to implode. "What's our next move? We're running out of time."

The problem was they'd also run out of leads. Micah wanted to bash a hole in the wall with a fist. He'd never felt so desperate, had always acted cool under fire, and enjoyed the challenge. But, not today. All he cared about was the women. *His* woman.

"Get out here!" Dupré shouted through the crumbled wall. "We've got a witness!"

Micah was first out, reaching for the handcuffed guy who sat in back of a cruiser. He hauled him to his feet. "Where are they?"

"I dunno, man!" The guy was dressed in rags and reeked of whiskey. His eyes were wild. He looked stoned to the gills. Still, he was the only eyewitness they had. "They took off! I was waiting 'til they left so I could get inside to sleep. Then you guys roared up."

Jeez, Micah wanted to shake him. Surely, he knew something that would help them. "What were they driving?"

"Dunno that either, man. All I know is they had wheels...something big. A van maybe?"

"I don't suppose you caught the licence plate?"

"No, sorry dude."

Micah dropped him back in the cruiser and closed the door. His head spun, his eyes searching the night sky. They had something, although it was a shot in the dark. He turned when Sully approached. "You know anyone who owes us a favor high up in the military?"

"I'm on it." Sully dialed, waiting until someone answered at the other end. He identified himself. "I need satellite images of the following coordinates over the past few hours. No, Colonel, I don't have time to go through regular channels." He listened for a beat before giving him the longs and lats. "Yes, sir, this makes us even. We're searching for a lone vehicle...it could be a van. We need an enhanced image of the license plate and the direction it's headed. We're talking life or death. Every second counts."

REMY SAT STRAIGHT LEGGED in the back of the cage. Her shoulder throbbed. Blood dripped down her back. She told herself to ignore it. She'd been hurt worse in the swamp. She took in a breath of fetid air and released it, trying to center herself. Prepare for battle. She had skills and she would use them.

Her eyes flew open when something slithered nearby. Her gaze cut to a glass aquarium through the mesh wall of their cell. Snakes writhed and coiled, bumping the lid. It wobbled and settled again, thank God. Fear backed up in her lungs. Her body trembled. She'd been brought here to die with the others. With no hope of rescue—the GPS tracker left on the floor of the garage with her shoes.

She had to save herself.

"This sackcloth itches like crazy," Melena murmured beside her, scratching a hip.

"I don't think our comfort is high on the sons of bitches' priority list." Billie banged the side of their enclosure with a hand. Chinked metal vibrated. The snakes thrashed again. "And I doubt we'll be wearing these rags much longer."

Not when killers want us naked to rape and torture. Remy prayed for guidance. She had to break free.

A single light bulb swayed overhead, making it impossible to see much around them. A stiff breeze blew through the space, rattling what sounded like chains. Melena jumped up, peering into the shadows. "Mother of God, what was that?"

"I don't want to know." Remy pulled to her feet. "Help me find a way out of here."

Melena paced to the other end of the pen. "What are we looking for?"

"Start by searching for weaknesses in the mesh." Billie gripped the wire every few inches and tugged. "It's what we do at the ranch. Test for metal fatigue."

"Exactly, and look, the wire is almost rusted through in places." Remy wrinkled her nose. "This place stinks. I think it was a chicken coup. The frame is secured to the floor with metal clamps. And mesh covers the top, most probably to keep the chickens from flying out."

"It makes sense. I'm guessing we're in a barn." Melena stared overhead. "Check out the rafters?"

"Planks and beams," Billie said. "That's exactly what it is."

"And it's old." Remy turned in a circle. "There's moonlight shining through cracks in the walls. That's where the wind is coming from."

"So?" Melena slumped against the mesh. "What good does it do us?"

"Listen," Remy whispered. "If we can pry up a couple of floorboards, we can hide under the barn until it's safe. The wood is probably rotten, so it shouldn't be difficult to loosen the planks."

"We'd need tools to do that." Billie scanned around them. "Wait a second. Look at this."

Remy dropped down where Billie pointed. "The frame isn't anchored to the floor clamps with screws."

"They used nails and they look rusted out." Melena squeezed between them, easing a nail up with her fingers. "Almost...yes, I've got it!"

Billie leaned in, wiggling the clamp back and forth. Twisting it from side to side until the nail at the opposite end popped free. She stretched her fingers through the wire and grabbed it. "It's the clamp we want, but we have to hide the nails."

"Hold onto them. We'll use them as weapons." Remy stared at the floor. "There's a problem. You can see where we removed it. The wood's a different color."

"I'll cover it up." Melena reached through and moved dirt around. "Okay, now what?"

"We use the clamp to pry up the floorboards," Billie said. "Walk around and see if any of them feel loose under your feet."

Remy heard footsteps. "Shh! Someone's coming. Quick, hide the nails and clamp!"

Each of them took one, concealing it up their sleeves before floodlights snapped on. The Swamp Killer strode into the barn, followed by other men. Remy focused on him, not on the instruments of torture she could see on a workbench beyond the cage. Not on the oversized hot tub gurgling a few feet away. Not on the long tables, straps and buckles hanging from the corners. And not on the spurs and whips on the wall. Oh, she saw them in her periphery, but she used them to feed her anger, not her fear. "Micah and his team will find you and kill you if you don't let us go."

"Don't you worry your pretty head about it, Remy Rose." Swamp Killer guy chuckled as if she'd said something funny. He stood a couple of inches from her on the other side of the chicken wire. Scraping a penknife under his fingernails, he cleaned the beds. "He'll be the guest of honor at our little soirée. I wouldn't think of starting without him."

"You're lying." Of course he wasn't, she could see it in his eyes, in the confidence of his body language. Terror gripped her heart and squeezed.

What have you done to Micah? No, no, you're bluffing, just trying to scare me.

"Micah won't waltz in here to be part of your sick plan. He'll tear you apart. And he won't come alone. You'll all die!"

Now the other men grinned, one of them tapping the Swamp Killer on the shoulder. "Guess Remy here underestimates the power of her charms, Sig."

Sig? She remembered that name from the swamp. It's what the man she'd killed had called him. She glanced at the Sig Sauer on his hip and understood. He liked to play with guns.

"You're right, Dentist." Sig finished his manicure and pocketed the knife. "You see, Remy Rose, Rivera figures he owns you. That kind of man doesn't like others touching his property. He'll come alone because I say so, figure he can flex his muscles and I'll hand you over."

"He's a fucking loser." The Dentist held a drill in his hands. He squeezed the trigger, listening to its whir. "By the time I begin your...dental restorations, he'll be hanging by chains on a meat hook."

"With his knees blown out," Sig agreed. "Your man's a muscle head, Remy Rose, just like the rest of his team. But he'll add to our enjoyment."

Stand tall, don't play his game. She knew Micah. He was smart. He was strong. He'd have a plan and he wouldn't come alone. "I can't wait, you slime sucking bastard. He'll eat you alive."

She felt Billie touch her arm, her hand jumping when the man with the bloody bandage wrapping his fingers leaned forward and snarled. "That's it Sig. Give me the keys. We're starting now with her big mouth."

"You'll wait until I give the order, Snake." Sig glared at him, unsnapping his holster.

The man who had stabbed her pushed forward, baring his teeth. "The bitch is asking for it. For Christ's sake—"

"Stand down, Ice-Pick. All in good time."

"I could open this door in about two seconds flat." Another man wrapped his hand around the padlock. He was chunky but not with muscle. Remy thought she could take him, but she wasn't sure about the others, at least not in close quarters, and not at the same time. He swept his gaze over Billie and Melena. "What about those bitches then? At least let us work on them until Rivera shows up."

Melena slipped her hand into Remy's, her fingers shaking. Remy stepped in front of her, using her body as a shield. If the lock came off that door, she'd fight to the death before she'd let the men take either of them.

"I said no, Keyhole." Sig pulled his gun. "Now back the fuck up, all of you. You'll wait until I say different. Get the hell out of here, and stay sharp!"

The men turned to leave the barn. Sig strode behind the others with the gun still in his hand. Someone shut down the floodlights, their voices raised in a shouting match.

"Oh, my God, Remy." Melena leaned against her taking in shuddering breaths. "I don't know how long I'll be able to hold out. If Theo doesn't come—"

"He'll be here. They'll all come. You'll see." Remy shot Billie a desperate glance. "Come on, we have to get the floorboards up."

Billie nodded. "Let's do it."

"I hate that bastard," Remy grumbled. "I hated him in the swamp and I hate him more now." She tested each plank until she found a loose one in the center of the space. It sagged when she stood on it.

Billie worked the clamp into a seam. Melena and Remy clawed at the edges until their fingers bled. *Almost, we're almost there.* The board creaked and tipped up on one side. She worked her hands underneath it and heaved. It popped with a groan. About six feet long and sixteen inches across, Remy eased it out. The next board came easier. There was enough space now for them to squeeze through.

Melena stared into the hole. "There's a crawl space down there, maybe a couple of feet high."

"Okay. Take out the nails so the planks lay flat when we slide them back over us." Remy stood on an end, pressing down with her weight to push the nail heads up through the wood. She changed ends, repeating the movement while Billie worked on the other plank.

"Remy Rose! You have pressed my last goddamn nerve!"

She shrieked, her eyes snapping to...Sig. His voice was different, familiar and yet it reminded her of someone else. Why and who? And how had the freaks sneaked back in without her hearing them? The floodlights came on. The guy called Keyhole opened the lock and the men roared into the cage. Lightning fast, Sig smashed her jaw with a fist before she could get to her feet. She fell on her side. He grabbed her arms, someone else pinning her legs. She saw Keyhole and Snake tackle Melena. Ice-Pick had Billie by the hair, an arm twisted behind her back, shoving her toward the door.

Sig dragged Remy out of the cage. Flashes of light streaked her vision as he hauled her across the floor. *He's heading for a table!* The wound in her shoulder raked the planks, jagged splinters piercing her robe. Her jaw pounded in agony. She struggled but couldn't use defensive moves. He hauled her up, tossed her on a table. Another punch to her face and he shackled her hands. She kicked out with her feet. The Dentist grabbed one of her flailing legs and Sig caught the other. They tightened restraints around her ankles. Billie shrieked her name. Remy turned her head, saw Ice-Pick strap Billie face-down on the table beside her. Melena cried out. Keyhole and Snake lifted her between them and threw her in the hot tub.

God, God, it's really happening! Please help us!

Sig pulled out his cell phone and dialed, waiting for someone to pick up. "You want to see Remy Rose again? Come to this location and come alone." He gave the directions. "You've got thirty minutes. I'll try to keep her alive until you get here."

He kept the line open. The Dentist squeezed down on her finger with pliers.

Remy screamed.

MICAH STOOD OUTSIDE the empty garage pacing inside his head. Checking and rechecking his weapons. He almost had everything he needed to find Remy. Only one piece of the puzzle remained. Satellite feed had netted him the licence plate on the van, but not its present location. It was a rental, thank Christ. Now came the easy part—or maybe the hardest—waiting for GPS coordinates for the van's position from the rental company. Hawke smooth-talked the rental agent like a pro, using his RCMP creds. Hell, he practically offered to father her children. And she still hemmed and hawed. Micah worried she'd demand a freaking warrant and prayed she wouldn't. They didn't have time.

Come on! Come on!

Hawke finally disconnected. "Got it. The van's parked about twenty minutes from here."

"We'll be there in ten." Whistling for Sergeant Dupré, Micah scrawled the data from Hawke's phone on a piece of paper. Dupré climbed out the hole in the garage wall and hustled over. He'd been inside supervising evidence collection. Micah handed him the paper. "These are the GPS coordinates for the van's location. Don't use the police band—use your cell phone to contact your people. I want every available unit and medical personnel sent to these coordinates STAT. Tell everyone to stay off the radio, and make sure they go dark. No sirens. No lights. Wait for my signal to move in."

Dupré nodded and broke for his cruiser to make the calls. Micah boarded the ambulance for the second time that night. Hunt drove, the others on the team piled in back. Hawke gave directions. No one else made a sound, not even to break the tension. Asphalt hummed under the tires. Wind whistled through half-open windows. The smell of pine carried inside on the breeze. That was it, nothing and no one diverting attention from what lay ahead. Only Law worked a screwdriver to kill the inside lights.

The ambulance pulled off the highway and hit gravel. They went dark, both inside and out. Hunt pulled over a couple of kilometers down the road. "It's over there. I can see the farmhouse. Barn's on the left behind it."

Micah leaned forward to scan the area. "Looks like they've got a good view from up there. Everyone stay low."

The doors eased open without a sound. Boots hit the ground as soft as ballet slippers. Men and weaponry crawled through a ditch and started up through a field. Micah took point, hearing nothing behind him. Alone and not alone, he was one killer of eight that included Joe. Part of a matched set of lethal, kick-ass operatives who would destroy the enemy. Love, hate—it was all the same to him right now. The love was for Remy, and hate came easy for those who'd taken her. For those who hurt her. His instincts sharper than they'd ever been because of that love, hate equalled annihilation of those who wanted to destroy her. No remorse. No compassion. Destruction guaranteed.

He whispered into his mic. "Theo, you see a good nest up there for your sniper rifle?"

"No need. I won't be using it tonight, Mic." Theo paused for a beat, his breath rasping. "Up close and personal is more my style today."

"Excellent. I'll take the sniper toys." Law said. "I'm betting there's a good view from the farmhouse roof."

"I'll tag along as your spotter." Hunt went silent for a couple seconds. "I just scoped the house. Lights are off inside. I'll clear it first."

"Sounds good." Micah rolled under the fence to the paddock. "Three hostages and six of us. Sully, you're with Theo."

"Wouldn't have it any other way," Sully said. "I've got your six, bro."

"Like always," Theo answered.

"You want me with Rocket, Mic?" Hawke asked.

"Roger that."

"Hawke." Micah heard the raw edge to Rocket's voice. "Be ready for anything."

"Looking forward to it."

"Joe's with me. On my count—" Micah's cell phone vibrated in his pocket. "Hold up. I've got a call."

The screen flashed 'Unknown Name.' He punched the connection, waiting for a voice at the other end. He already knew who it was.

"You want to see Remy Rose again? Come to this address and come alone." The prick spit out directions. "You've got thirty minutes. I'll try to keep her alive until you get here."

The line stayed open. *Jesus, God, Remy's screaming!*

He didn't need the phone to hear it. The sound echoed through the barn ten feet in front of him. He raised a hand. "Go!"

One hit with the battering ram and he was inside. Glock raised, he scanned the layout. Remy strapped to a table. The man bent over her with pliers, doing his damnedest to twist off a finger. Holstering the gun, he raced forward. Hooking two of his fingers, Micah drove them into the guy's trachea. The freak dropped the pliers to claw at his throat. "Yeah, it's tough breathing through a crushed windpipe."

Micah nodded to Joe. "Cut Remy loose. Get her off the table."

"Micah, the Swamp Killer—"

He couldn't look at her. Not yet. Not until this was over. "One minute, Trigger."

"Don't worry. I've got ya." Joe scooped her up and turned her away. "Your man's got to take care of business."

Micah flattened the guy's digits on the table. Pinning the wrist, he rammed his KA-BAR home. Hand impaled, air whistled through the bastard's throat when he tried to scream. Micah felt nothing. The cops could deal with the rest of him.

His sixth sense told him someone hid in the shadows behind him. He twisted sideways as the Sig Sauer fired. The Swamp Killer. He recognized the bastard. Micah kicked out and the gun flew. Grabbing by the throat, he threw him on the ground and frisked him, finding a penknife. He flex cuffed him to a table leg. "Don't go anywhere."

Micah moved onto the next table. Hawke stood off to the side holding Billie. She wore Rocket's T-shirt, and Hawke kept her face pressed into his neck. Good thing, too. Rocket had her tormentor strapped face-down. He pulled off the prick's cowboy boots with the spurs, ripped the back off his shirt and took the spurs for a ride, up and down his spine. He finished off with ice-picks, nailing his feet to the table. The asshole screamed in agony. Rocket leaned in. "Thanks for the use of your tools, Ice-Pick."

"Hawke, give Billie to Rocket." Micah aimed his Glock. Theo and Sully had their hands full with two guys in the hot tub. Melena huddled in a corner of the tub coughing, her robe tangled around her. "Get Mel out of there."

"Looks like the fuckers tried to drown her." Hawke moved in and pulled her into his arms. "I'll take her to Joe and Remy."

"No. You and Rocket watch them. Tell Joe I need him." Micah's gaze caught the aquarium and the water moccasins inside. He remembered the women in Europe who had died from snake bites. Figured Melena would have been the next victim. "Theo, Sully, get out of the water."

"Can't. They're still breathing." Theo shot him a back-off glare.

"Too bad. There's a couple of water moccasins over here you might be interested in." Micah turned when Joe walked up beside him. "Can you shoot snakes with that bang stick of yours?"

"Course I can. And I won't miss."

Theo hopped out of the hot tub after belting the guy in front of him. "You saying they planned to use those on Mel?"

"Maybe."

"Fuck." Theo grabbed gloves and a snare pole. Opened the lid and hooked a snake. "Sully! Get out now!"

When his brother was clear, Theo tossed one snake, and then the other. He threw down the snare pole and pulled his gun. "You assholes have a choice. If you stay in the tub and get bitten, you might survive. Get out and I'll kill you where you stand."

"Don't let the snakes get loose," Micah told Joe. "Use your bang stick."

Joe grunted and moved closer to the action. Micah tapped his mic. "Hunt, Law, anything outside?"

"Nothing but the cops lining up down the hill," Hunt said. "Do you want them to move in?"

"Not yet. I'll let you know." He strode over to Remy and took her in his arms.

"Micah!" She leaned into him, wounded and terrified. He wanted to carry her out of there. But he couldn't. Not yet. "Honey, it's not finished. There's still the Swamp Killer to deal with."

She stared at him with frightened eyes. "What will happen to him?"

"I can't let him live, Trigger." He let out a breath, wasn't sure if she'd understand. "I won't take the chance a deal could be made. He won't get the death penalty if the FBI wants closure for the families of the victims. There are probably a lot more dead women out there and they'll want the locations of the bodies."

"And if he doesn't get the death penalty?"

"He could bargain for an insanity plea, end up incarcerated in a psychiatric facility he could escape." He kissed the top of her head. "It ends here."

Remy nodded, placing her hand in his. "I want to see."

"You sure?" Micah walked toward the Swamp Killer. "I don't want to add to your nightmares."

She shot him a tremulous smile. "No. You want to give me peace."

Micah did it quick, snapped the bastard's neck. Remy held a hand out. "Please give me your gun." He did as she asked, had already guessed where this was going.

Remy gripped it between her hands, looking at the lifeless body. "This is for all the women you killed."

She fired at his crotch, a look of satisfaction in her eyes. "Micah? Look at his face. There's something strange about it."

He hit his haunches beside the body, touching the cheeks. Putty came off in his hands. So did the sideburns and a wig. He poked around in the guy's mouth and pulled out rolls of cotton. "Jesus. It's Winston Templeton, the guy renting the cottage next door."

"But that's impossible." Remy touched his shoulder, her hand shaking. "He was inside the clinic when we saw the Swamp Killer in the pickup. He pointed a gun at me through the window, remember? And Winston threw himself on his kids to protect them."

"We'll figure it out tomorrow, Trigger." He knew they were both done in. Well past the point of making sense out of anything. "It's been one hell of a day."

Micah rose to his feet, lifted Remy in his arms, and strode outside. He buried his face in her neck when she curled into him. Thanked God for giving him the chance to hold and love her again. It was more than he'd dared hope for, and nothing else mattered.

Chapter 15

C haos surrounded Remy—the bright lights, confusing sounds, and antiseptic smells doing nothing to calm her fears. She hated hospitals. The nurses were overworked and cranky. The radiologist positioning her hand to take X-rays was all business. No gentleness in his approach. No compassion for her mangled finger. She cried out when he touched it, shaking so badly she couldn't keep her hand still. He scowled at her and tried again. God, why couldn't she stop quaking?

A police officer stood tapping a foot in the doorway, impatient for the hopsack robe she still wore. She kept checking her watch as if she was on a tight schedule. Remy had nothing else to put on and wasn't about to strip for anyone, especially not after being attacked and tied down in the barn. Unable to cope with the memory, tears began to fall. Softly at first, but try as she might, she couldn't stop the flow.

Micah appeared suddenly and took control. "Sorry, I was filling out hospital forms. Are the X-rays done?"

The technician checked the digital readout on his computer screen and nodded. Micah glared at the crime scene tech. "Hand me the evidence bag and wait here."

"But—"

"Come on, sweetheart." Scooping Remy up from the cold metal stool, he carried her down the hallway. When they reached the examination room, he strode through, slammed the door, and set her down. She wobbled on her feet. Holding her close, he steadied her, making her feel safe, helping the tremors fade until she settled once more. Lifting the robe over her head, he tossed it in the paper sack. Then he held up a small bundle. "Look what I found."

Hospital scrubs, so much better than a stupid gown with her butt hanging out. He dressed her, picked her up again, and sat on a padded table with her in his lap. Paper crinkled beneath him. He reached over, tugged a thermal blanket from a shelf, and wrapped her in warmth, making sure her injured hand peeked out of the folds.

All Remy could do was tremble, her body taking on a will of its own. God, she was freezing. She couldn't control the tremors or stop her teeth from chattering. Micah curled her around him, brushing his lips against her forehead. "It's shock, honey. Your body is trying to process what's happened and deal with your injuries."

"I-I was so afraid," she whispered.

"So was I, baby." Micah cradled her swollen cheek in his palm, gazing into her eyes and making her feel safe. He kissed the corner of her mouth. "So was I."

Someone knocked on the door.

Remy jumped. A second later, the policewoman barged in the room. She noticed the sack on the floor and shook her head, crossing her arms. "It's not enough. I have to process the victim."

"The victim?" Micah snarled. "She's a person and not a dead body. We know where the attack took place and you have enough evidence at the crime scene. You need anything else you can read the medical report. Now take the bag and get out."

She left in a hurry. After the door closed, Remy sighed. "That's telling her."

"Yeah, well, Sully was right when he said Dupré's team lacks experience in the field." He shifted on the table, tightening a hand on her waist. "And no one's touching you without good reason."

A short time later, a burly technician with a two-pack-a-day smoker's voice walked in. He angled his chin at Micah. "You can leave. I have to draw her blood."

"Be my guest," Micah said. "But I'm not going anywhere."

"What's the matter with you people?" The guy clunked his caddy of glass vials and needles on a small desk, fisting his hands at his hips. "I got the same answer from the gorillas glued to the other two patients who came in with you. Do I look like an ogre to you?"

Honestly? He scared Remy to death, although she refused to say it out loud. Not when he was about to poke her with a needle.

"Yeah, you do, and I take care of what's mine." Micah met the man's gaze, glare for glare. "So go ahead and take the blood while I watch. And you'd better have a soft touch with the needle."

Micah towered over the technician even while sitting down. And he was still in warrior mode, the Glock riding his hip doing nothing to lessen the effect. Remy saw fear in the tech's eyes. He drew her blood, gathered up his supplies, and beat it for the door as soon as he was done.

"Am I?" Remy asked when he was gone.

"Are you what, honey?" Micah tipped her chin, holding an ice pack to her cheek, which made her tremble more. Not from the cold, but from the man who held her, a man so gentle he caused her heart to ache.

"You told that man you take care of what's yours. I want to know...am I really yours?" Remy licked her split lip, afraid of his answer. Was it only a turn of phrase or did his words hold meaning? He'd told her he loved her once, but that was before she'd pushed him away.

"You really have to ask me that, baby?" He removed the ice pack, lowered his head, and found her mouth, covering it with his own. He loved her with the soft press of his lips, his strength surrounding her. She felt the power of his restraint as he held back. And saw desire in the depths of his eyes. "You're my world, Remington Rose Renaud, and I love you."

"I love you too, Mic." She touched her forehead to his, tears spilling over her bottom lashes. "I'm just too emotional right now to show you properly."

Micah winked. "I'll let you off the hook for tonight, but you owe me."

The doctor came in the room, looked at them, and smiled. "I already know, don't ask the big guy with the gun to leave."

"It's the way it's going to be, Doc." Micah shook hands and tossed out a grin. "I'm sorry if it's against the rules."

"Don't worry about it." The doctor bandaged Remy's finger and splinted it. "Now let's get a look at your shoulder. Yep, it could use a couple of sutures."

Two stitches and a dressing, a shot of penicillin, and some pain meds later, and she was ready to leave. Joe and Stella waited for them in the lobby, Stella crushing her in a bear hug. "You're staying at my place tonight. You can tuck yourselves into bed as soon as we get there."

"Are Mel and Billie okay?" Remy asked, wanting to make sure.

"Oh, sweetie, they're better than okay. They've got their men fussing over them, just like you." Stella patted Micah's shoulder as he swept Remy up in his arms again to take her to the car. Stella turned with her hand in Joe's and walked out the door.

Remy knew Stella was right. Whatever happened in her life from here on in, she would have Micah by her side and they would face any hard times together.

REMY SAT BESIDE MICAH gazing up the hill. The sun rose over the mountains, dappling the bones of the panic room in shadow and light. Nothing else remained of his cottage except for charred wood and ash. A breeze came off the water blowing the scent of devastation in the opposite direction, thank God. It was almost too much for her to handle. He had lost such a wonderful place. Tubbs lay on the ground beside them, his head resting on her feet.

Micah wrapped his arm around her, gently kissing her swollen cheek. "You look pretty good for someone who's been to hell and back.

That's if I ignore the bruises, the puncture wound in your back, and your mangled finger."

"A girl's gotta have some fun, soldier." She snuggled against him, wrapping her arms around his waist. "I'm sorry about your house. It was beautiful here."

"And it will be again. I'll rebuild it." He pushed a hand through his hair, smoothing it back. "The important thing is you, Mel, and Billie are okay."

"I heard Joe talking to Rocket this morning." She touched a finger between his brows, smoothing a frown line. "Those men...is it true?"

"Yeah, they're all dead."

"I thought Ice-Pick was taken into custody."

"He was. He hung himself in a holding cell. Sully and Dupré cut him down this morning."

Micah stood up, found a ball lying in the grass, and tossed it in the lake. "Get the ball, Tubbs." The dog ignored him, groaned, and rolled on his side.

"What will happen to the bodies of those men? Will they be sent back to Florida?" Remy was worried, especially about Winston Templeton's body. She shouldn't have shot him, although he was already dead. But she'd needed vindication for the other women he'd killed and buried. Some of them would never be found.

"No. Doc is doing the autopsies and then they'll be cremated. Even Chloe didn't want her husband's remains back." He had a faraway look in his eyes. She wondered what he was thinking, if he was holding something back.

"Mic, are you in trouble for smuggling Joe and me across the border?" God, she hoped not. He'd only done it to protect her.

"Nope. I spoke with Graciella earlier. She sends her regards and says Pete's doing fine, by the way. She's also with the Miami-Dade Police Department. Apparently, she and Hawke were able to work something out after the fact between Miami-Dade and the RCMP."

"Seriously? So hunting the Swamp Killer became a joint venture, at least on paper?"

"Right. And I was following orders bringing you across the border to smoke him out." His mouth tipped up at the corners. "Evidently, the powers that be are indebted to us."

"Because you caught Templeton?" Remy burrowed closer. Thinking about the Swamp Killer still frightened her.

He nodded. "He murdered a lot of women in Florida."

"What about the other killers?"

"Still being identified, although Inspector Gauld of Scotland Yard is real happy the guy nicknamed Snake is dead. He's from Belfast, and Gauld thinks he tag teamed with the Spider guy. The other three could be from anywhere, and the investigation is far from over. Serial killers don't come together to hunt unless they know each other from somewhere else. I think we only found the tip of the iceberg, but at least our job is done."

"I still don't understand how Templeton was in two places at once. Standing beside us at the clinic as himself, and outside in the pickup, as the Swamp Killer."

"I think I can shed some light on that." Doc paddled his canoe into shore behind them and climbed out. He sat down on a nearby log. "I spoke with Chloe at the morgue when she identified her husband's remains during the night. She said Templeton belonged to a theatre group and was an expert with stage makeup. I'm guessing he put his disguise on someone else that day to throw you off, Mic."

"And it damn well worked." Micah shook his head in disgust. "I should have figured it out, but background checks on the cottage rental tenants all came back clean. Plus he used his family as a smokescreen."

"Chloe also said it was Templeton who beat the crap out of her when you found her in the woods that day. I don't think she knew what he was, but she had her suspicions. She was definitely a battered wife.

Said she was glad he was dead." Doc heaved to his feet. "Well, I'd better get going. I've got a full day of autopsies to get through."

Tubbs woofed when Doc left in his canoe. He got up on all fours and actually plodded into the water. A couple minutes later, he came out with the ball and plunked it at Micah's feet. Then he shook, soaking both of them.

"I'll miss this silly dog when he goes back to your friend," Remy said. Reaching out to pat his head, she took the ball and sent it sailing again.

"Tubbs is staying. I talked to Rizzo this morning and convinced him the dog belongs with you."

"With me? But—"

"No buts honey. The three of us make a good team."

Remy gazed into his eyes and liked what she saw. "Is this your way of asking me to move in with you?"

He kissed her then. Wild, sweet, and full of promise. "That's only for starters. We could end up rocking on a porch together when we're old and gray."

"I hope so, Mic. I really like that idea." She laid her head on his chest, feeling his heartbeat beneath her ear. "And I hope that porch is here at the cottage."

THANK YOU FOR READING this book. I hope you enjoyed it but even if you didn't, please take a few moments to go back online where you purchased it and leave an honest review. Authors absolutely depend on reviews to know how readers feel about their books and series. Thank you, it's appreciated.

For a free book, please hop over to my website at **https://www.kallielane.com**

A word about the author...

This is me in a nutshell. I was raised in Montreal and still have a home there, although most of my thriller and suspense novels come alive in my writing den, at a small cottage I love in the mountains. I guess I've always been a country girl at heart.

My constant companions these days are a Rottweiler, an American Bully, and a cat rescue. I'm widowed and have two adult sons who, I'm sure, worry about what trouble I'm getting into on a daily basis. Case in point; I've managed to break a few bones and dislocate others over the last few years when 'playing' with my dogs. While they are advanced obedience trained and a pleasure to have, I sometimes roughhouse with them a little too much. I also enjoy taking the boat out in the wee hours of the morning to see the stars and the night sky at the cottage. But, yes, I always have my cell phone handy. I'm sure if I didn't answer, someone would call 9-1-1.

I worked in the pharmaceutical and biotech industries for several years, and now I can finally enjoy writing as my real job, which I've dreamt about doing since I was a teenager. Wowzers! How lucky can a girl be? My spare time is shared with family and friends, including writer friends, and I work out to keep myself in shape, rather than dog wrestling! I'm an avid reader and spend more time with a book or tablet in my hands than watching television. Oh, I also like to travel, whether it's for business or pleasure, but I'm mostly found at the keyboard fulfilling my passion for writing.

I love to hear from readers, so please drop me an email at kallie_lane@ymail.com and I promise I'll message back. Lastly, I hope you enjoyed what you read. I would love it if you would leave a review where you purchased this book. It matters to me (and all authors) how you feel about our stories. Wishing you the very best!

To learn more about Kallie, visit her website at **https://www.kallielane.com** or follow her on Facebook at **http://www.facebook.com/KallieLaneAuthor**

Here's a sneak peek at book 1 in the Murphy Thriller series, available wherever you purchase books online...

Grave Compulsion

Chapter 1

Tuesday

Mary Giles mumbled to herself as she sipped a drink in the biker bar on the outskirts of Fort Myers. "This cheapskate must be on a really tight budget to bring me here, and stupid me for agreeing to come with him."

It always amazed her how much men would normally spend to have a piece of eye candy make them feel like God's gift to the universe. Drinks, dinner, and dancing; that was what they paid for and that was all she gave them. Still, why did this one bring her to a dump to show her off to his pals, especially when the place was deserted except for the bartender inhaling from a blunt the size of a small cigar? It made her feel cheap and sleazy, as if she was giving her date more than she should, perhaps even a piece of her soul.

She consoled herself because although she wasn't seated in a fancy bar or restaurant tonight, this guy was the last in a long line of men she'd had to entertain before being inducted into the sorority. Hazing was a pain, for sure, but it still existed under the radar. There was no way of getting around it, not if she wanted to join Alpha Chi Delta. She had to pay the price of admission, just like the other wannabes. So, Mary had placed an ad on tourist boards offering to show single, older gentlemen the night life of Fort Myers.

She reminded herself again this was supposed to be fun. All she had to do was provide the photos of her ten, so-called admirers. The membership committee would have a good laugh and that would be the end of her hazing.

Soon, Mary, soon, she consoled herself silently, feeling a bit unsteady as she finished the last dregs of a bitter-tasting mojito. By this time tomorrow, I'll be hazing other women into the group and loving the craziness.

"It's time to go," her date said. She startled, knocking over her glass when he whispered in her ear. She smelled his cheap aftershave, felt his fingers grasping her elbow and hauling her to her feet.

"But weren't we meeting your fwends?" she slurred. He wrapped an arm around her as they walked down a dirty hallway. She felt her legs go numb and knees begin to buckle as he hustled her out the back door into the night.

"There's been a change of plans," he said. "You've had too much to drink and I'm taking you home."

"I'm fine... only had one dwink... just a little dwizzy." Besides, there was no way she would tell him where she lived. He could drop her off on the beach for all she cared, but not at home.

Mary did not understand what was happening as he half-dragged her across the parking lot to his van. Her sluggish brain didn't register the engine was already running. She was more concerned with how she would snap his photo to provide proof of their ridiculous date and then get rid of this loser. Neither did she comprehend being bound and gagged by someone else after being tossed on a vile-smelling mattress in the back of the van. The long drive out to the middle of nowhere must have happened after she had passed out.

It was the sharp stab of a cattle prod on her naked thigh that jolted her brain back to life. And in that instant of agony, the wooden slab she was strapped to became her new, terrifying reality.

The days that followed of unbearable pain had absolutely nothing to do with sorority life, not when her focus was narrowed on torture, repeated rapes and chokings, her starving belly, her almost frozen and paralyzed limbs.

Life as she knew it was over. All she could do was pray to die, for God to take her. Because she knew there was no other way of escaping the monster and the other one watching from the shadows. It was far too late to pray for rescue, or for her body to heal.

With her final intake of breath, Mary closed her eyes and hummed a few bars of the comforting Sunday school hymn she had sung as a child. Jesus Loves Me.